The Love Shack

Tina K. Burton

CROOKED CAT

First Crooked Cat Love Cats Edition, Crooked Cat Publishing Ltd. 2015

Discover us online:
www.crookedcatpublishing.com

Join us on facebook:
www.facebook.com/crookedcatpublishing

Tweet a photo of yourself holding
this book to **@crookedcatbooks**
and something nice will happen.

For my daughter, Davina
With love, always,
Mumma xxx

About the Author

Tina started writing seriously ten years ago when she began a creative writing course. Within the year, she was selling short stories to women's magazines, and articles to various other publications.

Her first novel, Chapters of Life, was released in August 2013, and made it into Amazon's top 100 best-sellers list for its particular genre. The Love Shack is her second novel, and she's currently working on her third, a time slip story about a girl who dies suddenly and finds herself back in the thirties. She's also started the sequel to Chapters of Life.

When she's not writing, Tina loves to take her rehomed greyhound for walks through the forests in Devon, where she lives with her husband.

Find Tina at **http://tinakburtons.blogspot.co.uk**

Also by Tina K. Burton:
Chapters of Life

Acknowledgements

I'd like to thank my husband, Paul, for his continuing love and encouragement; my daughter, Davina, for being an excellent proofreader; my various friends – especially Liz and Sarah – for their kind support; and my publishers, Crooked Cat, for their great book covers.

The Love Shack

Chapter One

Daisy Dorson pushed open the glass doors of The Love Shack, and stomped across the floor to reception.

She hadn't stomped the first time she'd visited the dating agency. She'd sashayed, because there were a couple of fit looking men sitting in the waiting area, probably on the lookout for a potential mate. But a lot had happened since then, and the mood Daisy was in now, made her feel like stomping.

The smartly dressed woman behind the reception desk was busy tapping away at her computer, but she looked up as Daisy approached and said, "It's Miss…Dorson, isn't it?"

Daisy huffed. She bloody well ought to remember her, this was the sixth time she'd been in.

She was about to tell her so, but the phone rang and the woman held up a black nail-varnished finger to stop Daisy speaking, before answering in a husky voice, "Welcome to The Love Shack dating agency where you can find your perfect match, how can I help you?"

Daisy stalked off to the waiting area and sat in one of the plush chairs to wait for the woman to finish.

Just as she picked up a magazine, a door to her left opened and a man came out. He loosened the tie around his neck then glanced across at Daisy. She thought she recognised him as the agency head man – there'd recently been an article about the agency with a photo of the owner in the local paper – so she got up to meet him.

"Can I have a word?" she asked, stopping him from walking any further.

The man looked at his watch. "Well, I am terribly busy." He tried to scoot around her.

Daisy looked at the clock on the wall behind him. It was

quarter past twelve, lunch time in fact, and she suspected that he wasn't busy at all. He was probably on his way to the local snack bar.

She narrowed her green eyes, sidestepped so that she was standing in front of him again and said, "You're not really busy, are you?" She looked down at his name badge – Gregory Hanson, yes, he was the owner of the agency – then back up at him.

"Gregory…you're just on your way to lunch."

Gregory opened and closed his mouth like a goldfish, then looked at his watch again. "Good heavens, is that the time? I thought it was much earlier." He tried to backtrack, but it wasn't working.

Daisy, fed up with being messed around by the agency, snapped, "Look, quit trying to get out of it. You were lying. I want to have a word with you about how useless this agency is, so we can do it here," Daisy swept her arm around the foyer, "or somewhere quieter, it's up to you. If you're happy for everyone to hear what I have to say, then we can stay here."

She took a deep breath and released it slowly. She usually hated confrontation, so was quite proud of herself, but she was shaking a little inside.

Gregory looked around. Apart from Stella on reception, there was no-one else there. Perhaps he could listen to this obviously mad woman, get rid of her, and still have time to grab a sandwich.

But then the doors opened and two people walked in, so Greg said, "Come into my office, Miss?"

"It's Dorson; Daisy Dorson."

"Miss Dorson. Right, follow me." Greg turned to walk back through the door he'd just come out of, and as an afterthought, said to Stella, "Two coffees, when you're ready."

"I drink tea, not coffee," Daisy said.

Gregory rolled his eyes. "A tea and a coffee, Stella, please."

Once in the office, he said, "Do take a seat, Miss Dorson. Right, how can I help you?"

Daisy took a deep breath and exhaled again. She'd worked

herself up to having a good rant, but now all the bravado left her. She smiled weakly. "I'm not happy with your agency."

Gregory rested his chin on his clasped hands. "Okay, why not?"

Daisy was about to answer when the door opened, and Stella brought in a tray containing their drinks, milk and sugar.

Gregory waited for her to leave. "Help yourself, Miss Dorson."

"It's Daisy, and thanks." Daisy added a drop of milk to her tea.

Gregory added milk to his coffee and sat back in his chair. "And call me Greg, not Gregory. Now, please tell me, what's wrong?"

Daisy wanted to shout at someone, not sit drinking tea. This wasn't going how she'd imagined. But then she thought of the money she'd wasted and her anger returned.

"I'm upset about how ineffectual your matchers are. I've been 'matched' with six different men, all of them utterly useless." She'd made quote marks as she said the word matched.

"Useless? In what way?"

"Well, it says quite categorically on my profile that I'm an animal lover, so when I got the profile for Martin, I was quite excited because it said he liked animals too."

Greg frowned. "So, what was the problem?"

"He liked animals all right – stuffing them, he's a taxidermist. I was horrified when he took me back to meet all his pets as he calls them. Ugh, those dead eyes, all staring at me." Daisy shuddered and Greg was about to say, "How could they have been staring at you when they were dead?" but saw how distressed it had obviously made her, and said instead, "I'm so sorry, that must have been a horrible experience. But our matchers can only go by what they're told. If someone states on their profile that they like animals, how are we to know otherwise?"

"But it must have said what his occupation was."

"Hmm, yes, it should have. Let's see."

Greg put his coffee down and tapped on his keyboard. "I'll

have to get up your profile, is that okay?"

"Go ahead."

He found her details. "Right, you only took out the standard service, but you were matched with several men. Okay…Martin…Jones…" Greg scrolled down. "Ah got it. Profession – taxi driver."

"What? No, that's wrong, it's taxidermist. See, I told you, your matchers are hopeless."

"Oh dear, I am so sorry. I can only apologise and promise to have a word with the person concerned. I'll make sure it doesn't happen again."

"But that's just it, it has, six times," Daisy wailed.

"What? You've been wrongly matched six times? I find that hard to believe. We pride ourselves on being one of the best agencies around. All of our couples are hand-picked. We store your profiles on the computers, our matchers read through them and choose a partner who has similar interests."

"Maybe if it was all done by computer it would be better. I'm sorry, Greg, but your employees are rubbish at their job."

Greg was starting to think that maybe Daisy was just too fussy. They'd never had complaints before…well, only a couple.

"Are you sure it's not you being…erm, well, a bit too particular?" he asked as he leaned back in his chair.

"No, it isn't!" Daisy snapped.

"Okay, tell me about the others."

"Well, I also said that I liked watching period dramas, you know Downton Abbey, Mr Selfridge, that sort of thing."

"And?"

"They matched me up with Tom."

"And what was wrong with him?"

"Nothing, if you like to spend your weekends tramping round muddy fields."

Greg frowned again. "I'm not with you."

"He dresses up in medieval costumes, re-enacts battles and does jousting tournaments."

"But that's better than watching it on the telly, I'd have thought," Greg said with a puzzled look.

"Not when it's raining and you end up covered in mud. That's all he does every single weekend."

"Okay, you didn't like Tom, but that's hardly our matcher's fault."

"Look on his profile; does it say he likes watching period dramas?"

Greg scrolled through the computer again. "No, it says he's a multi-period re-enactor. I guess the matcher thought it would be the same thing. You can see where they were coming from."

"It's not the same." Daisy folder her arms across her chest and pursed her lips.

Greg sighed. "Okay, what about the others?"

"I said I appreciated a man who cared about his appearance and they sent me Rupert. He was late for our date – it was because he couldn't decide what to wear – then he spent the whole time talking about what fake tan he uses and the best way to shape your eyebrows. And when he suggested we go for a walk after dinner, he kept stopping to look at himself in shop windows. He even bent down to look in a car mirror."

Greg tried not to laugh. "Now that can't be our matcher's fault, can it?"

He looked through Rupert's profile and all it said was that he liked to keep himself in shape.

"Okay," Daisy conceded, "I was just unlucky there. But so far, all the men I've been sent have been unsuitable. I said I wanted someone I could have an intelligent conversation with, and got Pete. He was so stupid; when we were talking about the new pope, he asked how many of the popes over the years have been Catholic."

Greg laughed out loud at that one and Daisy suppressed a smile. "It's not funny. I don't think your matchers are doing a good job. They aren't pairing suitable people together. I want my money back." She crossed her legs and Greg noticed how slim and shapely they were. He tore his eyes away.

"I can give you a refund, it's not a problem. Maybe you should have taken out our premium service and got your own personal matcher. It's a hard job pairing people up."

"I couldn't afford that, and it isn't difficult if you read their profiles properly, maybe question them further and use a bit of common sense, I could do it blindfold. Well, I couldn't, because I wouldn't be able to read their profiles, but you know what I mean." Daisy folded her arms and raised her eyebrows.

"You reckon you'd do a better job, do you?" An idea had just popped into Greg's head.

"Yes, I would," Daisy said defiantly.

Greg ran his hand across his chin and looked at her. "Okay, prove it."

Daisy raised her eyebrows in surprise. "What?"

"I said, 'prove it'. I'm offering you a job."

Greg had been looking for a new matcher. One of his employees – the girl he'd had complaints about, and probably the one who'd been matching Daisy – had left the previous week, but he hadn't got round to placing an ad yet, and now this gorgeous girl had turned up claiming she could do the job, surely that was fate?

"But what if I already have a job I'm happy with?" Daisy asked.

"Do you?"

"Well, no…yes. I mean, I have a job, but I don't like it much."

"So, come work for me." Greg gave her the full benefit of his smile.

Daisy cocked her head on one side. "Depends on the package. I want more than I'm being paid now, holidays and a pension."

"Whoa. How about we sort that out properly when we know you're going to A – like the job, and B – be any good at it. For all I know, you could be worse than our current matchers. How about a three-month trial?" Greg then went on to mention an initial salary figure.

Daisy pretended to think about it, but in truth, she couldn't believe her luck. She'd come in to complain and ended up being offered a job. She hated her current work situation and had wanted to leave for ages. She wasn't stupid – she'd left uni with a degree in design – but just couldn't find a decent position anywhere. She was only working in the call centre to bring in some money, but had been there for a couple of years and needed a change. She liked people and surely couldn't do any worse than the present employees. Yes, she'd give it a go.

"You're on," she said and leaned across the desk to shake hands with her new employer.

Later that evening, she was telling her flatmate Kristof about her day.

"The only downside is that I now can't be on their books." She picked up a cushion and hugged it to her chest. "Oh, Kris, I'm never going to find Mr Right."

"Sweetie, I don't know why you even joined a dating agency in the first place. You're a gorgeous girl, you don't need an agency. I keep telling you, the right man will come along when you least expect it. Your soul mate is out there, fate will bring you together when the time is right. It brought us together, didn't it?" Kris took the cushion from Daisy and put his arm around her.

Daisy snuggled into him and sighed. "Why can't I find someone like you? Just my luck, I find a sweet, caring guy, and he's gay."

Kris laughed.

It was true though. Daisy was so glad she'd met Kris, he was her BFF, she loved him to bits, and fate had brought them together.

She'd gone to a new hairdresser for a trim and was moaning to the stylist that she couldn't find a reasonably priced house share. Kris – who was having his hair dyed a striped combination of pink and purple – overheard her and said, "Girlfriend, it's your lucky day."

They then had an interesting discussion where Daisy found out several things. One – he was gay, although that was obvious, two – he was studying drama and wanted to be an actor, three – his real name was Christopher Taylor but he thought it sounded too boring so changed it by deed poll to Kristof. And, most importantly, he was looking for a flatmate.

They went for a coffee after the hairdressers to discuss things, and Daisy moved in that weekend. They'd been blissfully happy living together ever since.

But, the only thing concerning Daisy was, she didn't have a boyfriend. Her nights out were usually with Kris. He often took her to his favourite gay bar where she had plenty of propositions, but they were all from women. She didn't fancy any of the men where she worked – she found most of them too immature – and anyway she didn't mix business with pleasure, so meeting a potential mate wasn't easy, which was why she'd joined The Love Shack. Now that she was excluded from that, she didn't know what to do.

"I suppose I could join one of the other agencies, but I'd feel a bit disloyal."

"Ooh, that would be quite interesting though; you could find out how they do things then report back to your boss."

Daisy was an honest person, and looked horrified at the thought of spying. "I couldn't do that, it's almost industrial espionage."

"Nah, you're right, you haven't got it in you to be underhand. Stop worrying, sweetie, as I said, the man of your dreams will turn up when you least expect it."

"I hope so. It doesn't help that every time I go to see my gran, she asks if I've got myself a nice young man yet. The other day she said she hoped to have a great grandchild before she popped her clogs." Daisy gave a big sigh and her eyes filled with tears.

"Oh, poppet, please don't get upset, you'll start me off and I look abs frightful when I cry, it's not a pretty picture."

Daisy sniffed and smiled. "I'm not asking for much though, I just want a man who will adore me. I eventually want kids and a nice family home… I don't want to become a lonely old maid."

Kris shook her. "Stop it. For heaven's sake, you're only twenty-four. Anyone would think you were fifty-four the way you're carrying on. And the next time your grandmother asks, tell her you're a lesbian so she can stop hoping. That'll shut her up."

Daisy laughed. "Ha ha, she'd have a fit. You're right though. I'm going to concentrate on my job and leave it up to fate. But if I'm still single when I'm thirty, then I'm going to join every dating agency in the area."

***

Two weeks later, Daisy sat behind a desk in her new office. Well, it wasn't just hers, there were five other people working at desks in the same room – three women and two men – but it was bliss after working in the call centre with literally hundreds of other people.

Greg had given her a tour of the place and explained a few things, but Daisy had grasped it already – it wasn't that difficult. They offered two services – standard and premium. For the standard, clients uploaded their details onto the company's bespoke website, and the matchers just had to read the profiles, highlight specific areas of interest, and link it with any other profiles who enjoyed the same thing.

The software they used even let them know when new profiles were added, by playing a few notes from the wedding march tune, which was really annoying after you'd heard it for the hundredth time. Daisy had worked out how to change it to one short ping instead. Once she'd found a potential match, she checked to see if they lived in the same area. It was always best to match people who were geographically close to each other. If there was more than one match, she'd whittle it down to a short list. When she'd finally decided on the best pairing, she'd call the two people concerned to set up an initial date.

The premium service was more exclusive. Each client was given their own personal matcher, who interviewed them at a venue of their choice – the agency, a restaurant, or even their own home if they wanted. Their details weren't put on the website, it was all private and discreet.

Daisy had also asked the one question she'd been curious about. "How did The Love Shack get its name?"

Greg had smiled and said, "It's a bit corny actually. I'd been listening to the song by the B52s, and decided that was going to be the name of my new agency."

"I hoped it might be because of the song. It's one of my all time favourites. You just want to get up and dance every time you hear it," she'd said with a grin.

Daisy went and got herself a drink, and had just sat back at her desk, when a new profile flagged up on her screen.

Sipping her tea, she read it through. "Christ on a bike," she yelled, then blushed as the other matchers stared at her. "Sorry, just read one of the profiles that's come in."

She ducked her head down at her screen again. It was from a young woman who was studying taxidermy. Heart racing, Daisy searched through her computer for Martin Jones' details.

"Please let him still be single," she prayed, as she scrolled through the Js. Alan, Daniel, Frederick… Frederick? How old was he? She had a quick look at his profile. Aww, bless, he was seventy-nine years old. Daisy loved elderly people. She'd come back to him later and see what she could do for him. She read down the list to the Ms. Aha – Martin. Fab, he was still single.

"Why am I not surprised?" Daisy mumbled. But, with any luck, he wouldn't be single for much longer. She looked through his profile and that of the new member – Skye. Bloody hell, they were made for each other. As well as taxidermy, they both liked rock music and visiting museums.

"Yeah, checking up on all the stuffed animal exhibits I expect," Daisy muttered. She reached for the phone.

"Martin? Hi, it's me, Daisy Dorson. What? No, I don't want to give us another try, thank you. But I work for the agency now and I think I've found the girl of your dreams."

After chatting to Martin a bit longer, she then called Skye, who was delighted a match had been found so quickly. Daisy was curious to know why Skye had joined the agency, but wasn't allowed to ask. Greg had said that everyone had different reasons, and it was none of their business. All they were interested in was finding their members a suitable love match.

However, Skye offered up the reason herself. She said that she'd had a few relationships, but they couldn't tolerate her potential career choice, so she'd decided to join an agency in the hope of finding a like-minded man.

"Well, I think I've found him. Now, when would you like

12

to meet up? He only lives about twenty minutes from you, so you could meet somewhere central. We suggest meeting in a public place to start with, like a restaurant or wine bar. The museum? Yes, I don't see why not."

Details finalised, she called Martin again, who was delighted with the choice of venue.

Daisy was just replacing the phone, a huge smile on her face, when Greg entered the office. She noticed how the other women looked across at him with admiring glances.

He perched on the edge of her desk. "So, how's it going?"

"Brilliantly, as a matter of fact. I've just matched up two people who I think are perfect for each other. It's the taxidermist I was matched with. A new profile came in, and she's studying taxidermy too."

Greg looked surprised. "Really? I mean, well done."

"You didn't think I could do it, did you?"

"I didn't doubt you for a second; why do you think I offered you a job?"

"Because you needed someone."

Greg looked caught out. "Oh."

Daisy laughed. "I know all about one of the matchers leaving suddenly to go to France with her parents. Handy me coming in to complain, wasn't it? Saved you placing an advert too."

"Ah, well, yes, I did need a new employee, but, erm, that's not why I asked you…"

"So, it was my sparkling personality that won you over?"

Greg beamed. "Exactly. I could see what an asset you'd be and would have offered you a job even if I hadn't needed anyone."

"That's bull and you know it." Daisy laughed at the look on Greg's face. "Oh, stop waffling. Whatever, I'm glad you did. I think I'm going to like it here."

Greg smiled, and for the first time, Daisy looked at him properly. He was actually rather attractive, with that little dimple in his cheek and those dark flecks in his light blue eyes. She mentally shook herself. You don't mix business with pleasure, and you're supposed to be concentrating on your job.

13

Greg stood up. "Well, keep up the good work and let me know how your clients get on."

"I will." Daisy watched him leave, so did the other women, and one of the men.

Chapter Two

As Daisy went to lunch one afternoon – she brought a packed lunch but liked to sit in the park, getting some fresh air – Stella, the snooty receptionist, was getting herself a drink.

"Hi, Stella." Daisy tried to make conversation. She got the feeling Stella didn't like her much, but she had no idea why.

"I can't stop to chat; I have to get back to the desk," Stella said brusquely.

"Okay, see you later." Daisy gave her a big smile. She was darned if she was going to let the woman intimidate her.

The spring sun shone in an almost cloudless sky, so Daisy removed her jacket, but replaced it again because it was a little chilly. She walked to the park and looked for a free bench. There was one by the pond, but a man was sitting there. Daisy shrugged. It wasn't solely his, she could sit down too.

"Okay if I sit here?" she asked as she approached and the man looked up from the book he was reading.

He nodded and shifted up a little so they wouldn't be too close to each other.

Daisy stole a look at him. He wasn't bad looking. Not her type, but okay. She opened up her lunchbox and took out a sandwich.

He shifted position again and as he did so, she spotted the title of the book he was reading, but trying – not very successfully – to hide. Dynamic Dating. How to Find and Keep a Partner. Daisy's heart raced. Could she recruit him for the agency? She was used to cajoling people, her job in the call centre had taught her that, although nine times out of ten she'd had the phone slammed down on her.

She cleared her throat. "Lovely sunny day, just right for

sitting in the park, isn't it?"

The man looked across at her and smiled, but didn't answer.

Oka-a-ay, he was probably shy, hence the book. How could she approach this? She decided to just be upfront.

"Sorry for interrupting you, but I noticed the title of your book."

The man looked at Daisy in alarm, and blushed redder than the tomato in her sandwich.

"I'm sorry," she apologised again, "but I work for a dating agency – The Love Shack – have you heard of it?"

The man shook his head, then relaxed a bit. "I'm new to the area and…well, I'm quite shy and not sure how to meet women." He turned to face Daisy. "How does one meet members of the opposite sex? I don't go to pubs and bars, I don't drink…" He tailed off and looked at her helplessly.

"Well, it's your lucky day. What's your name?"

"Malcolm."

"Well, Malcolm, it's your lucky day. As I said, I work for The Love Shack, which is the best dating agency in the area. We have a ninety percent success rate." Daisy mentally crossed her fingers at the lie – she was usually so honest – but what did a few numbers matter?

"I'm not sure about an agency, aren't they horrendously expensive?"

"Malcolm, what price can you put on finding your soul mate, the love of your life? Actually, we're reasonably priced for the service you get. We have a couple of packages. Our premium service is unlike other agencies. We personally interview you, then create a profile and keep your details on a private database. We don't put your photo on our website, it's all nice and discreet, and you have your own private matcher. We are the best. You've just said you don't drink and don't go out to clubs or pubs, which would make finding a girlfriend rather difficult. We'd be ideal." Daisy smiled in what she hoped was an encouraging way.

Malcolm closed his book and ran his hand through his hair. "I didn't think people used dating agencies any longer."

"They use them more than ever. People lead such busy lives nowadays; they often don't have time to go out socialising, so an agency takes all the hard work away from you, and matches you with people who have similar interests. How long could it take you to find a woman who enjoys the same things as you? We have a database of hundreds of members, many of whom could be a potential match."

Daisy could see that Malcolm was wavering, and plunged in with something to ensure the deal. "I tell you what, sign up with me and if I haven't found you a match within six months, I'll give you a refund. Now, you don't have anything to lose, do you?"

"With an offer like that, I can't refuse, but I only want to deal with you."

"Not a problem." Daisy inwardly high-fived herself, then hoped Greg wouldn't be angry with her for promising a refund.

Malcolm said he could leave work early that afternoon, so Daisy arranged an appointment, and agreed to interview him herself. She looked at her watch. "Oops, time to go, see you later."

She ate the rest of her lunch as she walked back to work.

Once there, she went into Greg's office and asked if she could speak to him.

He waved her to the chair opposite. "What can I do for you, Daisy?"

"I've got us a new client."

"Well done, how did you manage that?"

"I shared the same bench as him in the park, so I recruited him."

"What just like that? You just asked him, do you want to join a dating agency?"

Daisy laughed then told Greg about seeing the title of the book Malcolm had been reading.

"Excellent. I'm beginning to see that it was worth taking you on," Greg beamed at her.

He looked very attractive when he smiled. Aware that she'd been staring at him, Daisy quickly spoke.

"There's just one small thing." She held her thumb and

finger together to imitate something tiny, and bit her bottom lip.

"Ah, okay, go on."

"Well, I kind of promised him a refund if I haven't found him a match in six months."

She looked down into her lap, waiting for the blow up, but it never came. She looked up.

Greg was looking at her, his mouth a thin, tight line.

"Say something; shout at me or whatever," Daisy said.

Greg sucked in his breath. "Did I give you authority to promise him that?"

Oh crap, she was going to get the sack. A few weeks in the job – a job she really enjoyed – and she'd blown it. She realised Greg was waiting for an answer.

"No, you didn't, but I was using my initiative," she brazened.

"Good, I like an employee who uses their initiative."

Daisy smiled. Phew, she was going to be okay.

"But, not at the company's expense." Greg raised his voice a tad.

Daisy's face fell again.

"So," Greg went on, "if you haven't suitably matched him within six months, the refund will come out of your wages."

Daisy gulped. A thousand pounds was a lot of money, almost a month's salary.

The agency charged their clients a thousand pounds for six months on the premium service, or if they signed up for a year, they got it for one thousand eight hundred pounds. For the standard service, it was seven hundred for six months or twelve hundred for a year.

"But I can't afford to lose a thousand pounds."

"You better hope you find him a match then. Off you go, back to work."

Daisy slunk out, feeling stupid, but also determined to find Malcolm a match, whatever it took.

Greg watched her go and grinned. She was going to be a real asset. The truth was, he'd been thinking about a similar scheme for the company, but with the people who took out the yearly service. He'd offer them another six months free if they hadn't had a successful match after a year. But he wasn't going to let Daisy know yet, he wanted to see how hard she worked at finding her new recruit a partner.

During the interview with Malcolm, Daisy realised that finding a match for him was going to be more difficult than she'd thought. He worked for a funeral directors, suffered with OCD, was shy and – in Daisy's opinion – had one of the most boring hobbies she'd heard of. She didn't even know what campanology was until he explained that it was ringing bells. He travelled to different churches to take part in their bell ringing sessions.

"So, apart from that, do you socialise at all?" Daisy asked.

Malcolm shook his head.

"There must be something else you enjoy – going to the cinema, theatre?"

"Nope."

Daisy tried not to sigh, and fixed a smile on her face. "Okay, what do you do when you're not working, or ringing bells?"

Malcolm thought for a while. "I watch TV or read."

"What do you read?"

"Books about aircraft. Military aircraft mostly."

Oh, heck, she was never going to find him a partner.

"Okay," Daisy said, "we have a few things we can work with. But I have to be honest and say it may take a while as you're a bit more…erm, unusual, compared to most of our clients."

Malcolm blushed and looked down at his hands, which were clasped in his lap. "You mean boring."

Daisy saw how sad he was, and instantly felt sorry for him.

"No, not boring, just different that's all, so it'll take a while to find someone who enjoys the same things as you. But there's someone for everyone, and I'm sure we'll find her."

She gave him a big smile, and this time it was genuine. She really wanted to find someone for this rather pathetic, shy and lonely man. Someone who'd love him and bring some much needed light into his life.

She finished the interview and promised she'd get in touch when the right person came up.

Daisy wished he'd taken out a yearly service. She didn't think she'd find someone within six months. But, she reasoned, you never knew who could walk into the agency. The woman of his dreams could turn up that very afternoon.

Greg caught up with Daisy just before she left to go home.

"So, how was your newest recruit?"

Daisy crossed her fingers behind her back. "Oh fine. I'm sure I'll find him a partner quite soon."

Greg wasn't fooled. He'd seen the look that flitted across her face as he asked the question. Ha, he hoped this was going to be a challenge for her, it would serve her right for giving a proviso that she wasn't authorised to give.

"I hope you do, Daisy, otherwise you're going to be out of pocket by quite a bit of money."

"We'll see, Greg. I'm off, have a good evening."

Greg held the door open for her. "Yep, you too, see you tomorrow."

Stella had been watching their exchange and seen Greg's gesture. She narrowed her eyes. Daisy was younger than her, prettier, and had a better figure, and Stella felt threatened. From the moment Daisy had been employed, Stella decided she didn't like her. She had no grounds for it other than jealousy. Daisy was always friendly and pleasant, the other employees liked her and Greg had remarked that she was a perfect addition to the agency. However, Stella had made up her mind that she wouldn't be taken in by Daisy's affable nature, and would remain professional but distant.

Daisy told Kris about the difficulty in finding a match for Malcolm as they sat on the sofa that evening, eating supper.

"I've been through most of our database, and at the moment there's just no-one suitable. The other matchers are looking for me too, but so far, a big fat zilch. I need to find him someone," she wailed, "I can't afford to give up a thousand pounds."

"Don't worry, sweetie. If the worse happens, I'll fund you until you get paid again." Kris delicately nibbled a slice of pizza. He could probably have eaten half the world's food and not put on any weight because he was always on the go, but he rarely ate a full meal. He put the pizza down and looked at it as if it was going to jump up and attack him.

"You not eating any more of that?" Daisy asked.

"No, my tummy's gurgling, I don't think it agrees with me."

"Kris, your stomach is gurgling because it's complaining. It needs fuel. There's nothing wrong with the pizza."

"I think it might be off, that cheese is a bit odd."

"It's goats' cheese, and it can't be off, it was a freshly cooked frozen pizza. If you don't want it, I'll have it." Daisy helped herself to another slice.

"Girlfriend, you'll get podgy and spotty, with greasy hair, and then no-one will fancy you."

"No-one fancies me anyway so I might as well get my enjoyment out of food." Daisy waved the pizza slice at him then took a huge bite and chomped on it. "Nom nom nom, delish."

Kris laughed. "So, back to the problem of Malcolm. Seriously, sweetie, if you do have to pay back the money, I'll fund you, so don't worry. You don't really think Greg would make you pay, do you?"

Daisy stopped chewing and thought for a bit. "Yes, I think he would. He owns the company and takes the running of it seriously. He can't afford to lose money, so, yep I think so."

"Well, if he does, I'm going to march right in there and tell him he's a big fat meanie."

"Don't you dare. Thanks for offering to fund me; I'd do the same for you, anytime. But I know you can't afford it, you get even less than I do. If it happens, we'll just have to eat beans on toast for a month until I get paid again."

"And, sit in the dark with candles, to save electricity."

"And, not have showers, to save water – euww, we'd stink." Daisy laughed.

They then spent ten minutes thinking up stupid ways to save money, and ended up in a fit of giggles when Kris said they could use Daisy's celebrity magazines as sheets of loo roll.

"I won't be buying any magazines if I have to give my wages up."

"Oh, I was looking forward to wiping my bottom on the faces of the celebs I don't like."

Daisy laughed so hard at the image that conjured up, that she had tears rolling down her cheeks.

"I love you; you always know how to cheer me up." Daisy hugged her friend. "Go sit down whilst I tidy up."

She cleared away the plates, then settled down on the sofa with Kris to watch the soaps.

Chapter Three

One morning, a few weeks later, Daisy was out in the foyer putting some new brochures on the tables. She'd put the hunt for a mate for Malcolm on hold for the time being; she and the other matchers had now searched the whole database, but there was no-one suitable.

The front doors opened, and a little old lady entered.

Daisy looked across at Stella, who was 'busy' filing her nails, so Daisy walked up to greet the woman.

"Hello, can I help you? Are you lost?"

"Oh no, dear," the elderly lady said, "I think I'm in the right place."

Daisy tried not to laugh. "Well, this is The Love Shack dating agency."

"In that case, I'm definitely in the right place. Now, dear, I'd like you to find me a man. I can pay you, look." The lady opened up her cavernous bag to reveal bundles of cash.

"Bloody hell!" Daisy looked up but Stella was still filing her nails and hadn't noticed. Guiding the old woman by the arm, Daisy said, "Close that bag and come with me." She led her into one of the interview rooms, then went out and made them both a drink.

The lady's name was Marjorie Williams. She was seventy-five-years old and had been a widow for two years.

"I'm fed up being on my own," Marjorie explained. "I go to weekly bingo but it's full of old ladies."

Daisy smiled and wondered if Marjorie had looked in a mirror recently.

"I want a man to wine and dine me, and a bit of 'how's your father' would be nice too," Marjorie said with a twinkle in her eye.

Daisy almost choked on her tea, then burst out laughing.

"I thought that would get you," Marjorie said. "Now, do you have anyone on your books for an old crone like me?"

Daisy sat in thought for a few seconds, then remembered something from a few weeks back. Oh, what was it? Her mind went into recall as she pictured the scene. She was scrolling through the computer, looking up names of... Jones. That was it, ah, Frederick. She wasn't going to let Marjorie know straight away though, she didn't want to get her hopes up.

"I'm sure we'll have someone. Now, what sort of service can we offer you?"

Daisy felt a bit at odds dealing with Marjorie. On the one hand, the agency were providing a service, which people rightly had to pay for, but Daisy didn't like the idea of taking money from a pensioner. But then Marjorie had shown her a bag full of cash. Daisy was worried about that. The old lady shouldn't be carrying money around, she might get mugged.

"Marjorie, why are you carrying a bag of money around with you? You should be careful, you know, you could get attacked."

"Tsk, I'm not daft, dear. I don't usually carry it around, it's kept at home, but I'm not telling you where."

"I don't want to know, but I hope it's in a safe, or somewhere locked up, and not under the mattress?"

Marjorie looked at Daisy with her steely blue eyes and raised her eyebrows.

Yep, it was under the mattress. "Why don't you keep it in the bank?" Daisy asked.

"What's the point? You don't get any interest anymore, and I want my money where I can easily get it. I don't trust the banks, especially with so many of them going bust. Now, if you're worried about taking money from an old bird like me, don't be, there's plenty more where this came from. So I can afford it."

"Hell's bells, Marjorie, what did you do, rob a security van?"

Marjorie laughed. "No. My Arthur never trusted banks so

he had a post office card account and always drew his pension in cash. We paid for everything with cash – never owed a penny – and that's how I like to do things now. He wasn't short of a bob, so don't you worry."

Daisy relaxed. She liked this quirky old lady, and hoped she'd be able to help her.

"Okay, but please at least get somewhere lockable for your money, don't keep it under the mattress. Now, what sort of gentleman are you looking for?"

"I'm not too fussy, dear. As long as he has teeth and some hair, I'll be happy."

Daisy laughed out loud. "Well, seeing as you're not super fussy, I think our standard service will suit you. Do you want six months or a year?"

"I may not be here in a year, my dear."

Daisy pushed out her bottom lip and made a sad face. "Oh, don't say that."

"But it's true. When you get to my age, all your friends start dying around you. You don't know if each day will be your last. So I try to enjoy every day as much as I can. So, let's say six months. If you haven't found anyone and I'm still going, I can take out another six months. But, I hope you find me someone sooner rather than later, I want to start having some fun now – if you get my meaning." Marjorie winked.

"Marjorie Williams, you are a wicked woman, do you know that?" Daisy laughed.

"I do, and I'm going to continue for as long as I'm able. Now, let's get this done so I can pay you and go to my zumba class."

Daisy's eyes widened. "You do zumba?"

Marjorie giggled. "Ha, ha, your face. No, I'm having you on. But I do swim. Got to do something to keep the old joints flexible. I'll be no good to any gentlemen if I can't manoeuvre my body into various positions, will I?"

Daisy cringed. "Too much information, Marjorie. Okay, let's start with your hobbies and interests."

Daisy discovered that Marjorie was interested in lots of things. She liked swimming, ballroom dancing – although her late husband wouldn't dance so Marjorie had to be content with watching rather than doing. She painted – not well, but she enjoyed daubing paint on a canvas – and she liked baking. Daisy took it all down and told Marjorie she'd prepare a profile and contact her if she found any suitable matches.

Marjorie opened up her bag and took out several bundles of cash. She counted out seven hundred pounds. Then counted out another forty and told Daisy that was her tip.

"Oh, Marjorie that's really kind of you, but I'm only doing my job, which I get paid for, and I haven't found you anyone yet. I can't take this, you keep it."

"But you've been delightful, helping an old dear like me, and I want to thank you."

"I tell you what; you can thank me if and when I find you a match. Buy me a box of chocolates. Maltesers are my favourite."

Marjorie sniffed, then brightened and agreed.

"Can you hang on here a bit? I just need to speak to the boss."

Daisy went to Greg's office and knocked at the door.

"Come in. Oh hi, Daisy, what can I do for you?"

Greg was looking rather good that morning she noticed. He had on a shirt that matched the blue of his eyes. "Nice shirt."

"Thanks. What's up?"

Daisy explained about Marjorie paying with cash. Their clients usually paid by debit or credit card, so they weren't used to handling lots of money.

"I'm not quite sure what to do."

Greg got a receipt book out of his desk drawer. "Write her a receipt and ask Stella to fill out the form and take the money to the bank when she goes on her lunch break."

"Oh, I can do that."

"No. It's Stella's job. I know she's the receptionist, but she does banking and other little jobs too. Get her to do it."

"Okay. Marjorie tried to give me a tip too, bless her."

"Tried? Didn't you accept?"

"No, I didn't. I can't take money from an old lady."

"Daisy, if she can come in here with a bag of money and

26

pay seven hundred pounds for our service, then I'm sure a little extra for a tip is nothing. Older people are used to giving tips; you probably offended her by refusing."

"I don't care. I'm not taking money from an old lady. I said she can buy me a box of Maltesers if I find her a match."

Greg grinned. "Hmm, chocolate lover, are you?"

"Yep, I can't get enough of the stuff. Right, thanks. I better get back; she's waiting to go swimming."

When Marjorie had gone, Daisy went and sat at her computer. She'd put the cash into a big envelope and stashed it in her desk drawer to give to Stella later. She scrolled through the database of names until she got to Jones. There he was, Frederick. Seventy-nine years old. Daisy read his profile and squealed with delight. He and Marjorie were made for each other. Among his list of interests were ballroom dancing and painting. In fact, he was a retired art tutor who still gave private lessons. Wow, that would be perfect. She reached for the phone.

After an interesting conversation with Fred, who seemed as eccentric as Marjorie, Daisy waited until she thought Marjorie would have arrived home then called her to set up their initial date. They were going to meet in the local museum's art section and both be carrying a red scarf so they knew who each other was. Daisy hoped it would go well for them.

Remembering the money in the envelope, she got it out and went out to reception.

Stella was reading a magazine but she quickly put it away as she saw Daisy approach, and looked at her computer screen.

"Hi, Stella, Greg says can you please bank this money when you go for lunch."

Stella snatched the envelope from Daisy and said, "If there's a queue I'm not wasting my lunch break."

"Oh, well, I did offer to do it, but Greg said banking was one of your jobs…" Daisy tailed off at the unfriendly look on Stella's face.

Then, trying to be helpful she said, "Look, I'm not busy, I can sit on reception for a while if you want to do it now, that way you're not wasting your lunch break."

"And what if the boss comes out and sees you here?"

"I'll tell him I offered to sit here so you could go to the bank." Daisy smiled.

"Right little teacher's pet aren't you," Stella said nastily.

"No, just trying to be helpful. Stella, have I done something to upset you?"

Stella didn't like being challenged so backed down and said, "No, I've got a bit of a headache today, sorry. Thanks, I'll take the money now."

Daisy handed it over.

"It's not good to have it lying around," Stella said as she counted out the money and filled out a banking slip.

When Stella had gone, Daisy went behind the desk and thought she ought to tell Greg, just in case anything happened. She picked up the phone and buzzed through to him.

"Yes, Stella!" Greg snapped, which threw Daisy for a second, she'd never heard him speak so roughly before.

"Erm, it's not Stella, it's me, Daisy."

"What are you doing on reception?"

"I said Stella could go to the bank now. She was worried about there being a queue and wasting her lunch break, so as it's quiet, I offered to sit in for her."

"You shouldn't have done that, Daisy. It wouldn't have hurt her to go during lunch; she doesn't exactly work hard as it is. I'm not stupid; I've seen her reading magazines and stuff."

Daisy didn't quite know what to say, so she stuck up for Stella. "But, if there's nobody here, there's not much for her to do, so it doesn't matter if she reads a magazine now and then, does it?"

She heard Greg sigh at the other end of the phone. "If you were on reception, and it was quiet, what would you do?"

Daisy didn't hesitate. "I'd make sure the foyer was clean, tidy up and change the magazines, check the coffee machine…"

"Exactly. You wouldn't sit reading a magazine or filing your nails."

He was right.

"I just wanted to let you know."

"Thanks, but don't do it again."

Greg hung up and Daisy was left feeling that instead of

doing someone a favour, she'd made another mistake. That was twice now she'd pissed Greg off. First, by offering Malcolm his money back, and now with this. She was worried because her three-month trial was up soon. Would Greg keep her on? Or would he use these mistakes as an excuse to get rid of her? She hoped not, she loved her job.

When Stella came back, she asked Daisy if Greg had seen her sitting on reception. Daisy could truthfully say, no, he hadn't. She didn't admit that she'd buzzed through and told him.

"Thanks, Daisy. It saved me wasting my lunch break."

Daisy, who was happy when people were pleased with her, went back to the office. At least someone was grateful for her help.

Chapter Four

It was Friday night and Daisy was out with Kris, but instead of his usual favourite venue, they'd gone to a new wine bar that had recently opened up.

"No offence, Kris, but I'm never going to find a boyfriend at a gay bar, am I? It's okay for you, you don't want a steady relationship, you just want to hang around with your mates, get pissed occasionally and have fun."

"F.U.N is the name of the game, girlfriend." Kris swigged another mouthful of his drink and said, "Sweetie, chill. I thought you'd decided to concentrate on your job instead?"

"Yes, except I may not have a job after next week. Oh, Kris, what if he sacks me, that's twice I've messed up." She got off the bar stool she'd been perched on.

"Baby D, he won't sack you. You're probably the best matcher he's got. If you ask me, the person he needs to sack is that Stella. She sounds like a right bitch."

"She wasn't too friendly initially, but since I did her that favour she seems to have thawed. She's okay, just a bit stuck up that's all." Daisy looked sad for a moment. "I hope I don't lose my job, I'll really miss it. I like Greg too, he's a great boss."

Kris looked at Daisy and cocked his head to one side like a puppy. "Do I detect something here? You like Greg as in, like, or fancy?"

"I don't fancy him." Daisy gulped her drink.

"Girlfriend, look at me."

Daisy wouldn't look.

"You do, you fancy the boss."

"I so do not. Okay he has a nice personality, he dresses well and he's got lovely eyes. But that doesn't mean I want to shag him."

"If you think he's got lovely eyes, you fancy him." Kris then danced around, singing, "Daisy fancies the boss man, Daisy fancies the boss man."

"Stop it. Kris, stop it." Daisy giggled as Kris grabbed her and twirled her around.

When he let her go again she admitted, "Okay, I do fancy him a bit, but he's miles older than me and anyway, you know my rule about not dating anyone I work with, I never mix business with pleasure."

"How old is he?"

"I dunno. Early thirties, I think. Ancient."

"That's not old; and anyway I think you'd suit an older man. You want to settle down, an older man would too."

"Kris, it ain't happening. He's my boss, end of. Now, get me another drink whilst I nip to the loo, then after this we'll go to the club, there's no-one remotely interesting here, and I want to dance."

The one thing Daisy liked about the club Kris took her to was the music, and the huge dance floor. She and Kris had a right laugh dancing together. He'd dramatically twirl her around and do all sorts of stupid John Travolta moves. He was the best person to go for a night out with.

As she made her way to the ladies, she overheard a woman who was rather tipsy and shouting instead of talking, say to the woman sat beside her, "I'm never going to find someone at this rate. Who on earth would want a woman who likes ringing bells?"

Daisy's eyes widened. She stopped and pretended to look in her handbag so she could hear more.

"I know you think it's boring, but it's something I've loved since I was a child. We lived beside a church and I used to lie in bed listening to them practise on Tuesday evenings, and get up to hear them ring properly on Sunday mornings. One Tuesday, my father took me in to watch them, and I was fascinated. I've been hooked ever since."

"BRILLIANT!" Daisy shouted, making the woman jump. Daisy laughed, then said, "I need to nip to the loo, but can I talk to you when I come out?"

The woman looked puzzled, but nodded.

Daisy came out, went and got her drink from Kris – promising she'd only be a few minutes – and sat down at the woman's table.

"You aren't going to believe this, but I work for The Love Shack dating agency…"

Daisy introduced herself and found out the woman was called Geraldine. She went on to explain that she had someone on their books who might just be ideal for her.

"But will I have to join the agency?" Geraldine asked.

"Oh, yes you will." Daisy hadn't thought about that aspect of it, she'd been so excited to find someone who might be a match for Malcolm."

"How much is that going to cost me?"

"Well…" Daisy explained the two services, standard and premium.

Geraldine looked doubtful.

"My client took out the premium service. He's serious about finding someone. He's a little shy, but quite good-looking. I think you'd get on well."

"What else does he like doing?"

"I'm afraid I can't give you any more information. It's private. You'd have to join to have that access. But, if you do join and he isn't suitable, we'll keep your details and seek other matches for you."

At that moment, Kris came over. "Come on, Baby D, I want to go dancing."

Daisy realised it was unfair to do work stuff on a night out with Kris, so she reluctantly got up.

Geraldine was talking to her friend, but she looked up and said to Daisy, "Okay, I'll pop in to see you on Monday morning, will you be there?"

"Yes. Just ask for me at reception." Daisy delved into her handbag and produced one of the agency's business cards. "Here, just in case you forget. See you Monday, hopefully."

When they got outside, Daisy jumped up and down yelling, "YES, YES, YES."

"Do you want to tell me what that was all about?" Kris pouted like a little boy at being kept out of things, so Daisy told him. He picked her up and whizzed her around. "Woohoo. That's serendipity for you."

"Serenwhat?"

"Serendipity, unexpected luck, a fortunate accident, that sort of thing."

"Never heard of it, but I like the word. Anyway, hopefully, they'll get on and I won't have to give up a month's wages. Ah, that's brilliant. I'm starting to think you're right, there is something in this fate stuff."

"As I keep telling you, girlfriend, your destiny is written in the stars, you're supposed to meet certain people when the time is right."

Kris linked arms with Daisy and, giggling, they skipped down the road to the taxi rank and on to the club, where they got extremely drunk, and danced the night away.

***

Monday morning, Daisy got to work early as she wanted to run something by Greg. She'd learned not to say anything to clients now without asking him first.

She knocked at his office door. There was no answer so she hesitantly pushed the door open to be confronted with Greg half dressed. He was in the middle of putting his shirt on.

"Oh, I am so sorry," Daisy spluttered, but she couldn't take her eyes off his tanned, rippled chest. She willed her racing heart to slow down as she started to back out of the door.

"It's okay, come in now you're here, but that's why I didn't answer. What if you'd had a client with you?" Greg scolded.

"I'm truly sorry. Because you didn't answer I thought you weren't here so was going to leave you a note. Erm, why are you only just getting dressed?"

"I spilled coffee down my shirt. Just as well I always keep a spare here." He gave her a rueful grin as he put his jacket on.

"So, what brings you into work so early?"

Daisy told him about meeting Geraldine.

"Well done again. You do seem to have a knack of meeting potential clients, are you sure you're not just bribing people to join up?"

Daisy laughed. "No, it's just bizarre coincidences. But, what I wanted to run by you was this. Geraldine doesn't really need to join for six months as I've already got a match for her, so, how about we introduce a new one-off service for people we already have a potential partner for? She pays us a fee and we introduce her to Malcolm. If it works, great, if not, she can then join the standard or premium service."

Greg thought for a bit. "Okay, how much were you thinking of charging?"

"Well, it wouldn't work out as cheap as joining properly; we still have to make a profit, so I was thinking something like two hundred and fifty pounds?"

Greg ran his hand over his chin, and leaned back in his chair.

"Okay, here's how we'll do it. We won't advertise this new feature, because we'll just get people wanting to join up the once. But, yes, if you are in this position again, you charge them two hundred and fifty pounds for setting up the initial meeting with the proposed partner. If it goes well and they continue the relationship, then they've got their money's worth. If not, they can then join up for six months and we'll knock off half the initial fee – a hundred and twenty-five pounds. What do you think?"

"I think it's a great idea. Right, we'll need new contracts. Shall I mock one up from our current ones? I'll just change the fee and dates etc. It shouldn't take me too long."

"Yes, please, Daisy. Email it across to me when you've done it, will you – before you give it to Miss…what's her name?"

"Geraldine. I'll get on to it right away."

Greg stood up to see her out of the door and as she went, he put his hand on her shoulder. "Well done, Daisy, great idea and good job. Let's hope they hit it off, it'll save you some money."

Daisy made a face at him. "I told you I'd do it."

Stella had just arrived for work and was watching them. Daisy smiled at her and Stella smiled tightly back.

Daisy worked on the new contract and emailed it across to Greg, who replied five minutes later. "All looks good. Print off several copies and keep them in your desk. Thanks again, great work. G"

Daisy printed off the copies and kept one out for Geraldine. She hoped the woman would actually turn up. Maybe she'd got so drunk that she'd forgotten, or she'd lost or threw the business card away. Daisy imagined all sorts of scenarios. "Oh, please turn up," she muttered. "I have a lot riding on this."

Sure enough, at eleven am, Geraldine walked into the agency. Stella buzzed through to let Daisy know.

"Geraldine, I'm so pleased you turned up," Daisy greeted her. She was more pleased than Geraldine would ever know.

Daisy took her into an interview room and offered her a coffee.

She explained that for the one-off fee they would give her details of the potential match and arrange a meeting if she liked what she saw. But they would need payment first.

Geraldine was happy to part with the fee, explaining that she hadn't had a boyfriend for years and she was sure it was her hobby that put men off.

"Well, no worries about this one as he's a campanologist too," Daisy smiled.

"What other interests, if any, does he have?" Geraldine asked.

"Let me see." Daisy scrolled through the list on the computer screen. "He works as an undertaker, does that put you off?"

"Not at all. My grandmother used to prepare bodies, it was one of her first jobs. She told me lots of crazy stories when she was still alive."

"Excellent. Okay, he likes reading, but mainly non-fiction books about aircraft."

"Bloody hell. Are you serious?"

Daisy was dismayed. Oh no, that's blown it.

But Geraldine was smiling. A huge grin on her round face.

"That's a good thing?" Daisy asked.

"You bet. I love aircraft. I went to the Imperial War Museum at Duxford with a friend once, and spent almost two hours looking at this one aircraft. It's called a Blackbird, or Lockheed SR-71 to give it its proper name. Do you know, it had special paint that changes colour to avoid detection by radar, and it held the record as the fastest, and highest flying jet."

"Really? Fascinating stuff. I think you two would get on well. I have to warn you though, he's rather shy, so may not talk much."

"That's okay; I can talk enough for the pair of us – as you can tell." Geraldine grinned again. "When can I meet him? As soon as possible please. Oh, I'm so excited."

Daisy was excited for her. She prayed they'd hit it off. "Take a seat outside and I'll phone him now. Help yourself to more coffee."

Daisy settled down and phoned Malcolm. He was surprised to hear from her as he'd all but given up hope. But he sounded delighted that she'd found a match. The only slight problem was arranging where to meet. Because he didn't drink, he didn't go to pubs, clubs or wine bars. Then he suggested the big bookshop, Merrilies, in the high street of his local town Bewford. Daisy thought that was perfect. The only other thing was how to recognise each other. Daisy liked her clients to have a common item so they'd easily identify one another. Sometimes it was wearing a specific piece of clothing in a particular colour, other times it was what they carried, such as a scarf or book. It was no good carrying a book to meet in a bookshop, almost everyone would be holding one, but Malcolm suggested they carry a bell.

"Hang on a moment, Malcolm, I'll be two ticks."

Daisy ran out to Geraldine. "I don't suppose you have a bell, do you? I don't mean a huge one, but a small ornamental one?"

"Of course, I don't know a bell ringer who doesn't have one – or several."

"Excellent. How do you feel about taking it with you so that Malcolm will know who you are?"

Geraldine laughed. "I think it's a great idea, where are we meeting?"

"Tell you in a moment."

Daisy ran back to the interview room. "Malcolm, yes, she has a bell and thinks it's a great idea. Yes, I'll tell her, seven pm Thursday, the shop stays open late. Okay, bye, and best of luck."

Daisy hung up and called Geraldine back in. "Okay, do you know Bewford?"

Geraldine nodded. "One of my friends lives there."

"Great. Malcolm suggested meeting in Merrilies bookshop at seven pm on Thursday. The shop stays open late. He said you could go for a meal after. I'll ring him back if it's not convenient."

"Thursday evening is perfect. Oh, I'm so glad you overheard me on Friday. I must remember to take my bell. What a fab idea." Geraldine impulsively hugged Daisy, her eyes shining.

Daisy had to agree. "Malcolm said once he's there, he's going to ring the bell and see if he gets an answering ring. Ha ha. I must say when I met him he was rather shy, but on the phone just now he was quite enthusiastic. The best of luck, I hope you hit it off. Please let me know how you get on."

"I will. Thanks again, Daisy, I'm going to recommend you to all my single friends. It's already the best money I've spent, and if it doesn't work out with Malcolm, I'll be signing up with you."

"Aww, thanks, Geraldine."

"Please call me Geri, you're a friend now."

Daisy was really touched. This was the best part of her job, making people happy. She saw Geri out then went back to the office and emailed Greg. "Went well, Malcolm and Geraldine meeting on Thursday evening. D x"

She pressed send then read it back. Oh, crap, she'd put a kiss. Why did she do that? It was force of habit, she put one at the end of all her emails and texts, but she usually only emailed or texted Kris, her sister or mother. Oh, bloody hell. So, did she now email back saying she didn't mean to put a kiss, or ignore it and hope he wouldn't spot it? She opted for ignoring it; otherwise, it was drawing attention to it. She got out her phone and texted Kris. "Just emailed the boss man and put a kiss at the end. How embarrassing. D x"

Kris texted back, "That's because you fancy him, lol. K"

Daisy replied, "Maybe, but how mortifying. It's because I always put a kiss when I text you, my sis or mother. Gotta go, see you tonight. D x"

Kris replied "X"

Daisy laughed out loud. Kris had a great sense of humour.

A few minutes later, she had a reply from Greg. "Well done, let's hope they hit it off. You didn't quite finish your email, but I can't think what word starts with X. G"

Damn, he had noticed. Daisy flushed beetroot, then decided to tell him how it had happened. "Really sorry, force of habit, always put a kiss at the end of emails and texts, but they are usually to my flatmate, sister or mother. D"

Seconds later, she got a short reply of a smiley face.

Phew, hopefully he understood. She didn't want him to think she was coming on to him. Her three months were up at the end of the week, she hoped Greg was pleased enough with her work to keep her on. She'd worked hard for the company so far. Okay she'd made a couple of mistakes, but one of those was soon rectified if Malcolm and Geri hit it off. Ah well, she'd just have to wait and see.

Chapter Five

Friday morning, Daisy was just getting a cup of tea, when Stella answered the phone with her usual, "Welcome to The Love Shack dating agency where you can choose your perfect match, how can I help you?" She held the phone out. "It's for you."

"Put it through to my desk please, Stella. Who is it?"

"Someone called Geraldine."

Daisy gasped and rushed into her office. She put her tea down and picked up the phone. "Geri, hi."

She couldn't get a word in for the next ten minutes as Geraldine told her how wonderful the evening had gone, how much they had in common and how it seemed they'd fallen in love at first sight.

Daisy sighed blissfully. "Geri, I am so pleased for you. When are you seeing him again? Tonight, and every evening this week? Aww, that's excellent news."

She hung up, feeling overcome with emotion, and had to stop herself from crying, but they were tears of happiness for two lost souls who'd been brought together by her own doing. She wanted to tell Greg and was about to email him, but decided to tell him in person.

She knocked at his door.

"Enter."

She went in. "Enter? That's a bit stern, you usually say 'come in'." Daisy laughed.

"Oh, I thought it was Stella with my coffee. What can I do for you – you look like the proverbial cat that got the cream."

"Guess what? Geraldine and Malcolm really hit it off last night. They have loads in common and are seeing each other again tonight and every night this week." She couldn't stop beaming.

"That's great news. So, you won't have to pay back any refund after all."

Greg saw the shine in Daisy's eyes, and realised it wasn't all about having to give up her wages, she genuinely liked helping people.

"This wasn't just about the money, was it? It was about bringing two people together. I can see it in your face. Well done, Daisy, I'm proud of you. In fact, this is a good time to talk about your future here."

Daisy gulped and looked at Greg, the smile disappearing from her face.

Greg went on. "As you know, your three-month trial is up, and I'd like to offer you a permanent position with us, if that's what you'd like. I've been really impressed with your dedication, Daisy. This isn't just a job to you. I've watched how you relate to people, you genuinely like helping them, and have put more into your work these last three months than some of our matchers have in years. So, I'm also promoting you to head matcher. But we'll call it something fancy like 'senior consultant'. It will come with a pay rise of an extra one hundred pounds a month, and I'll clear out that junk room so you can have your own office... Daisy, what is it?"

Greg rushed out of his chair to Daisy's side as she'd burst into tears. Just as he was comforting her, Stella walked in with his coffee. She put it on the desk and Daisy, who was wiping her eyes, saw the venomous look she gave Greg as she walked out.

Daisy sniffed. "I'm sorry, I'm just so relieved. I thought you were going to sack me because of the two mistakes I made a while ago. I'd be devastated if I lost this job – I love it. I'm also a bit emotional about Geri and Malcolm. Sorry for being a wuss." She sniffed.

"Daisy, you're not a wuss, you're just a big softy, and I'm glad because that's what makes you so good at your job. Now back to work, I'm not paying you a fortune to sit around crying you know." Greg winked at her. "You'll have a name badge with your new title on it by Monday, and your higher salary will start next month."

Daisy went into the ladies to sort out her blotched face. Whilst she was there, Stella appeared. "Everything okay, Daisy?" Stella secretly hoped Daisy was crying because she'd been sacked, but she put on a concerned face and patted Daisy's back in what she thought was a comforting manner.

Daisy laughed. "Yes, I'm fine, thanks. Just got a bit emotional over a couple I recently matched, and with relief that I'm now a permanent member of staff."

"You've been taken on? Wonderful news, you must be thrilled."

"Yes, I am, especially as it comes with a new title and pay rise."

"New title, what's that then?"

"Senior consultant. Sounds posh but it just means head matcher." Daisy laughed and rubbed at a splodge of mascara underneath her eye.

"That's really great news, Daisy, well done." Stella was fuming. She'd hoped Daisy would be dismissed, not kept on and promoted. "I must say I was a bit shocked when I brought Greg's coffee in as I thought you two were in a clinch."

So that was why Stella had given Greg a filthy look earlier. Daisy smiled. "No, he was just comforting me because I stupidly burst into tears."

"Yes, I realised it must be that. I mean, he wouldn't be in a clinch with you." Stella emphasised the word 'you' as if suggesting Daisy was an alien or something.

Daisy was confused. "What do you mean, 'with me', what's wrong with me?"

Stella gave Daisy a questioning look, then she laughed. "Oh, honey, you don't know?"

"Know what?" Daisy frowned.

"Gregory is gay."

"Greg, gay? No, really?"

"Yep. I thought you knew. Everyone here knows, but please don't let on that I told you. One of our previous matchers saw him out with his male friend in a gay bar, and Greg asked him to keep it to himself. He worried that it might affect the reputation of the agency, and give the wrong impression. The guy told us all, but made us promise to keep it to ourselves, so I'm telling you to prevent you making an embarrassing slip up at some point."

Daisy was stunned. She lived with, and mixed with, gay men, and would never have thought Greg was homosexual. Her gaydar was way off course.

"Thanks for letting me know, Stella, and yes, it could have been embarrassing at some point. Good job you told me, don't worry, I'll keep it to myself."

"No problem, congrats again on the job," Stella said sweetly and went back to reception.

Daisy went back to the office. She was astounded. She just couldn't believe it. But why would Stella lie? Should she ask the others? No, she better not, if Greg knew she'd been asking about his personal life, he wouldn't like it and she'd promised Stella she'd keep it to herself.

She felt like a fool now, as she'd found Greg rather attractive, especially that time she'd caught him with his shirt off. No wonder he'd not made anything of it. And she'd admitted to Kris that she fancied him. When he heard this, he'd laugh his head off. Daisy sighed. At least it meant she could stick to her rule about not mixing business and pleasure. Not that Greg would have fancied her, even if he was straight. He was older than her and probably too professional to get involved with a colleague.

She mentally shook herself. She'd get on with her job and forget about her love life. She should listen to her BFF, he'd got it right.

Daisy was determined that from now on, she was going to concentrate on her job during the day, chill out with Kris in the evenings, and party hard at the weekends.

"I just can't believe it," she told Kris as she tucked into the macaroni cheese he'd made for their dinner that evening. "Mmm, this is delish, by the way."

"Thanks, it's my special touch that does it. A little sprinkle of cayenne pepper."

"You're a great cook. I want to marry you." Daisy laughed.

"Ha ha. Hey, here's a suggestion, if neither of us are married by the time we're forty, then we marry each other."

"You're on," Daisy said, and clinked her water glass with his.

"Oh, hang on," she added, "it'll have to be earlier than that, I'd like kids. How about thirty five?"

"Okay. It'll be a turkey baster job though – no offence."

"Ha ha, okay. Actually, you'd make a great dad. You're funny, kind, caring."

"Yeah, maybe one day. Now about the boss man. Why can't you believe it?" Kris buttered his roll.

Daisy swallowed a forkful of food. "Well, I'd swear he's straight. I've mixed with enough of your friends now to know when someone is gay. I don't think Greg is."

"Sweetie, you can't always tell by looking at someone. I know a few of us are overtly flamboyant so it's pretty obvious, but there are the quiet ones. How many times have you heard that a celeb is gay and would never have known?"

"Hmm, not often. Except for that guy in the film we saw the other night. Oh, and that gorgeous man in the new serial we've started watching… Yeah, okay, I get your point."

Daisy tore off a piece of bread from her roll and wiped it around her plate. Kris watched her. "Girlfriend, I don't know where you put all that food. You eat like a horse, but are super slim, I hate you."

"Got good genes, I guess, either that or it'll all start piling on when I hit my thirties and I'll look like a telly tubby."

She popped the last bit of bread in her mouth and chewed thoughtfully. "I guess it would make sense that he wants to hide the fact – it would possibly give a different impression of the agency if people knew it was run by a gay man. I just never expected it. I've not seen one hint."

"But you wouldn't see any signs if he's trying hard to hide it. Anyway, you're just annoyed because you fancy him. Daisy fancies a gay man, Daisy fancies a gay man," Kris teased.

"Oh, shut up, you." Daisy threw her napkin at him. "It wouldn't be the first time. I really fancied John Barrowman, and I knew he was gay."

"Ooh, good taste, he's gorj. I think lots of men and women fancy him."

"Anyway, with Greg it's fancied, past tense. Finding that out sobered me up pretty quickly, I can tell you. Well, at least I can fully concentrate on my work now without any distractions. And I won't stand there drooling if I catch him with his shirt off again."

"Sweetie, can you do me a favour?"

"What?"

"If you do catch him with his shirt off again, call me, I'll be round there in seconds."

"Ha ha, you are so amusing." Daisy stood up. "I guess seeing as you cooked, it's my turn to do the dishes."

"Nah, we'll do them together, then we can watch that film I recorded last night."

Chapter Six

When Daisy arrived at work Monday morning, she saw a plaque on the door of the old junk room. Daisy Dorson. Her new office! Greg must have either stayed late on Friday to clear it, or done it over the weekend. Daisy went in. It was minimally furnished with a desk, chair, filing cabinet, computer and wall clock, but on the desk were two envelopes, a bouquet of flowers and a box of Maltesers.

She sat down and started to open things. In one envelope was a lovely card from Martin and Skye – the taxidermists. They were still seeing each other and wanted to thank her for bringing them together.

"Ah, how lovely," Daisy said aloud. The next envelope had a hand-written letter in shaky writing and fifty pounds. She knew who that was from. It was Marjorie, thanking her and giving her the tip she'd offered when she'd first met her.

So, who were the Maltesers from? Daisy picked them up. No card or message on them. Hmm, that was odd.

The flowers were from Geri and Malcolm. They were beautiful. A big round bouquet of pink roses and white carnations with sprigs of green leaves and gypsophila.

None of the other matchers, nor Stella, were in yet, so Daisy couldn't ask if they knew who'd left the chocolates. She'd noticed the light on in Greg's office so sent him an email.

"Got some lovely thank you gifts this morning, how wonderful, but don't know who sent a box of Maltesers. Did you see who left them? D"

A few seconds later, she got a reply. "Welcome to your first day as senior consultant. Did you not see the post it note on the box? G"

Daisy picked up the box – nope, no post it note, then she saw a luminous yellow piece of paper on the floor by her chair and picked it up.

"Remembered you liked these, just a thank you for your hard work. G"

They were from Greg. Aww, fancy him remembering she liked chocolate, especially Maltesers. She emailed him. "Thank you, they're my favourites, that was kind of you and appreciated. D – oh PS, do we have a vase anywhere?"

She heard a bit of noise, then a few moments later Greg appeared in her doorway holding out a vase. "Will this do?"

"Ah, perfect thank you. I want to put these in water. Can I take them home later or shall I keep them here?"

"Of course you can take them home. Well done, people obviously like you. Great thinking on my part that day offering you a job." He grinned.

Daisy laughed. "Yes, it was. I love it here and can't imagine working anywhere else now."

"But you have a degree in design; don't you want to do something with that?" Greg sat on the edge of Daisy's desk, something that would have made her heart beat faster last week, but now, knowing he was gay, his closeness didn't affect her – well, not much.

Daisy shook her head. "Nope. I did at the time. I was really arty at school and going to uni to study design seemed like a good next step, but I couldn't find a job when I left and ended up in the call centre just to earn money. But I really love this job. I think my calling is in helping people, not in art."

"Maybe you'll go back to it in the future?"

"I don't think so; I haven't done any design since I left. I think it was just something to do at the time. I'm happy where I am now."

"Good, because I'd hate to lose you." Greg gave her a warm smile. "How do you like your new office?"

"I love it; thank you so much." Daisy frowned. "You didn't spend your weekend clearing the room out, did you?"

"Only some of Friday night and part of Saturday morning. I wanted to get it ready for you. Sorry it's sparsely furnished, add whatever you like in the way of pictures etc."

"I will. You shouldn't have given up your weekend though. I could have waited, and even helped clear it."

"No, I should have done it ages ago as I had boxes of old files and all sorts of junk that needed sorting through. Still, it's done now. Nice to see the room being used."

"Well, it's great to have my own office, thanks again, I appreciate it."

"And I appreciate what you've done since you started here, so we're quits."

Daisy smiled. She picked up the envelope from Marjorie. "Remember the old lady who tried to give me a tip?"

Greg nodded.

"Well, she sent it in a letter, but, she gave me fifty pounds this time. I still don't want to take it. I was just doing my job."

"Keep it, Daisy. If she couldn't afford to give it to you, she wouldn't have. And you better get used to accepting tips and presents, I have a feeling there'll be a lot more coming your way. Oh, before I forget, here's your name badge."

Greg took it out of his pocket and handed it over. Daisy was quite chuffed to see 'Daisy Dorson Senior Consultant' written on it.

"Put it on."

Daisy pinned it to her jacket and then made herself feel ill trying to look down at it. "Ooh, that made me feel weird." She blinked rapidly and shook her head.

Greg laughed. "You can't read it upside down, silly. It looks great. Right, we better do some work. Catch you later." He got off her desk and returned to his office.

Daisy went out and filled the vase with water, unwrapped the flowers and arranged them in it, then put the vase on top of the filing cabinet. She stood the card on her desk and put the envelope from Marjorie in her handbag. Bless her, she must phone to say thank you. In fact she could do it now whilst it was quiet. Then she wondered if it would be classed as a personal call. Personal phone calls were forbidden at work. She wasn't even supposed to use her own mobile whilst working, but she did text Kris now and then when it was quiet.

She didn't want to do anything to jeopardise her job, so she sent another email to Greg. "Is it okay to phone Marjorie and thank her for the money? Not sure if that's classed as a personal call? D"

He replied immediately. "Go ahead, if you're phoning clients for whatever reason, it's work related. G"

Ah, good. She looked at the clock on the wall. Ten to nine, hmm would Marjorie be up yet? Daisy's gran was always up early so she decided that maybe elderly people didn't sleep in and picked up the phone. Marjorie answered on the third ring.

"Hi, Marjorie, it's Daisy here from the agency. I just wanted to say thank you for the letter and money. You really shouldn't have, but I appreciate it."

"Oh, my dear, you are most welcome. I can't thank you enough for bringing me and Fred together. A real life Cupid, that's what you are. I'm having a whale of a time. I didn't think at my age that life could be so good, but I'm having more fun now than I've had in...oh, years. Not that I didn't have fun when my Arthur was alive, but he was a more reserved man. Fred is so different, we are having a ball. Do you know, he's teaching me ballroom dancing. It's wonderful. And he's teaching me to paint; he's such a clever, patient man."

And so she rattled on for a good fifteen minutes more. Daisy didn't have the heart to end the conversation. Marjorie was so thrilled with Daisy's service, thanking her over and over. She'd seen Fred almost every day since their initial meeting, and they were talking about taking a little holiday together.

"I must say I'm looking forward to it, but am a bit nervous. I've never been on an aeroplane before, the furthest I ever got to with my Arthur, was Scotland on a camping trip when we had our caravan."

When Daisy eventually got off the phone, she smiled at the thought of Marjorie never having flown before. That was something they had in common, as Daisy hadn't been in an aeroplane yet either. She could be excused as she was only in her twenties, but Marjorie was in her seventies. She supposed there must be plenty of older people who'd never flown though. She was so pleased that things seemed to be working out well for the elderly couple.

Daisy went out and got herself a cup of tea. There was a coffee machine in the foyer, and there used to be just ordinary teabags. Daisy didn't drink coffee, and she liked different teas such as Earl Grey and green tea, so she'd started bringing in her own. Greg had caught her taking an Earl Grey out of her bag one day, and asked what she was doing.

"We only have ordinary teabags." Daisy had wrinkled her nose and whispered, "Stella buys cheap supermarket own brand tea."

Greg had looked across at Stella and sighed.

"You shouldn't be bringing in your own tea. I'll provide it from now on."

True to his word, he'd bought several different boxes of tea, so they could now offer their clients and callers a variety of drinks.

As she waited for her tea to stew, she looked across at Stella, who was reading a magazine again. Greg was right, she didn't do a lot of work.

If it was quiet, Daisy knew she'd find things to do, like dusting the reception desk and emptying bins. They was really the cleaner's jobs, but if it wasn't busy, Daisy would do them. She wondered why Greg didn't say something to Stella, or even replace her if she wasn't doing her job properly.

She did do her reception job though, and it wasn't her fault there were quiet times. And, you couldn't sack someone without good reason, so she supposed they were stuck with Stella for the foreseeable future.

Stella saw Daisy watching her and raised an eyebrow. Daisy smiled. "Would you like a drink, Stella?"

"No, thank you, I had one just now."

"Okeydoke." Daisy smiled sweetly and went back to her office.

Stella narrowed her eyes. That little Miss better not start getting high and mighty now she'd been promoted. Stella knew Daisy had been watching her, but she wasn't her boss, so couldn't say anything. Stella smirked and continued reading her magazine.

The rest of the day passed uneventfully. Daisy got a few pings to say someone new had joined the standard service so she read their profile and noted key interests. Then around three pm Stella rang through to her.

"Daisy, there's a gentleman out here who's interested in joining up, but if you're busy, I'll call one of the other matchers."

"No, it's okay, I'll be right out."

Daisy stood up, brushed down her skirt and walked out to the foyer.

Daisy's gaydar was working again; she felt sure that the man standing there was gay. Ah, now what should she do? She didn't even know if the agency dealt with same sex matches, she hadn't thought to ask. The best person to deal with this was Greg.

Daisy smiled and took the man into an interview room. Before going into too much detail, she explained the two different services and, not wanting to assume, she asked him who he was hoping to meet. When he said a man a bit older than himself, that confirmed her thoughts.

"Can you hang on here for just a few moments please, Mr Walsh, I'm just going to have a word with my boss."

Daisy knocked at Greg's door, and went in before he'd said 'come in'. He was on the phone, and Daisy heard him saying, "Dinner sounds good, see you later, Robin. Yep you too, bye."

He looked annoyed that Daisy had caught him on the phone because he frowned and pursed his lips.

So the rule about not making personal calls at work obviously didn't apply to him! But then he was the boss, so could do what he liked.

"Yes, Daisy, what can I do for you?"

"I've got a gentleman in that I think you'd be better dealing with."

Greg raised his eyebrows. "Oh, why?"

"Because he's looking for a man."

Oops, she didn't mean to say it like that. Now he'd know that she knew he was gay. And, he'd want to know how she knew, which would then get Stella into trouble. Damn. Think,

think.

Daisy realised Greg had spoken and was waiting for an answer. "Sorry, what did you say?"

"I asked why you thought I'd be better at dealing with him."

Oh crap, now what could she say? She had a brainwave.

"Because, I don't even know if we deal with same sex dating. It's not something I thought to ask, and you haven't discussed it with me."

Greg looked flustered. "Oh, sorry. Well, we don't, but I know an agency that does. Send him in. What's his name?"

"Mr Walsh. I've already covered the service we offer with him, which of course he won't need now because we don't do it…" She realised she was babbling. "Right, thanks, I'll send him in."

She hurried back to the interview room. "Mr Walsh, so sorry to keep you. The agency owner Mr Hanson is going to help you, please come this way."

She showed the man into Greg's office then ran to her own and sank into her chair. Bloody hell, that was close, she'd almost messed up. She was pleased at how she'd covered it up, but knew she'd have to be more careful in the future. At least it confirmed one thing though. Greg was gay. He'd been talking about having dinner with someone called Robin, and how else would he know an agency that dealt with same sex dating? Perhaps he'd been on their books?

It didn't occur to her that most agencies knew about each other. They made it their business to find out how other agencies worked, what they charged, what their packages were etc.

When Mr Walsh had gone, Greg called her into his office.

"Daisy, I'm sorry for not covering same sex dating, it was very remiss of me. I should have been more thorough. We don't deal with it here, but, if anyone comes in again and asks, this agency does. They specialise in same sex matching and are very good, apparently." Greg handed her a brochure for the Union Dating Agency.

She took the leaflet. "Thanks, sorry for disturbing you, but

I didn't know what to tell him and didn't want to look unprofessional."

"No worries, you did the right thing. But you'll know for next time."

"Yep. Thanks." She went back to her desk wondering just how he knew the agency were good – first-hand experience? Was that where he'd met Robin?

When she was in the park at lunch time, eating her sandwich, she texted Kris. "Confirmation, Greg is def gay. He's having dinner with Robin, and knows of a gay dating agency. D x"

Kris texted back. "Ah never mind, you said he was too old anyway. I've been chosen to play Puck in the drama school's version of A Midsummer Night's Dream. Talk tonight. K xx"

Daisy smiled. Puck was the perfect character for Kris to play because he was mischievous, clever and funny, a bit like Kris. Aww, he'd be full of excitement later that evening. Thinking about Kris always made Daisy smile. She loved him, really loved him. He was like her brother, sister, and best friend all rolled into one.

Chapter Seven

Spring gave way to summer, and Daisy settled well into her job. It was like she'd been there for years, but she wasn't complacent. She still worked diligently, and often more than was required. She'd meet clients in their own homes and go that extra mile to help them. It was a serious business finding a life partner, and Daisy wanted to make sure she matched people properly. She hated the thought of someone getting all excited, and then feeling let down because the person they'd met wasn't who they'd expected.

It was inevitable that it happened occasionally, but Daisy did her best to try to make sure the matches were perfect.

She'd started covering reception when Stella went for her lunch breaks. They worked it so that Stella went for lunch at twelve, Daisy sat in for her and then went for her own lunch at one. They were only supposed to take half an hour for lunch, with a mid morning and mid afternoon break of ten minutes. But Stella abused Daisy's kindness, often taking forty-five minutes for lunch.

Daisy knew that if Greg found out, he'd be furious. He didn't mind Daisy covering reception, in fact, he preferred it because he said Daisy did a better job, but if he knew Stella took longer than her allowed time, he wouldn't be happy.

But, Daisy was one of those people who liked to help everyone, and hated any kind of friction, so she kept quiet. Unfortunately, those people were often the most put upon because people knew they wouldn't make a fuss.

So, she was sitting on reception one lunch time, when Marjorie and Fred arrived.

"Hello, how lovely to see you both." Daisy beamed at

them.

"Hello, dear, we have something for you." Marjorie handed Daisy an envelope.

"Not more money, Marjorie?"

"Open it and see."

Daisy opened the envelope to see a cream and silver embossed invitation. She opened it and gasped. "A wedding? You're getting married? Oh that's wonderful."

She got off her chair, ran around the front of the desk and hugged them both in turn.

"My first ever wedding. I'm so pleased for you both, I really am…" She stopped talking to wipe the tears that had appeared in her eyes. "Sorry." She laughed. "I'm such a cry baby, but I really am delighted for you both."

"And it's all thanks to you, lovely Daisy," Fred said and hugged her again. "If it hadn't been for you, we'd never have met."

"Yes you would, one of the other matchers would have paired you up because you have the same interests."

"Not necessarily," Marjorie said. "I think you're good at your job and maybe the others wouldn't have looked so hard for an old fogey like me. You were kind, caring and interested. Not everyone has time for us elderly folk. Especially people like Miss Frosty Knickers who usually sits on reception, I'm glad I didn't have her."

Daisy laughed at Marjorie's description of Stella, and explained that Stella was the receptionist so wouldn't have dealt with Marjorie anyway.

"Ah, good. So, will you come?"

Daisy looked at the invite. It said she could bring a plus one. She'd take Kris. Or should she invite Greg? After all, it was his agency. The wedding was being held at a lakeside hotel in the Oxfordshire countryside. What a lovely place to get married, especially for an older couple.

"I'd love to, thank you so much. Do you mind if I tell my boss?"

"Of course not, we hoped you would. We've recommended the agency to lots of our now single friends, and when you get to our age, there's quite a few."

"Aww, bless you." Daisy went behind the desk and buzzed through to Greg, to ask him if he'd come out for a moment.

Daisy let the couple tell him their good news, and he was delighted for them, shaking Fred's hand and kissing Marjorie on the cheek.

"I have something for special occasions like this; I'll just go and get it. Would you mind if I also took a photo of you with Daisy? I'd like to put a piece in the local newspaper."

"Ooh, hear that, Fred, we're going to be in the paper." Marjorie was thrilled.

Daisy wasn't sure she wanted to be in there though, but she saw the happy faces of the couple and decided she couldn't refuse really.

Greg came back out with a bottle of champagne – not cheap cava, the real thing – tied with a white bow, and presented it to them.

Marjorie was overwhelmed. "Oh, how wonderful."

"Now, if you both hold that, and Daisy, if you stand beside Fred, that's it, I'll get a nice photo," Greg said.

He clicked away with a digital camera, taking several shots, then showed them all afterwards, and let them choose the ones they liked best for the newspaper.

"Now then, ah…" Greg stopped speaking for a bit then carried on. "I was going to ask if you had a computer so I could email the photos to you, but…"

"Hey, just because we're old, young man, doesn't mean we aren't up with technology. I've got an iPad and a desktop computer," Fred said.

"Excellent, write down your email address and I'll send them to you in a moment."

Marjorie nudged Daisy. "Guess what, he's even got me online. He's been teaching me how to use the pad thingy. Ruddy amazing it is. I like playing Scrabble; it keeps my old brain active." She lowered her voice, leaned towards Daisy and whispered, "the rest of me is being kept active enough, if you know what I mean."

Daisy pretended to be shocked. "Marjorie Williams, you're

terrible." She smiled. "I truly am so pleased for you."

"I won't be Williams for much longer, I'll be a Jones soon. That'll take a bit of getting used to; I've been Williams for over fifty years."

Daisy suddenly realised that actually it must be quite hard for both Marjorie and Fred, getting used to a new partner after a lifetime – longer than Daisy had been alive – with their previous spouses. It must be a huge adjustment. So despite how happy and jolly Marjorie appeared to be, at times it was probably all a bit difficult for her. Daisy thought about her own grandparents and how her gran would feel if gramps died. She quickly changed her train of thought, before it made her cry.

Greg promised he'd get Daisy to phone the couple and let them know when the piece was going to be in the paper, congratulated them again and went back to his office.

"Right, I better get back to work as well. Thank you so much for inviting me to your wedding, I'm looking forward to it."

"We couldn't get married without you there. We'll raise a toast to you tonight." Marjorie held up the bottle of champagne. "What a kind man for giving us this. We'll definitely keep in touch. Bye, dear."

The couple left and Daisy whooped with delight. Her first wedding! She couldn't wait to tell Kris in her lunch break. She picked up the phone and called Greg.

"Yes, Daisy?"

"I just wanted to say what a wonderful touch, giving them a bottle of champagne. Did you just happen to have it in your office or something?"

Greg laughed. "No. I keep a couple of cases specifically for occasions like this. It's not every day our clients get married, and little touches like that mean a lot. It helps to make it extra special. And we always put a piece about an agency wedding in the local paper. I know the editor – Frank – we play golf together actually, so I get mates rates."

"Ah, well, I thought it was a lovely thing to do. Great champagne too."

"Only the best for our clients. So you know your

champagne?"

"A little, it's my favourite alcoholic drink, I just can't afford it. I don't know much, but I do recognise certain names."

"Well, if you're a good girl, you may get a bottle on your birthday. Is Stella back yet?"

Daisy realised Stella had been longer than half an hour again, but she saw her walking up the street so said, "Yep, she's here now."

"She's late, again. I'll have to have a word with her, she's taking liberties. Send her into my office would you."

Oh heck. Now Stella was going to get told off.

"Please don't have a go at her, it's probably my fault she's late. I forgot my sandwich this morning and asked her to get one for me. I expect she was stuck in a queue," Daisy flustered.

"So, if I go into your office, your lunchbox won't be sitting on your desk, will it?"

Damn, she'd forgotten about that.

"Nice try, Daisy but you're not a very good liar. And stop covering for her. I know you've done it before, and I let it go, but I'm not having her take liberties. She doesn't do a lot of work as it is. Send her in please."

"Okay, just go easy, please, for me?"

Greg hung up.

Daisy hung up too and turned to Stella who'd been standing there and obviously heard most of what went on. "I'm really sorry; I tried to cover for you. He wants to see you in his office."

Stella rounded on Daisy and snapped, "Oh bloody great! How did he know I was late in the first place? Tell tales, did you?"

Daisy was outraged. "NO! Stella, you know I wouldn't do that. The elderly couple I matched came in with a wedding invitation and Greg came out to congratulate them. He took photos and...and..." Daisy started to cry. She felt awful, but none of it was her fault.

"It's okay. Stop blubbing. I know you didn't tell him deliberately, but you called him out, and therefore he noticed the time." Stella straightened her shoulders and went into

Greg's office.

Daisy wiped her eyes. That was so unfair. She hadn't done anything wrong and even tried to cover for Stella. It wasn't her fault Stella took liberties and was lazy. She wasn't even a nice person. Daisy wondered why she put up with her. Because she just wanted everyone to get on and be happy. She blew her nose. She could hear Greg's raised voice. She'd never heard him shout before, so knew he must be really angry.

Life was strange. Just now she was so happy to hear that Marjorie and Fred were getting married, and now she was upset and felt as if she was in the wrong, when all she'd done was try to help Stella out, yet again.

Stella flew out of Greg's office, her face like thunder. "Thanks, Daisy, I'll take over now."

"What happened? Are you okay?"

Stella was about to snap, "Do I look like I'm okay?" but with Greg's voice still ringing in her ears, she took a deep breath and said, "I'm fine."

"So you've still got your job?"

"Yes." Stella didn't tell Daisy that she'd already received a verbal warning and was now going to get a written one, but she did acknowledge that none of it was Daisy's fault, so she muttered a perfunctory, "Thanks for trying to cover for me, and for asking him to go easy."

"That's okay. I just want us all to get on. I love my job and don't want anyone falling out or being unhappy."

"Yes, well, life isn't always all pink and rosy, Daisy." Stella sighed at the look on Daisy's face; it was like kicking a puppy when it was already feeling poorly. "Look, I'm okay, you can go back to your office now."

Daisy went and sat down. She was kind of angry with herself for being so soft. Why didn't she just tell Stella it was her own fault she'd been shouted at? That she was lazy and didn't do her job properly? But Daisy wasn't like that. She was a soft, kind girl and even if she did have bad thoughts sometimes, she never voiced them.

It was her time for a break now so she grabbed her lunchbox and set off for the park.

Being out in the sunshine always lifted Daisy's spirits, so she wasn't down for long. She sat on her usual bench and watched the people walking around the park. She loved people watching. She'd sit there and imagine how they'd got together or wonder what interests they had, and if they were with their soul mate or if that was still yet to happen. She leaned back against the bench and turned her face up to the sun, enjoying its warmth.

Her phone bleeped with a text. She rummaged in her bag, knowing it was Kris, he usually texted her at lunch times.

"Hey, Baby D, how's things going today? K xx"

Daisy smiled and replied, her thumbs working speedily. "Great ta. The old couple I matched are getting married, so sweet! D x"

Kris replied. "Aww fab news, Tell me all about it tonight. Stuffed chicken breast okay? I'm being adventurous. K xx"

"Mm delish, can't wait, see you l8r. D x"

Daisy finished her sandwich and threw the crusts to the birds. A duck waddled out of the pond right up to Daisy and quacked at her. She laughed. "You want some bread, do you? Here you go."

She broke a bit off and bent down, holding it out. The duck snatched it from her, went back to the pond and dipped it in the water before gobbling it up. He turned to look at Daisy and with another quack, came waddling back. He sat by her feet, looking at her expectantly.

"Looks like you've made a friend there," a voice said, and Daisy looked up at a man standing by her bench.

He was around the same age as her, with light brown hair. She couldn't see his eyes properly because he had sunglasses on. He was dressed in a suit, so she guessed he was probably on his lunch break too.

"Yes, it seems I have. But he's out of luck; I don't have any more food for him."

"Here, take mine. I've got to get back to work anyway."

The man handed her a bag of duck food.

"Oh thanks. Erm…"

"Simon." The man smiled and took off his sunglasses. He

had brown eyes, rather nice ones."

"Thanks, Simon, I'm Daisy."

"Nice to meet you, Daisy, sorry I've got to rush."

"No problem, thanks for the food."

She watched him walk off. How kind to give her the duck food. Any man who cared about animals was okay in Daisy's book.

The duck was still sitting by her feet and now gave an impatient quack. She laughed. "Okay, okay, here you go." She poured some duck food into the palm of her hand and held it out.

The duck greedily pecked it from her, not in the least bit afraid.

"Ouch, hey fella, be a bit more gentle, will you." He'd nipped the skin on her hand as there was no food left. She poured the rest in and the duck pecked it all up.

Daisy shook the bag out and got up. "Okay, mate, I have to go back to work." She picked up her lunchbox and walked off in the direction of her office. She heard a quack and turned around to see the duck following her. Oh heck.

"No, you can't follow me. Shoo, off you go." She flapped her hands at him and he jumped back a bit. She carried on walking and the duck followed her once more.

Daisy stopped again. "Go away. Go on, off you go." She felt mean shooing him away, but she couldn't have a duck following her to work for goodness sake.

The duck stood looking at her with his little beady eyes and Daisy felt awful.

"Oh, I'm sorry. I probably shouldn't have fed you, but you can't follow me. I don't have any food left. Go back to your friends or family."

She knew that ducks mated for life – ha, they didn't need a dating agency. "Go back to your mate, you must have one, go on, off you go." She flapped the empty bag at him, but he thought it was food and tried to grab it.

An elderly couple passing by, laughed. The woman stopped and said, "We have some bread, let's see if he'll come to us instead." She took out a piece and offered it to the duck, who eagerly accepted it.

"Traitor," Daisy laughed.

"Okay, make your get-away now whilst he's distracted," the woman said, and Daisy quickly left whilst the duck was dunking the bread in the water.

As she entered the agency foyer, Greg was just coming out of his office.

"You look happy; did you have a nice lunch?"

"Yes thanks. I made a new friend."

"Oh?"

Daisy smiled. "A duck. I stupidly fed him with my crusts, then a man gave me the rest of his duck food, and I couldn't get rid of him. He tried to follow me back to work."

Greg looked alarmed. "The man?"

Daisy laughed. "No, the duck."

Greg laughed too. "See, even the wildlife are taken in by your charms. I'm not surprised though."

And Greg meant it. Looking at Daisy standing there with a happy smile on her pretty face, he realised what an attractive girl she was. She had such a nice nature – wouldn't harm a fly and always saw the best in everybody – and a great figure too. Small but firm looking breasts, and shapely legs. Greg was shocked to find himself thinking of her like that. What on earth had come over him? She'd been working there for months now and he'd never thought about her in that way before. Well, not often. He did sometimes watch her as she walked out of his office, that pert bottom swaying from side to side. He gave a little shake. He'd better stop that; she was his employee, and a valuable one too. He coughed, "Aherm, okay we'd better do some work. I noticed that a few new profiles have come in if you'd like to take a look at them."

"Okeydoke, catch you later." She beamed at him, and went into her office.

Over the next few days, Greg found himself watching and thinking about Daisy more and more. It was if a veil had been lifted and he'd suddenly realised what a goddess he had right in front of him. How could he not have noticed her before?

But, she'd never shown the slightest interest in him. He

didn't know much about her personal life – for all he knew she might have a boyfriend – and anyway, he really shouldn't get involved with a work colleague. But that didn't stop him thinking about her, watching her, looking forward to her little emails or phone calls. He wondered if he was having some sort of broody hormonal thing like women did. He was thirty-two and felt ready to settle down, but hadn't found the right person yet, maybe it was just his hormones making every woman seem like a potential mate? But then he thought about Stella on reception and shuddered. He certainly didn't fancy her. Okay, so that was one theory out the window.

Greg didn't know what it was, but he knew he had to remain professional. He couldn't scare Daisy off; she was the best employee he'd had. Thinking about Stella brought up a problem he'd been mulling over for a while. He didn't like her and wanted to get rid of her. But one couldn't just dismiss an employee nowadays; you had to have good reason. She'd been given a verbal and written warning, he just needed one more thing and he could sack her.

Later that afternoon, Daisy sent Greg a quick email, "Getting myself a cup of tea, want a coffee? D"

"Yes please, was just going to come and get one. G"

Daisy poured a coffee for Greg and took it in to him. As she put it on his desk, he went to take it as well and their hands brushed. She almost gasped as she felt a zing pass between them and looked at Greg in shock. He'd obviously noticed it, as he was looking surprised too.

"Oh my goodness did you feel that static?" Daisy said and shook her hand.

Static? Of course, that's what it was. "Yes, I did," Greg said.

"Sorry, it's my fault; I often get a static shock from touching different things. I haven't had it touching another person before though, sorry." She went back out to get her tea and returned to her office.

Greg was glad she'd explained it as static. You heard those stories about people who's fingers brushed and a spark of electricity flew between them and they realised they were meant for each other... That's what it had felt like at first.

Bloody hell, he'd been running the agency for too long, it was turning him into a soppy fool. But he smiled at the memory of their hands touching, which then set him off on a daydream, wondering what it would be like to touch the rest of her.

"Stop it. You can't go there, and she's not interested," he scolded himself.

Daisy was also thinking about the spark that had flown between them. She was sure it was static; it had to be. It was true, she did suffer with static a lot, when she touched her car, escalators and other metal objects, but she'd never sparked off a person before, and was it her imagination, or did Greg look at her in a different way now? He seemed to brighten up when he saw her, and look at her with an interested gleam in his eyes.

She was just being stupid. She knew he was gay, so why would he be interested in her? Maybe he wasn't sure about his sexuality anymore. She decided to talk to Kris about it later and see what he thought.

"I know I didn't imagine it, because Greg felt it too," Daisy said over dinner that evening. Kris had excelled himself with their meal. Chicken breast stuffed with cheese and wrapped in Parma ham. It was delicious.

"Sweetie, like you said it was just static."

"But, I'm sure he takes more notice of me now. He seems to find reasons to see me – forms to sign, a question about a client, etc."

Kris poked at his chicken with his fork and said, "Look, babes, you've been there for ages now, he's probably just more relaxed with you. He's got used to you and is more at ease. He knows he can trust you, probably values your opinion, so wants to know what you think about certain things."

"Yeah, you're probably right."

"I am. Don't start getting fanciful about him again. As you said, he's your boss, he's gay and he's older than you. Now, tell me about this wedding."

"Only if you eat your dinner. Stop poking around at it Kris, it's delicious."

"I am eating it. I can't eat too much; you know I can't risk putting on weight, especially in my profession."

"Kris, you're as skinny as a snake, you're always on the go so burn off anything you eat anyway, and I hate to remind you, but you aren't employed yet, you're still studying."

"Yes, but agents and scouts come to watch our productions, I may be spotted, so I need to look my best."

"You won't put on weight just by eating all your dinner. Eat the chicken and peas and leave the potatoes if you must leave something."

Kris pouted, but cut a piece of chicken and popped it into his mouth. He chewed it then said, "It is really good, isn't it?"

"Yes, so eat up. Christ, I sound like your mother."

"Heaven forbid."

Kris pulled a horrible face and Daisy laughed, knowing how much he disliked his dragon of a mother. He hadn't had much contact with her since he'd plucked up the courage to tell her he was gay and she'd thrown him out.

Daisy sometimes felt really sorry for Kris. His father died when he was only a little boy, and his mother had disowned him. He didn't have any siblings, so Daisy was the closest person in his life and the person he classed as his next of kin.

"I'm watching."

"I'm eating. Now, tell me about your day."

Daisy told him all about Marjorie and Fred coming in with the wedding invite, and Greg giving them a bottle of champagne. "And, I'm going to be in the local paper."

"Ooh, get you. I'm hoping I'll be in the paper when I play Puck in our production. I can't wait, do you think I'll be any good?"

"You'll be brilliant. I couldn't think of a better person to play the role. I can take a plus one with me to the wedding, and I immediately thought of you, but then wondered if I should take Greg seeing as he's the agency boss?"

"Don't you dare. I want to go with you, I love a good wedding." Kris thought for a bit, then said, "I suppose you should offer, though, see what he says."

"I'll ask him tomorrow."

Chapter Eight

All thoughts of asking Greg about the wedding went out of Daisy's head because the following day it was really busy with people calling into the agency, and Daisy had lots of new online profiles to read. It took her a couple of weeks to sort them all out and arrange personal interviews with the ones who took out the premium service.

Then, one morning, as she came out of the ladies' loo, a policeman walked into the foyer and up to reception.

"I'll deal with this, Stella, thank you," Daisy said as she approached. Stella scowled at her.

"Morning, officer, how can I help you? Come to sign up, have you?"

"No, I haven't, Miss…?"

"Dorson, Daisy Dorson, senior consultant."

"I'm afraid I'm on police business, is there anywhere we can talk?"

"Of course. I better tell my boss – the agency owner. Come this way."

She led him to Greg's office and knocked on the door. Greg gave his usual 'come in' and Daisy entered then showed the policeman in.

The officer introduced himself as PC Bullock and asked if they had a certain Charles Smythe on their books, except that wasn't his real name.

"I don't recall anyone of that name, but it might have been before I started," Daisy said.

"Let's have a look." Greg searched through the agency database. "Ah, yes, Charles Smythe took out our premium service just before you joined, Daisy."

"Have you matched him with anyone yet? And what contact details did he give you?" PC Bullock asked.

Greg sat back in his chair. "Okay, before I give out personal information on one of our clients, I know you're in uniform, but can you show me some ID?"

The officer showed his ID and gave Daisy the telephone number of his station. Daisy went into her office and phoned to verify he was a real policeman. He was.

"I need to know if he's been matched with anyone. If so, I want her details as well."

"Of course, I'll check," Greg said scrolling through his screen. "Can I ask why?"

"It's just been brought to our attention that he's a conman. He's joined several agencies under different names, and persuades women to hand over substantial amounts of money before disappearing. Because he uses an alias, and a false address, they have no way of tracking him. I take it he paid for his service with cash?" PC Bullock asked.

Greg checked. He had.

He'd been matched only a month ago with a Mrs Hughes, who'd also joined their premium service.

"Right, thank you for the information. We'd better go and speak to her to find out if she's handed over any money, and if she hasn't, to warn her off."

"I'll remove him from our books immediately. He still has a couple of months left, what do I do about that?" Greg asked.

"Can you keep him for the time being, sir. We need to find this man, so we don't want him to know we're aware of his exploits."

"I have a mobile number; can you track him with that?"

"Yes, if it's on. We've only just found out about this and it seems he has a number of phones. The ones we've checked so far are not in use. He's obviously got what he wanted and moved on. Your lady might be next."

Daisy had been listening with interest. "I have an idea. If Mrs Hughes hasn't yet paid him, I'm assuming he's still going to try to get money out of her. She could arrange a date with him and you can find out where and arrest him."

"Nice idea, but we'd rather not risk her getting involved anymore. We'll find a way to track him down," the policeman said.

"I could do it."

Greg and PC Bullock looked at Daisy. "What do you mean?" Greg asked.

"How old is he?"

Greg checked. "It says thirty-five, but that could be a lie."

"That's about right, sir. All the women have said he's mid thirties."

Daisy was getting excited at the idea she had brewing. "And what age range is he looking for?"

Greg checked again. "Between twenty-eight and fifty."

"Okay, I'm four years younger, but could pass for twenty-eight. He doesn't know me, so, you could contact him and say you think you've found him a perfect match. Lay it on a bit to get him hooked. Say I'm the wealthy daughter of a lord or something, and that we've got a lot of interests in common. We can arrange an initial date – somewhere posh – and then the police can turn up and arrest him." She beamed at them both, pleased with her cleverness.

"No. Absolutely not." Greg was appalled at the idea. He didn't want to risk Daisy getting into any sort of trouble.

"Why not? It would work. If he's after money, what could be better than the daughter of a rich lord or whatever? He'll jump at the chance." She turned to PC Bullock. "What do you think?"

"I'm not sure, Miss. We'd usually get an undercover female officer to do this sort of thing."

"But I'd be much better. I know how the agency works. I know all the right things to say if he asks about why I joined etc. Besides, I won't have to be with him for long, will I? He'll order me a drink and your lot will turn up. Greg, you could take a photo of me and email it to this Charles so he knows what I look like, make it all look kosher."

"He'll take one look at you, and want to meet you immediately," Greg said. He held Daisy's eyes for a long moment, then broke off as PC Bullock spoke.

"It does sound in theory like an excellent idea, but it's not up to me to make the decision. I'll have to run it by my boss."

He said he'd get back to them that afternoon. They needed to work quickly to catch this man before he stole any more money from another poor unsuspecting woman.

In the meantime, Daisy said she'd phone Mrs Hughes to prepare her for a visit from the police, who'd be in plain clothes in case Charles was watching her house. They didn't want to frighten him off.

When the officer had gone, Greg turned to Daisy, his eyes soft and concerned.

"I'd rather you didn't put yourself in a situation that might cause you harm." He laid his hand over hers. "I don't want anything to happen to you, Daisy."

Again, she felt something pass between them. He was making her feel confused. Why was he looking at her like that? But then she realised he had a vested interest. She was his best employee; of course he didn't want to lose her.

"I'll be fine. Don't spoil my fun, I'm looking forward to this, it's the most exciting thing that's happened for ages. Thanks for the concern, but your star employee will be okay."

Greg was in turmoil. She had no idea at all. She thought he was just worried about losing her as a member of staff. Greg wanted to tell her she was so much more than that, but she obviously only saw him as her boss, and he didn't want to frighten her off. What if she left? He'd rather see her everyday as his employee, than not see her at all.

PC Bullock phoned early that afternoon as promised. His boss had agreed to Daisy doing it and they wanted to get things sorted out as soon as possible. They'd been to see Mrs Hughes, and thankfully she'd not yet parted with any money. At their request, she'd phoned Charles and left a message to say she didn't think their relationship was working out, and didn't want to see him anymore.

"So, he'll be looking for someone else now," Daisy said.

Greg decided they wouldn't say Daisy was a daughter of nobility, because Charles might try to look her up online, and wouldn't find her. Better to just drop in that she was a financially secure young woman – she'd been left a large sum of money by an elderly aunt or something.

He picked up the phone and left a message for Charles to call him back. He did so within ten minutes.

Greg said he'd just got someone on their books who Charles might like.

"A real stunner too, and wealthy by the looks of it. Money left to her by an aunt or something. She's young, only just twenty-eight, I hope that's not a problem?" He raised his eyebrows at Daisy as he spoke into the phone.

She smiled and nodded encouragingly. He was playing it really well.

"I can email a photo so you can see her, if that helps?" Greg gave Daisy the thumbs up. So far, so good.

"Just sending it now." Greg waited a few seconds until Charles had received it.

"Hi. Yes, she is beautiful. I thought you'd like her." Greg looked at Daisy, and again held her gaze for longer than usual. She blushed under his scrutiny."

"A date tonight? Oh I'm not sure, Mr Smythe, it may be a bit short notice for our client." Daisy was nodding her head, and Greg didn't know if that meant yes, it was too short notice, or yes, she'd do it.

He asked if Charles could call him back in about fifteen minutes and in the meantime, he'd phone Christina – Daisy's suggestion for the name – to see if she could make it at such short notice.

"Yes, I'll do it tonight," Daisy said. "Might as well get it over with. Maybe it's too short notice for the police though. I know they want to get things moving, but this is quite quick. Phone them and ask."

So Greg phoned and asked for PC Bullock, who put him on hold and then returned to say, if Daisy was willing to do it that evening, they'd go for it. They'd await her call telling them where she was going to meet the crook.

"Ooh, this is exciting, isn't it?" Daisy said, her eyes shining.

"No. Frankly, I'm against the whole thing, Daisy. I can't

believe you've put yourself up for this."

"Greg, I'll be fine. I promise. Think of the publicity we'll get – 'Agency helps find conman', that sort of thing. You can give the exclusive story to your editor friend."

Greg had to admit it would be good for the company. But he was more concerned about Daisy's safety.

"What if, when the police pounce to arrest him, he attacks you – he could have a knife or a gun even."

Daisy laughed. "Greg, I'll be in a posh restaurant. And if he's going to try to get money out of me at some point, I should imagine he'll be utterly charming."

"Just be careful please."

"I know we're not allowed personal calls, but can I please phone Kris to let him know I won't be home for dinner this evening?"

"Of course. Then once we've arranged the date, you can go home."

Daisy dialled Kris's number. His voicemail came on which meant he was busy so she left him a message saying she was out on work business that evening, and was leaving work now, to get ready.

She knew that would get his interest. Just wait until he found out, he'd think it was brilliant.

When Charles called back, Greg said that Christina was looking forward to their date, and she'd suggested they have dinner in a well-known, exclusive boutique hotel, which obviously suited the conman well. Neither needed to carry anything for recognition, because he'd seen a photo of her and she knew what he looked like. Greg arranged for them to meet at seven pm so they could have a drink beforehand.

Greg then phoned the police, who said they'd contact the hotel to let them know what was going on and would make sure a couple of plain clothes officers were there, posing as diners, as well as a couple more in the lounge area, who could be available if necessary.

"Are you sure you want to do this?" Greg asked Daisy as he hung up.

"Yes, I'll be fine."

"And you know what he looks like?" Greg moved his computer screen around so Daisy could look at Charles – or whatever he was called – again.

She had to admit he was rather hot. No wonder women fell for him.

"I might go as well, just to make sure you're okay," Greg said.

"No, don't. I won't be able to relax knowing you're there watching my every move. And won't he recognise you?"

"No. None of our photos are on the website and I didn't match him, the girl who left to go to France did, so he doesn't know what I look like." Greg didn't believe in putting staff photos up on the website, it left them open to potential contact from weirdos.

"Greg, I'll be okay. I'll phone you after if it'll make you feel better?"

"Yes, please. Okay, you can go now, and I won't dock it from your wages." Greg grinned. Then he stopped her and grabbed her hand. "Good luck, Daisy, please be careful."

"I will."

She collected her lunchbox and handbag, and walked out into the late afternoon sunshine.

It was just gone four pm, so she'd only left an hour early. She wondered if she should go for a quick walk in the park but decided to drive straight home. She was still confused over Greg's concern for her. It felt like more than a boss worrying about his employee, but how could it be when he was gay?

Kris got home just after five and was full of questions about what Daisy was up to that evening. She expected him to be excited about her bit of detective work, but he was horrified. He said much the same as Greg had.

"Baby D, you are not going. I simply cannot let you put yourself in danger like that." He dramatically held his hand against his chest.

"Oh for Christ's sake, Kris, don't you start as well. I had enough of it from Greg. I'm not putting myself in danger. Think about it. This guy thinks he's meeting a wealthy woman who he's going to try to persuade to give him money at some later date. He's going to be on his best behaviour."

"Yes, sweetie, until the police pop up, then he could go crazy. He'll blame you and what if he has a weapon on him? Oh I can't bear it." Kris sat down on a kitchen chair.

"I know you're studying to be an actor, but don't be so dramatic." Daisy stood looking at him with her arms folded.

Kris gasped. "Darling, so cruel. I'm hurt." He pretended to swoon in the chair, with his arm across his forehead like the old movie stars did, and Daisy giggled. He knew just how to make her laugh.

"Come here, you idiot."

He got up and went to her and she hugged him, then he sat on the nearest chair and pulled her onto his lap. She played with his hair and said, "It's so sweet that you worry about me but I'll be okay – promise. I've got it all worked out – what I'm going to say to the questions he might ask me. Where I was schooled, where I work and live etc. I'll phone you as soon as it's over. You can drive me in."

"Can I drive your car?"

"Yes, but drop me a little way away in case he's already there. Someone posh wouldn't be arriving in my little Toyota. So I'll walk in. If he asks, I'll say a friend dropped me off, which is true."

"Okay then. But let me know as soon as he's been arrested. Oh I wish I was there to watch it all."

"That's what Greg said," Daisy moved off his lap. "He was acting really weird though."

"In what way?"

"Well, really concerned. He held my hand and gazed into my eyes. I dunno, but more than a boss should, if you know what I mean."

"He probably cares about you. You're his number one employee, and he's a nice guy, so of course he wouldn't want you to get hurt."

"I suppose. Hey you'll never guess what happened in the park?"

And she told him all about the duck, and the man who'd given her his duck food.

"Ooh, maybe you'll meet him again and it'll be the start of a beautiful romance."

"Ha, I doubt it; he was just being friendly and needed to get rid of his duck food."

"Darling, you are so practical."

Daisy laughed, then leaving Kris to make himself something to eat, she went and got ready for the evening ahead.

Chapter Nine

Daisy dressed in her best little black dress with an electric blue silk scarf draped casually across her shoulders, and her diamond drop earrings that her parents had bought for her twenty-first.

"Sweetie, you look a-maz-ing," Kris said when she came downstairs. "How could any man resist you?"

"Thanks."

She wiped her hands on the towel hanging over the kitchen cupboard. "I'm a bit nervous now."

"You can always call it off; you don't have to go through with it."

"I'll be fine. Get me a quick drink to calm my nerves."

Kris poured her a small glass of wine. "Not too much, you haven't eaten, and you need a clear head. By the way, I made some pasta for you. You probably won't get around to eating, so you'll be starving when you get home."

"Thanks, Kris, what would I do without you?"

"Cry for the rest of your life, I hope."

Daisy laughed. She looked at the clock. Six thirty. "Okay, you better drive me in. I'd like to arrive a bit early, it gives a good impression."

And, with her heart pounding, she got into the car, ready to put 'operation Christina' into practise, and praying it would go well.

She was glad Kris had dropped her around the corner from the hotel because it gave her a few minutes to gather herself and take some deep breaths. She paused outside the hotel, smoothed down her dress and went through the doors.

She walked into the lounge and saw that Charles was already there, seated at a table in front of the windows, facing the lounge entrance, obviously, so that he could look out for her. She noticed there was an ice bucket containing a bottle of champagne on the table. Charles raised a hand in greeting.

Daisy stopped herself from looking around to see if she could spot any plain clothes police, and with a smile, walked over. Charles stood to greet her, and kissed her on both cheeks.

"How lovely to meet you, and can I say how stunning you look."

"Thank you, you look nice too." She returned the compliment.

He pulled out the chair beside the one he'd been sitting in. He moved it so that it wasn't too close to his and Daisy sat down. As she put her clutch bag on the floor, another couple arrived and sat at a table to her left. Daisy wondered if they were the police, or just an innocent couple having a romantic night out.

Charles sat down, and poured her a glass of champagne. "Cheers."

Daisy accepted the drink and clinked her glass with his. "Cheers, here's to a good evening."

"So," Charles asked, "why is a beautiful girl like you with a dating agency?"

"Because I wanted to meet a more discerning type of man. I find many of the men my age are just too immature."

She took another sip of champagne, playing for time, and went on, "I like the finer things in life, not a pizza with a bottle of beer." She gave a little laugh. "I also wanted to meet someone with similar interests and tastes."

"I totally agree." Charles smiled. "There's such a lack of sophistication in young people nowadays. Now, tell me all about yourself, where do you work?"

Daisy was glad she'd already decided on her answers, and went on to tell him that she'd studied design and now had her own company. She said she made one-off, exclusive fabric coverings for a wide range of items. She told him she'd been in Country Life and a few of the other magazines.

Ha, she was good. She tried not to giggle. Never mind Kris studying drama, maybe she ought to as well.

Charles was obviously impressed, as he hung on to every word she said.

"And what about you?" Daisy asked.

Charles gave her a sexy smile. "Never mind me; I'd rather hear more about you." He sipped his drink and gazed into her eyes.

Just at that moment, Daisy was aware of some movement. She instinctively looked up, to see two men approaching. The men stopped in front of them. One showed his identification and said, "Charles Smythe? Police. We'd like a word with you."

Charles panicked and stood up, ready to make a dash for it. The police were in front of him so he went sideways, but Daisy, who had also stood, was in his way. He pushed her, just as one of the policemen moved in that direction. Daisy staggered and fell, hitting her face and head with a sickening thud on the metal legs of the table beside her.

***

Kris checked his watch, and the clock. Eight pm. Surely Daisy was out by now. The police wouldn't have made her sit with him for an hour, they'd want to pick him up as soon as possible. He couldn't wait any longer so dialled Daisy's number. Her phone was answered by a male voice.

"Who's that?" Kris asked.

"I'm John, one of the A&E nurses at the city hospital."

"Oh my God, what's happened to Daisy? Is she okay? OH MY GOD, I KNEW SOMETHING WOULD GO WRONG," Kris shouted hysterically.

"Please, calm down, sir, who's calling?"

"I'm Kris, her flatmate, we're best friends."

"Okay, Kris, Daisy's had an accident. She'll be okay, but she's hit her head pretty badly and we're keeping her in overnight for observation."

"I'm on my way."

Kris flung the phone down, grabbed his keys and ran out to

the car.

He was at the hospital in record time and hoped he hadn't been caught by any speed cameras.

He asked at reception where Daisy was and was shown into a side ward. He gasped when he saw her, and burst into tears. She had a nasty cut on the side of her face, from just above her eyebrow towards her ear, which had been stitched up, and her poor, beautiful face was swollen and bruised. She looked so small, pale and helpless lying in the hospital bed, that it broke Kris's heart.

"She looks a bit of a mess," the nurse said, "but she'll be fine with some rest. The bruising will fade and the scar won't show that much. She's got concussion – she was knocked unconscious – so we're keeping her in overnight. Don't get upset," the nurse said as Kris cried again, "she'll be okay. She just needs plenty of sleep so her brain can recover."

The nurse patted Kris's shoulder and said he could sit with Daisy if he liked.

Kris pulled a chair up close to the side of the bed and spoke softly. "Hey, sweetie, it's me, Kris. I'm here and I'm staying until you're allowed home. Oh, my poor baby." He gently smoothed back her hair from her forehead and as he did, she stirred and opened her eyes.

"Kris? Where am I?" Her voice was all small and wobbly.

"Shh, don't talk, honey. Just close your eyes and get better. I'm here."

"Champagne…designs…stop him…" She wasn't making any sense, but Kris supposed that was the concussion.

"Babe, you're in hospital. You fell and hit your head. I don't know how, or where, but you're okay. You've got a nasty cut on your face, and you'll be a bit sore for a while."

Daisy frowned and moaned in pain. "Got him?"

"I don't know. I don't care either. All I care about is you. Close your eyes. We'll sort everything out tomorrow."

"Police…"

"Shh, close your eyes, that's it, off to sleep."

Kris got up and pulled the curtains around the bed to give them some privacy. He was angry. Angry that Greg had allowed

Daisy to put herself in danger, and angry that he himself hadn't stopped her. She had assured him everything would be okay, but how could she have known that? It was a stupid idea, and one that had got his precious Daisy hurt. Greg should never have agreed to it, nor the police.

As Kris sat there holding Daisy's hand and occasionally stroking her hair back, a nurse came and said, "There's someone else who wants to see Daisy."

"Who?"

"A Greg Hanson."

"Tell him to get lost."

"He says he's Daisy's boss and is worried sick about her."

"It's because of him that she's here. Tell him to go away."

The nurse disappeared and returned a few moments later. "He says he's not going anywhere until he's seen Daisy."

Kris sighed. Best to let him see her, then tell him to sod off. "Okay, show him in, but he can see her, then go."

"He won't be allowed to stay long, even you shouldn't be here."

"I'm not going anywhere," Kris said, and he meant it. He'd already decided he was going to ask for a blanket and sleep in the chair beside Daisy all night.

Greg walked into the enclosed space and groaned when he saw Daisy.

"Yes, take a long look at her, because this is all your fault." Kris spat at him.

"You must be Kris? She's always talking about you." Greg stared across at Daisy. "I am so sorry. Poor Daisy."

Greg ran a shaking hand across his chin and looked as if he was going to cry and Kris felt a little sorry for him. He knew it wasn't really Greg's fault.

Greg moved closer. "Can I talk to her?"

"I want her to sleep, the nurses said it's the best thing for her, it'll help rest her brain – she's got concussion – but yes go on, just for a minute, then you'll have to leave."

Greg went up on the other side of the bed and tentatively touched Daisy's hand, then he leaned down and said, "Daisy, it's Greg. I am so sorry. Don't worry about work, you take as much time off as you need, we want you to get better. I'll see you soon." He wanted to lean down and kiss her, but with Kris watching his every move, he decided against it and just stroked her head then moved away.

"I tried to stop her, I swear. I told her it was a ridiculous idea and that I wouldn't allow it. But she was so excited. She said I was spoiling her fun and that it would be good publicity for the agency. I even said I'd go there as a customer so I could keep an eye on her, but she didn't want me to." Greg bit his bottom lip.

"I tried to talk her out of it too. I said the guy might have a weapon and she could get hurt, but she just laughed it off. Daisy has a mind of her own; neither of us could have stopped her." Kris stared at Daisy and sighed. "Thank God she's going to be okay – well, they say she'll recover. I hope so."

He looked up at Greg. "How did you find out? And do you know what actually happened? All I know is she's hurt."

"The police phoned me. When they approached Charles Smythe – they've got him by the way – he tried to run and pushed Daisy out of the way. She fell and cracked her head. The police took him away and the hotel called an ambulance for Daisy."

"She'll be pleased to know they've got him, that she didn't get hurt for nothing. I don't know when she'll be back at work, I'm going to look after her and make sure she's fully recovered."

"Of course. She can take as much time as she needs. I really am sorry. She means the world to me, I…" Greg was going to say that he cared for her a lot, but it wouldn't seem appropriate. As far as Daisy was concerned, he was just her boss, so he said he'd be in touch, and left.

Kris frowned and pondered on what Greg had said. "She means the world to me." Strange thing for a boss to say about one of his employees. And Daisy was right; he didn't come across as a homosexual man. Kris wondered what was going on, but didn't have time to dwell on it because a nurse came and said, "Right, my love, time for you to go."

"I'm not going anywhere."

"You've been here for ages now – you shouldn't really be here at all. Daisy needs to rest, and we need to do her obs. You can't be here."

"Please," Kris pleaded, "I won't get in the way or disturb her. I'm not leaving. What if something happens and she dies in the night? I want to be with her if she does."

"She's not going to die."

"You know that for absolute definite, do you?" Kris challenged.

"Well, no, of course we can't be a hundred percent sure, but we're ninety-nine percent certain."

Kris folded his arms determinedly. "I'm staying."

"But where will you sleep?"

"In this chair. You could get me a blanket, I'll be okay. Please, she's my best friend ever; we love each other to bits. We're going to marry each other if we haven't found a partner by the time we're thirty-five," he stated, as if that would make her change her mind.

Funnily enough it did. The nurse looked at the young man and saw how much he cared for Daisy. If they kept the curtains around, no-one would know he was there and they could still do her obs, he wasn't really in the way.

She smiled at him. "I'll get you a couple of blankets. Would you like a cup of hot chocolate or something?"

Kris's eyes lit up, he loved hot chocolate. "Yes please. Thank you, I won't be in the way, I promise."

The nurse nodded and went to get him a drink and some blankets.

Kris leaned down to Daisy. "I'm still here, sweetie. I'll be here all night long, so just you rest, and hopefully you'll be better in the morning."

***

When Greg got indoors he poured himself a large whisky. He was distraught at what had happened to Daisy, and angry with himself for letting her go ahead with the stupid plan. As her boss, he should have put his foot down and said she couldn't do it. But he didn't have any right to stop her. It wasn't in company time, so he had no grounds for refusing. She was an adult and knew her own mind. It was just extremely unfortunate that she'd got hurt.

Greg sat on the sofa, his head in his hands, then he took a huge gulp of his drink and waited whilst the alcohol worked its way through his system. He needed something to take the edge off; otherwise he knew he wouldn't sleep.

When he'd seen Daisy lying there looking all small and vulnerable, he'd just wanted to take her in his arms and make the hurt go away. He already cared about her, but finding out she'd been injured had caused him physical pain – the thought of losing her almost killed him – and he realised just how much she meant to him.

Her overprotective flatmate wouldn't have been too amused if he had swept her into his arms though. Actually, he was probably doing Kris a disservice, anyone could see how much he loved Daisy; the poor guy was in bits.

Greg decided he'd phone the hospital in the morning and find out how she was. She could take as much time off as she needed to recover – with full pay – and maybe, when she was better, he'd take her out to dinner and find some way to let her know how he felt about her.

Chapter Ten

Kris didn't get a lot of sleep, what with the nurses coming every couple of hours to do Daisy's blood pressure, pulse and temperature, so he was awake early the next morning when she opened her eyes and tried to look around her.

"Morning, sweetie. It's okay, don't panic," Kris said as Daisy looked alarmed. He reached out and stroked her forehead. "You're in hospital, you fell and hit your head."

Daisy closed her eyes, then opened them again. "Charles, he tried to run. Did they get him?"

"Yes, they did; he's under arrest and is probably now waiting to be questioned."

"Thank heavens." Daisy winced. "My head really hurts."

"I'm not surprised, babe, you gave it a hell of a knock."

"Do I look as awful as I feel?"

"You look a bit battered, but still beautiful."

She put her hand up and tentatively felt along the stitched up cut. "That doesn't feel good – ouch." She winced again, shifted and tried to sit up. "Ooh, my body aches too."

"That must be from falling over. I'm so glad to hear you talking. I was worried sick about you."

"What time is it?" Daisy moved her head to look at the ward clock. "Six am. Kris, you're here early."

"I've been here all night."

"All night long? Where did you sleep?"

"Right here, beside you."

Daisy's eyes filled with tears. "Oh, Kris, you didn't?"

"Yep. I wasn't going anywhere, girlfriend. If you were going to peg out on us, I wanted to be with you, so you didn't die alone."

At that, Daisy couldn't control the floodgates and she burst into noisy tears. A nurse came over to see what was going on.

"Are you okay, Daisy?"

Daisy wiped her eyes, moaned because it hurt, and said, "Yes, just really touched at this crazy idiot spending the night here."

The nurse smiled at Kris and said, "You've got a good one here. He refused to leave your side. He obviously loves you a lot."

"The feeling's mutual." Daisy smiled through her tears. "Thanks, Kris; I don't know what I'd do without you."

"Now, young lady, you're looking better, and much more with it. The doctors will be around later. Depending on what they say, you should be able to go home. I'll see if I can get you a cup of tea. And one for you too?" the nurse asked looking at Kris.

"Yes please."

Kris pressed the button that raised the back of the bed up, and put Daisy's pillows behind her to support her. "There you go, that's better."

"I think you've missed your calling, you should be a nurse instead," Daisy sniffed.

"Ha ha. You're obviously feeling better."

Daisy laughed then winced again. "Ouch, my face. Get my bag, Kris, I want to see."

"You sure? You looked a bit frightful, you'll scare yourself."

"Just get it…please."

Kris passed her bag to her, and she rummaged around for her compact. She opened it and studied her face.

"Christ on a bike! Oh, Kris, look at the state of me." She turned her head so she could see the stitched cut. "Thank heavens it missed my eye. A bit further over…"

"Yes, you could have been blinded. And you've got concussion. You weren't making a lot of sense last night; you were mumbling all sorts of weird stuff."

"Sounds like you after a heavy night out."

"Ha bloody ha. Seriously, babe, I'm so glad to see you

behaving a bit more like yourself."

"I have an awful headache, not surprising really. These bruises will disappear; I just hope the cut doesn't scar too much."

"I don't think it will. Whoever stitched it did a good job. If I ever see that Charles, I'll kill him for pushing you over."

"I don't think he meant to, I was blocking his escape route, he just panicked. I'm glad they've got him though."

"We should never have let you do it. I said you'd get hurt, didn't I?"

"So you're a psychic as well as a nurse. We?"

"What do you mean?"

"You said we should never have let you."

"Me and Greg. He came to see you last night. He felt really bad for not stopping you."

"Greg came here? I don't remember."

"You were asleep. I wasn't exactly friendly at first. I blamed him."

"Oh, Kris, it wasn't his fault any more than it was yours. I wanted to do it. So it's my fault. You shouldn't have taken it out on him." Daisy put her compact back in her bag and handed the bag to Kris.

"It's okay, I backed down. I realised it wasn't his fault, and he was worried about you." Kris put her bag beside his chair.

"Was he? How worried?"

"Very. He said you meant the world to him."

"Did he?" Daisy sighed. "Why do all the nicest men in my life have to be gay? Well, except my dad of course."

Kris looked perplexed. "Hmm, I don't know if Greg is or not. I really couldn't tell. I only spoke to him for a short time, but…I dunno."

"Well, I sometimes wonder, especially when I catch him looking at me or he says sweet things, but Stella told me he is, he knows about that gay agency, and I caught him arranging dinner with someone called Robin, so he must be. Anyway, I wonder when I can go back to work?"

"Daisy, you're not going back until you're properly well again—NO." Kris held his hand up as Daisy started to protest.

"I am definitely putting my foot down on this occasion. You've had a nasty bang to your head, with concussion. You are not going back until you're one hundred percent fit. It's all worked out. I'm taking a few days off – I told the drama school it's for personal reasons – and Greg said you can have as much time as you need. So, no arguing."

Daisy knew when Kris was serious. Besides, her head was banging, and she felt tired, so perhaps a couple of days off would be necessary.

When the doctors arrived later that morning, they checked Daisy's obs and asked her a few questions such as 'Where are you? What were you doing before you fell? Name the months in reverse order'.

Daisy managed to complete the tasks, and the doctor said she could go home. She had to have someone with her for the next couple of days, and was advised to get plenty of rest, avoid stressful situations and no alcohol.

"When can I go back to work?"

"When you're fully recovered," the doctor said. "That may be in three days, or it may be a week. But only go back when you feel completely well. Take paracetamol for the headache, but it should clear later today or tomorrow."

Kris drove Daisy home and settled her on the sofa with a blanket, cup of tea and packet of chocolate digestives.

"Now, just call me if you need anything. Are you sure you wouldn't rather go to bed?"

"No, I'm comfy here. I'll watch a bit of daytime TV. Thanks, Kris, you're the bestest friend anyone could have."

"You're welcome, sweetie." Kris kissed the top of her head and went into the kitchen. He was going to make her his macaroni cheese for lunch, and there was a garlic baguette in the freezer somewhere – they'd have that with it.

When he checked Daisy a little later, she was fast asleep. Kris turned the TV down and pulled the blanket up over her.

He wondered if Greg might phone. He didn't want the ringing to wake Daisy, so he decided he'd phone Greg and bring him up to date. He phoned the office and Stella put him through. He said Daisy was now at home and would be off for at least two days, maybe more.

"Not a problem, as long as she needs. I was wondering… erm, would it be okay to call in and see her? I'd like to bring some flowers to say thanks for what she did, and sorry she got hurt."

Kris agreed he could call in when he'd finished work.

Daisy slept for a couple of hours, and when she awoke, she said, "I'm starving." She looked around for Kris, then called out, "Mm what's that smell?"

Kris came out of the kitchen. "Macaroni cheese and garlic bread."

"Oh, you're an angel. I'm so hungry I could eat a scabby dog."

"Euww, girlfriend that is gross. Stay there!" Kris ordered as Daisy went to get up.

"Kris, I need the loo."

"Oh. Well, back on the sofa after, I'll bring your food in on a tray."

Daisy polished off her meal as if she hadn't eaten for a week, and was surprised to see Kris eat all his too.

"That was delish, thanks. And look at you, you've finished the lot."

"I haven't eaten since early yesterday evening, and for some reason I was ravenous. Must be the shock and stress."

"Same here. I feel tons better – my headache isn't as bad as it was this morning, I'm just tired. They say sleep and food is the best medicine." She stretched her arms above her head, then yawned. "I could sleep again though. Is it okay if I go to bed for an hour?"

"Of course it is, for as long as you like. If you're still asleep when the boss man calls, I'll tell him."

"Greg's coming round?"

"Yes, after work. He wants to bring you some flowers."

"Ah, that's sweet. Don't let me sleep for ages then, wake me up in time to make myself presentable."

"Babe, he saw you last night, I wouldn't worry how you look."

"But I can't have my boss seeing me look a mess."

"Whatever. Off you go, I'll wake you later."

Daisy slept for another two hours, and woke of her own accord. She lay in bed thinking over the events of the last couple of days. That morning her head had felt a bit woolly and she'd had to concentrate, but it was a lot clearer and she could think more easily now.

She didn't regret 'operation Christina'. It was unfortunate that she'd got hurt, but that was only because Charles had panicked. At least she'd helped put a stop to his scams. And Kris was an absolute darling for the way he was looking after her, although she felt guilty for the worry she'd caused him.

She then thought about Greg. Why would he tell Kris that she meant the world to him? It wasn't the sort of thing you said about your employee. But, those lingering looks he'd given her, those sparks of electricity that passed between them when they touched. She'd said it was static, but was it?

She wondered what Greg was playing at and decided that whatever it was, she'd find out. She was secretly looking forward to his visit later, even if she did look a mess.

The flowers Greg brought were fabulous. A huge bouquet that must have cost him a fortune, and three boxes of Maltesers. Daisy laughed when she saw them. "I can't eat all those, I'll get fat."

"No, you won't. And anyway it's a known fact that chocolate aids recovery," Greg joked.

Daisy's eyes twinkled. "Is it now? In that case you better bring me another three boxes."

Greg laughed. "I'll order a crate load."

He'd maintained an easy rapport so far, and hadn't said anything slightly unbosslike, and Daisy again wondered if she'd been imagining things. He was her boss, she was his employee, end of.

"So," she asked after they'd been chatting for a while, "when can I come back to work?"

Kris jumped in. "Not until you're completely better."

Greg nodded. "I agree. You stay home for another couple of days at least, Daisy."

Daisy folded her arms, which meant she was getting into seriously determined mode.

But Kris decided that for once, he was putting his foot down.

So he folded his arms and said, "Before you get stroppy – I know that arms folded stance – there's no point arguing or trying to worm round me. You are not, I repeat, NOT, going back to work for another two days at least."

Kris puffed out a breath and fanned his hot face. He'd never been so assertive in his life. Well, not in real life anyway. He did when he was acting, but that was different.

Before Daisy could object, Greg said, "I completely agree. In fact if you turn up for work, I will personally bring you home again, so I wouldn't even try."

Greg looked up at Kris, who said, "Nice one, boyfriend," and they high fived each other.

Daisy looked exasperated. "I don't stand a chance against you two, do I?"

"Nope," the two men chorused.

Daisy huffed. "But what am I going to do all day? I can't sit here watching daytime telly, it'll bore me stupid."

"You could read," Kris suggested.

Daisy thought for a bit. "Hmm, I do have a couple of paperbacks I haven't got around to reading. But I want to be involved in work. I love my job. Greg, you said there's a few new clients. I want to know who."

"You're just a nosebag." Kris laughed.

Greg rubbed his chin. "Okay, here's an idea. Do you have a laptop?"

"Yes."

"Right. If you promise to stay at home resting, I'll email the new profiles across to you. I can also set you up with remote access so you can get into the office system via your laptop. But, I don't want you sitting on it all day, Daisy, you're meant to be resting."

"Can you limit it?" Kris asked.

"Yes, in fact I can. Okay, how about a couple of hours a day? Say ten till eleven in the morning, and two to three in the afternoon, that way she'll get plenty of rest in between?"

"Good idea," Kris said.

"Great, my best friend and my boss ganging up on me," Daisy huffed.

"Take it or leave it," Greg said.

"I'll take it, thanks."

So for the next few days, Daisy rested at home, reading, watching a bit of TV – she'd found a channel showing repeats of old comedies, which she and Kris sat laughing at together – and reading through the new profiles. And, when she was able to get into the system, she checked recently added profiles. She knew the other matchers had probably already done it, but quite often, one would spot something the others had missed.

Greg called in again with another supply of Maltesers, which she and Kris shared as they watched TV.

Daisy ended up staying off for the rest of the week, and apart from being fed up with the way she looked – the cut was still evident and the bruising had gone from black and blue to greeny yellow – she was back to her usual, bright, cheerful self.

***

When Daisy walked into the foyer Monday morning, Stella looked up and asked her how she was.

"We were all horrified when we heard what had happened. Good job you weren't more seriously hurt. I have to say it was brave of you, I wouldn't have done it."

Daisy was surprised; Stella looked as if she actually meant it.

Greg stuck his head out of his door and beckoned Daisy into his office.

"So," he asked as she sat down opposite him, "how are you? All better?"

"Yep, all back to normal – well, apart from the cut, and green coloured face." She pointed to the green tinge where the bruises were fading. "I look like the Incredible Hulk's sister." She laughed.

"You look lovely, as always."

Daisy raised her eyebrows and Greg quickly cleared his throat.

"Erm, Daisy, now that you're better, I want to thank you properly for the work you've done and for putting yourself in danger like that. Would you like to have dinner in Rialto's one evening?"

Rialto's was an expensive Italian restaurant. Daisy had never been, but often wondered what it was like.

"Oh, Greg, that's kind of you, but I don't think."

"It's on me. Just as a thank you. I feel really bad about you getting hurt."

"But it was my decision to do it."

"Yes, but if you hadn't been working here, it wouldn't have happened, would it. So I am kind of responsible."

"You've already thanked me with the beautiful flowers and the endless supply of Maltesers."

Greg frowned. "Don't you like Italian food?"

"I love it." Daisy could see no reason to refuse, so she accepted. "Thank you, it's really kind of you."

Greg smiled, delighted that she'd accepted. Maybe away from work, and her flatmate, he could finally tell her how he felt.

They arranged to go on Friday evening, so that they could have a drink and not worry about work the next day.

Greg asked her not to mention it to the other employees though.

"I wouldn't, I don't discuss you with other members of staff."

As she sat in the park on her usual bench at lunch time, she wondered why Greg didn't want any of the other employees to know. Maybe he worried that they might get jealous and accuse him of favouritism. Especially Stella. Daisy knew there was tension between the pair.

She was just breaking her crusts into pieces, when a duck came waddling out of the pond and stood in front of her.

"I don't believe it. You're not the same duck, are you?" Daisy bent down to look at him. Yep he was. She remembered that he had a funny black streak on his beak, which looked like an exclamation mark.

"Surely you don't recognise me?" Then she laughed at her stupidity. Of course he didn't, she was just a person with food. "Duh, stupid me," she said.

"Hello again, Mrs Doolittle."

The voice startled Daisy and she jumped. It was the man who'd given her his duck food a few weeks ago.

"I'm sorry; I didn't mean to frighten you. Oh, what's happened?" He pointed to her face.

Daisy self-consciously touched her healing cut. "Long story. Short version, I got pushed over and bashed the side of my head. Ended up in hospital with this cut and concussion."

"Ah, that's why I haven't seen you." He frowned as he tried to remember her name. "Daisy, isn't it?"

"Yep, you have a good memory. I'm sorry, I can't remember yours."

"That's okay, you've had concussion. It's Simon. Are you better now?"

"Yes, thanks. I know it's daft talking to a duck, but I'm amazed to see it's the same one I was feeding last time we met. That was about three weeks ago, or was it four? Whatever, I was surprised he remembered me, then I realised I was being stupid. It's not me he recognises, I'm just someone with food." Daisy rolled her eyes.

Simon smiled. "Actually, he may well recognise you. Ducks have a pretty good long-term memory – they have to remember different navigational routes when they're flying – so it may not be as daft as you think. He'll certainly recognise you if he sees you every day."

The duck was growing impatient and with a quack, made a grab at the bread Daisy was holding.

"Oi, you." She laughed and fed him.

Simon sat down beside her. "So, where do you work? It can't be far if you have your lunch here."

Daisy told him where she worked and asked him about his job. He worked in the solicitor's office just a few doors down from the agency. He told her he was twenty-nine and had been qualified for three years. Daisy told him she'd only been in the job a few months.

"But I absolutely love it. It's not what I originally intended – I have a degree in design – but I couldn't imagine doing anything else now."

"You're obviously good with people." Simon looked at his watch. "Oh heck, I'd better go."

"Me too," Daisy said, standing up.

"We can walk back together if you like?" Simon was a bit unsure and Daisy liked that about him.

"That'd be good."

They walked to their offices, chatting companionably on the way. "See you tomorrow maybe?" Simon stopped as they got to Daisy's building.

"Sure. Enjoy the rest of the day," Daisy said with a smile, and went in thinking how nice Simon seemed, and hoping she'd see him again.

Later that afternoon she was looking through some new profiles, when one from someone called Cheryl caught her eye. Under 'Interests' Cheryl had put 1940s re-enacting. Something clicked in Daisy's mind and she tried to remember what.

That was it, Tom, the man who liked dressing up at weekends. Well, Cheryl obviously liked dressing up too, maybe they'd get on.

It took Daisy a while to find Tom because she couldn't remember his surname. It was Brooks. She was glad he was still a member.

Right, what did it say about him? She read his profile to refresh her memory. Yep, that was it, multi-period re-enactor. She wondered if Cheryl would be interested in other eras or if she was only into the forties.

Daisy gave her a call.

"Cheryl? Hi, I'm Daisy from The Love Shack. I've got your profile up in front of me, and just might have someone to match you with. Yep that was quick. We set to work immediately to help our clients find a partner – we are the best agency around."

She asked Cheryl if she'd be interested in other eras, and Cheryl said she would. She loved all periods in history, even though the forties was her favourite, and would be happy with a multi period enthusiast.

"Okay, the thing is, he's not just interested in dressing up, and he goes way back before the twenties and thirties." Daisy scratched her head, wondering how to delicately put that he liked stomping around in muddy fields re-enacting battles or jousting.

"Put it this way, you won't always stay nice and clean. He does battle re-enacting and jousting, even when the weather isn't good, so you might get a bit muddy at times."

Cheryl said that wasn't a problem, the thought of getting all muddy with a man was quite a turn on. Daisy covered the mouthpiece of the phone and laughed, then turned it into a cough. "Sorry about that, I choked on my tea," she fibbed. "I'll call Tom to see if he's happy to meet you."

The great thing was, geographically, they were only a couple of streets away from each other, but Daisy didn't want to give that information out yet.

Tom was definitely interested. He spent all his time at work and doing his re-enacting thing at weekends, so meeting women was really difficult. The few ladies who did the multi-period stuff were either older than him, or already married.

Tom said he could meet Cheryl the following evening in their local pub. He'd wear a fedora so she'd know who he was. Daisy phoned Cheryl back with the details. Cheryl said she'd wear a 1940s hat so that Tom would recognise her.

"There's nowt as queer as folk," Daisy said with a laugh when she finally put the phone down. She so wished she could turn up at some of these initial meetings. It would be fun seeing a man in a fedora and a woman in a 40s hat sitting together.

At home that evening, Daisy told Kris about meeting Simon again, and about Greg asking her out to dinner. "I said I didn't want to go, but eventually changed my mind."

"Girlfriend, what IS wrong with you," Kris screeched. "If someone invited me to Rialto's, I'd accept immediately, and offer them by body in thanks."

"Yes but you're just a shameful tart." Daisy grinned.

"You said it, babes."

Daisy scowled. She sometimes worried about Kris's lifestyle, but she knew he wasn't reckless, and since they'd been living together he hadn't actually had many dates or one night stands.

"Anyway," she said, "I just felt a bit uncomfortable about accepting. I mean yes of course I'd love to go to Rialto's, but, he's my boss. I shouldn't be going to dinner with my boss."

"Why not? Sweetie, if he wants to take you to dinner, let him. When else are you going to get the chance? I'm dead jealous; neither of us can afford to eat there."

"Aww, Kris, now I feel guilty. Maybe I ought to say I'll go on one condition – you come too?"

"Hmm, I don't think he'll agree somehow. No, you go and have a good time. Maybe he wants to discuss work business, but away from the office so the other employees don't hear. Hey, maybe he's going to promote you?"

"He's already promoted me."

"Well, whatever, he has his reasons. Bring me back a doggy bag. That's the only way I'll ever get to eat any of their food."

Chapter Eleven

The rest of the week passed by uneventfully. Daisy saw Simon again; they met every lunch time in the park. He seemed really nice – asking if she wanted his company or would rather be on her own – and making her laugh with different voices for the ducks. Daisy's special duck – who they'd named Gilbert – seemed to know when she'd be due and was already out of the pond waddling towards her as she approached her favourite bench. She looked forward to lunch times. She didn't fancy Simon, she didn't get that thrill when she looked at him or if their hands accidentally touched, but he was good company.

On Friday afternoon, Greg asked Daisy if she still wanted to go for dinner that evening.

"Of course, I'm looking forward to it," she said, smiling. She didn't tell him she'd never been anywhere that posh before so was quite nervous.

Greg arranged to meet her outside so she wouldn't have to walk in by herself.

"No need to pick me up, Kris will drive me in," Daisy told him after he'd suggested giving her a lift.

"Okay, see you at seven."

Daisy had tried on every outfit in her wardrobe at least three times. She sat on her bed and said to Kris – who was being her personal dresser, "I don't know why I'm bothering so much. It's not as if it's a date, he's only my boss."

"But you still want to look fabulous, sweetie. You never know who else might be in there. They get a lot of celebrities."

"What? Oh, great, I'm going to be really nervous now. I'm not ordering spaghetti; I end up with it everywhere." She suddenly squealed. "Eek, what if there's paparazzi in there and they take photos of a celebrity in front of me and there I am in the background, carbonara sauce dribbling down my chin?" She picked up the dress she'd just taken off and put it back down again. "Maybe I'll cancel, say I'm not well."

"Don't you dare. I'm living this evening out through you, so I want to go, even if you don't."

Daisy laughed and hugged Kris. "I so love you, do you know that?"

"Love you more."

"Love you most. Right," she stood up again, "what am I going to wear? Nothing too sexy – not that I have anything sexy. But nothing too conservative, just in case there are celebs there."

She finally settled on her white skinny trousers with a soft grey silk shirt and her high-heeled strappy silver sandals. She could take a jacket for when it cooled down. Although it was summer, it got a bit chilly in the evenings.

"Darling, wear a thong, you don't want VPL, especially with white trousers." Kris opened her knickers drawer and threw a skin coloured thong at her. She was wearing the unflattering big pants that she wore for work as they were more comfortable. Daisy reckoned that sitting in a thong all day, was like sitting on a cheese wire.

Kris turned his back as she changed her underwear. Then he turned round and helped her dress. He was a great personal assistant. He had a knack of knowing what colours went together – even ones she wouldn't have dreamed of – and was good at accessorising too. She always took him with her when she went clothes shopping.

"Now, I think you should wear your hair down. You always wear it up in a French roll or ponytail. I think you should leave it loose, over your shoulders."

He removed her grips, unrolled her hair, stood behind her and brushed it, then arranged it nicely around her shoulders. "You look totes amazeballs."

Daisy went to get up to check the result in the mirror.

"No, stay there whilst I get some hairspray." Kris ran to the bathroom and came back with the spray. He arranged a bit more hair, then sprayed it liberally.

Daisy coughed. "Ruddy hell, Kris, are you trying to poison me?"

"No, just making sure your hair stays perfect all night." He stood back to admire his handiwork. "Abs fab, darling. But you better not go near any naked flames; you'll set your head on fire. Okay you can look."

Daisy stood up and looked at herself in the full-length mirror. Kris had done a fabulous job on her hair, and she had to admit, she looked good. Her make-up had covered the slight bruising that still hadn't faded completely. She couldn't do much about the cut, but with her hair down it was less noticeable.

"Kris, you're a darling. Thank you so much. Okay, shall I have a little drink just to steady my nerves?"

"I wouldn't. You don't want the boss man to smell booze on you when you get there, do you?"

"No, you're right; he might think I'm a secret alcoholic. Okay, you sure about driving me in? I can get a taxi."

"I want to take you, I might see a celeb going in or coming out. I'll pick you up too, just phone me when you're ready."

"But that means you won't be able to have a drink all night." Daisy didn't want Kris to have a lousy evening because he had to act as her taxi driver.

"Sweetie, I never drink alone anyway, you know that."

"But I thought you were going to the club?"

"Not tonight, sugarplum. It's just me and a take-away."

"Oh, Kris, I feel bad about going out now. I'll stay in with you. Let me phone Greg…"

"Baby D, you'll do no such thing. Get yourself downstairs, it's time for me to act as your chauffeur for the evening." Kris pushed her out of the bedroom.

The truth was, since Daisy's accident, he'd become a bit paranoid about something happening to her and wanted to look after her as much as possible. You heard all sorts about young girls being attacked by taxi drivers. Kris couldn't bear it if anything else happened to her, so he'd planned to stay in until he could collect her and know she was safe at home with him again.

Kris was just dropping Daisy outside Rialto's, when he shrieked, making her jump out of her skin. "Omg, look who's just going in. It's her from Silent Witness, the pretty blonde girl, I'm sure of it."

Daisy caught the back of a blonde head disappearing through the doors. "I didn't see. I'll text you if it's her. I'll nip to the ladies and text you if there's any other celebs in there. Wish me luck." Daisy wiped the palms of her hands on the car seat. "I'm so nervous. I've never been anywhere this posh. Bet I make a right idiot of myself. I must remember my table manners."

"And start with cutlery from the outside."

"I know all that, I'm not a complete heathen. I just don't know much about wines."

"I'm sure the boss man will choose for you. Speaking of the devil, there he is. Now, away with you before I get told off for stopping. Have a fab time, call me when you want collecting." Kris kissed her and drove away.

As Greg watched Daisy climb out of the car and walk towards him, his body did all sorts of things. Wow, she looked gorgeous. He'd never seen her hair down before, and the way it was gently waving all around her shoulders and framing that beautiful face… He felt a stirring in his trousers and had to resist the urge to pull her into his arms there and then. She looked extremely shaggable. He was aware that she was standing there waiting for him to say something, so he pulled himself together.

"Hi, you look gorgeous. Your hair suits you down; you ought to wear it like that more often."

Daisy was pleased with the compliment. "Thanks, you look nice too." He had on a grey suit that almost matched the colour of her top, with a baby pink shirt underneath, no tie, so it was open at the neck.

He offered her his arm. "Shall we go in?" She giggled at his formality but took his arm anyway and they walked into the restaurant.

Inside, the place was packed and it was only five to seven. Daisy tried not to gasp as she looked around. Kris was right, it was the girl from Silent Witness, and she was with the bloke from Hustle. In fact, as Daisy looked, she saw it was the whole gang from Hustle, including the girl who looked like Kylie.

A waiter asked if he could take Daisy's jacket, and she handed it over.

"Would you like a drink here at the bar, or do you want to go straight to the table?" Greg asked.

"Can we have a drink here first?" Daisy wanted the chance to look around a bit more, see who else she could spot. There was a sign asking for all mobiles to be switched off and 'No photo taking, please respect the privacy of our diners.' Damn, no celeb photos then. She'd have to go to the loo to text Kris.

She was so busy looking around, she didn't notice the drink Greg put in front of her until he spoke her name. It was a glass of champagne.

"Oh, Greg, you shouldn't have."

"You said once it was your favourite alcoholic drink, so that's what I got you."

"But it'll cost a fortune."

"Daisy, stop worrying. It's on the company."

Daisy frowned. "But you own the company."

Greg laughed. "Stop worrying and just enjoy yourself." He clinked her glass with his. "Cheers, here's to you. Thanks for all your hard work, and I really am sorry you got hurt."

Daisy shrugged. "Forget it, I have."

"Yes, but you'll always have a reminder." Greg gently lifted her hair away from the side of her face so he could see the cut. "Actually it's healed nicely. You shouldn't have much of a scar at all."

He looked into her eyes. God, she was so beautiful, with those deep green, expressive eyes. Again, he felt that stirring below, and tore his eyes away from her face.

Daisy wished he'd stop looking at her like that. Even though he was gay, his scrutiny was making her heart do somersaults. She looked out at the diners, and to distract him – and herself – said, "Look over there, it's the people from that programme Hustle, and the girl from Silent Witness. Kris would faint with excitement if he was here now, he loves celebrity spotting."

Greg saw the group sitting at a side table. They were all having a good time, laughing and talking together. "They come in here quite often; it's a popular place for celebrities."

"How do you know they come here often? Have you been before?" Daisy asked her eyes wide.

Greg shrugged. "A few times."

A few times was an understatement. Greg dined in Rialto's every couple of weeks.

A waiter informed them that their table was ready, so Greg said, "Follow that man." Daisy did, then had to run back to the bar and retrieve her clutch bag that she'd left there.

She smiled embarrassedly. "Sorry. This is all a bit overwhelming for me. I've never been anywhere like this before," she hissed, keeping her voice down so nobody else knew what an idiot she was.

Greg smiled. Bless her; he loved her naivety and innocence. "Don't worry, relax and enjoy yourself. It's just a building and these are just ordinary people. Pretend it's the office and they're clients."

And that's exactly what they did. During the starter, and most of the main course, they pretended the other diners were clients, and had great fun seeing who they'd match up with who. Daisy was enjoying herself so much, she'd forgotten how nervous she was, and relaxed, as if she ate in this sort of establishment frequently. The alcohol also helped put her in a mellow mood. She suddenly remembered she'd told Kris she'd text him, so excused herself and went to the ladies. She fumbled in her bag for her phone and switched it on.

"Guess what, girl from Silent Witness here with the gang from Hustle, including Kylie lookalike. D x"

She laughed as she imagined Kris reading it and squealing.

Sure enough he texted back. "ARGH! So wish I was there. Hope you're having a fab time. K xx"

"Yep it's great, will tell all when you collect me. D x"

She turned her phone off again and went back outside.

"You okay?" Greg asked.

"Yes, I just texted Kris to let him know what celebs are here. Shame, he'd love eating here, but on our wages, it's something neither of us could do." Realising what she'd said, Daisy looked at Greg in alarm. "Oh, I don't mean that you don't pay me enough, I mean…well, with Kris studying, he doesn't have much spare cash, and it's not the sort of place I could spend my money in…oh, shut up, Daisy." She grinned at Greg and he laughed.

"It's okay, I know what you mean. Well, I give my staff a Christmas bonus if profits are healthy and they've done a good job, so maybe you can treat Kris with yours – if you get one?" Greg looked at her and held her gaze. God, those green eyes of hers.

"Oh, he'd love that. It'd be nice to treat him, especially after the way he cared for me when I was hurt. He's a real darling."

"You think a lot of him, don't you?"

"I love him," Daisy said simply. "He means more to me than anyone else in the world. He's like my sister, brother and best friend all rolled into one."

"I could tell he feels the same way about you. Well, we'll have to see what we can do about getting him in here one day."

"Greg, that would be lovely. Kris would be…oh, he'd be thrilled. He's like a big kid when he gets excited, he's so funny."

Daisy finished the rest of her main course, and because she'd stayed away from spaghetti dishes, she managed to keep her chin sauce-free.

She'd started with a simple rocket salad, topped with shavings of parmesan, and her main course was pollo al tartufo estivo, which was chicken breast – organic of course – stuffed with truffle cheese sauce, and it was absolutely delicious.

Greg had some sort of venison, which he ate was extremely good, but Daisy couldn't bear the thought of eating Bambi.

Apart from bars of chocolate, she didn't often eat desserts, but she loved cheese, so had the cheese platter to finish. It wasn't exactly Italian, but Daisy thought it sounded better when it was called formaggio.

Greg ordered coffees for them and asked if she'd like to take them in the bar area. He knew the staff would want the table as soon as possible for more diners. Daisy agreed.

She'd had a fabulous evening so far – good company, great surroundings and food, and a laugh trying to pair up the diners. She didn't want it to end.

As they waited for their coffees, and Daisy watched a couple entering the restaurant, Greg studied her. She really was gorgeous. He could look at her all night. She turned back and saw him.

"Thanks for a great evening, Greg, I've really enjoyed it."

"So have I, Daisy. In fact..." He stopped talking and his expression softened.

"In fact what?"

"Daisy, I can't wait any longer, I've been wanting to do this for ages." He leaned towards her, put his hand gently around the back of her head to bring her closer and kissed her. A long searching kiss.

Daisy was enjoying it until it fully registered what he was doing. She pulled away, her eyes wide in shock. "Greg, what the hell do you think you're doing?"

"Kissing you."

Tears sprang to her eyes and she slid off the bar stool. "How could you? How bloody could you?" she yelled and, grabbing her bag, she ran out of the restaurant.

"Shit," Greg muttered. He couldn't run after her because he had to settle the bill and he remembered Daisy had given her jacket to the waiter. He sat there feeling like a right idiot. He'd been about to tell her how he felt, but just couldn't resist kissing her. Now he'd really messed up. She didn't feel the same way about him, that was obvious. How could he have got it so wrong?

Daisy stopped running, tears streaming down her face and took out her phone.

Kris saw it was Daisy ringing, she obviously wanted him to

collect her. He answered, and heard her sobs on the other end. His heart started hammering in his chest.

"Daisy? What's happened? Okay, calm down, sweetie, I'll be there as soon as I can. Hang on, babe."

He raced out of the door and into the car. She'd sobbed that she was around the corner from the restaurant, could he collect her from there. Kris wondered what on earth had happened. Nothing good, that was for sure, Daisy had sounded distraught. And why wasn't Greg looking after her?

A horrible thought then struck him. If that man has harmed a hair on her head, I'll kill him with my bare hands. Kris banged his fist on the steering wheel.

***

Daisy took a few deep breaths to try and control her sobbing. What the hell did Greg think he was playing at?

Suddenly the penny dropped, and Daisy realised what was going on. He was having a sexuality crisis. That would make sense. Those lingering looks, telling her she was gorgeous, and now, kissing her. He was trying to find out if he was still gay. But how could he use her like that. Why her? Why not some random woman on a night out? Daisy cried even more, not caring about the curious looks she was getting from people walking by.

She was relieved when Kris screeched to a halt beside her. He went to get out but she shook her head and got in the front passenger seat.

"Sweetie, what on earth's happened? If Greg has done something to you, I'll kill him. Where is he?"

"Kris, just drive. I'll tell you on the way."

So, as he drove home, she told him that Greg had kissed her.

"He what? Why?"

"I don't know. Well, I do now, I've worked it out. He must be unsure about being gay and was using me to test it." She turned to Kris. "Does that happen? I mean, do people suddenly wonder if they're gay?"

"I don't know, babe. There was no doubt for me. I knew from an early age that I liked the same sex. I'm not sure a gay man would suddenly at the age of thirty-two start questioning it. I know youngsters are often confused about their sexuality, but you'd think by your thirties you'd know which way you swung. I guess stranger things have happened though."

"Well, you hear about men who've been married and had kids suddenly deciding they are gay, don't you? Maybe this is the reverse of that?"

"I don't think they suddenly decide they're gay – it doesn't work like that. It's not a lifestyle choice, it's who you are. I think those men were always gay but they tried to suppress it by doing the conventional thing – marriage and babies. But they couldn't deny it any longer."

"But look at that guy in the soap we watch. He was gay and now he's living with the girl across the street. So it obviously does happen."

"That's a TV soap, babe, not real life."

"Yes, but they do their research, they must have got the idea from somewhere."

They arrived home and Kris put the kettle on to make Daisy a cup of tea.

She flopped down on the sofa.

"Do you know the worst thing about it?"

"What?"

"I enjoyed it at first. I'd had such a lovely evening, and we were sitting at the bar waiting for our coffees. I caught him looking at me and he was going to say something, but then he just pulled me towards him and kissed me, and it was nice. Until I realised what he was doing. Grr! How could he." She punched the cushion.

"So, what does he kiss like?"

"Kris!"

"Hey, only asking. Go on, tell, what was it like?"

"It was soft and gentle and…lovely, but wrong and inappropriate. How am I going to go to work on Monday?"

Daisy's phone rang and she looked at the screen. "It's Greg." She switched it off and threw it on the floor. "If he thinks I'm going to talk to him, he can think again. I'll hand in my resignation on Monday."

"Don't be stupid, you love that job."

"But how can I work there now? It'll be really awkward for both of us – he's my boss."

"Sweetie, don't do anything hasty. Please. Think about it over the weekend. It'd be silly to give up your job. You need to talk to him."

"NO. I don't want anything to do with him." She folded her arms in her defiant stance.

"Right, listen to uncle Kristof. Stop being stupid. You need to clear the air."

Daisy went to speak but Kris stopped her. "I don't mean let him off. Tell him it was unprofessional and uncalled for, and that it was wrong to use you. Say it must never happen again, and that if he can't accept that, then you'll find another job."

Daisy looked doubtful but Kris could see she was thinking about it.

"If you can clear the air, in time you'll probably both laugh about it. You'd both been drinking, just call it a stupid mistake."

"At my expense." Daisy let out a deep breath. "Okay, maybe I overreacted a bit, and yes, we'd had a few glasses of champagne and wine. But it was still unfair to use me to test out his sexuality."

"Yes, it was, but have you never made a mistake? It's not worth losing a job you love over, is it?"

"No." Daisy pouted. "Okay, I'll go into work on Monday, but I don't know if I want to talk to him. I'll avoid him and give him the silent treatment if our paths cross."

"You can't do that, he'll want to talk to you. How embarrassed do you think he must be feeling right now? He's probably kicking himself."

"Good. I'm keeping my phone turned off all weekend. Let him suffer."

"You're a hard woman, Daisy Dorson," Kris teased.

She wasn't at all. Kris knew she was a great big softy, who was just putting on an act to cover up how upset she really was, and he hoped she'd come round enough to sort things out.

105

Chapter Twelve

Greg had tried to phone Daisy all weekend. But her phone was obviously switched off. He didn't want to leave a voicemail and he didn't want to phone the house phone and risk Kris answering. He wanted to speak to her. He replayed the scene over and over so many times, and mentally kicked himself so much, if he'd physically done it he'd be covered in bruises.

How could he have been so stupid? Why didn't he tell her how he felt first before kissing her? He'd have been able to gauge how she felt in return then. He'd thought she liked him too. He saw the look she'd given him that time she'd caught him with his shirt off, and knew she'd felt the spark between them when their hands touched. Had he really got it so wrong?

All he could do was wait until Monday, and call her into his office for a chat. He'd apologise profusely and promise it would never happen again. He was her boss, and shouldn't have acted so unprofessionally.

Greg was a good guy and was never too proud to apologise for his mistakes.

***

Daisy deliberately turned up for work later than usual on Monday, so that Greg couldn't collar her alone. So she was dismayed to see him hovering in the foyer when she arrived.

"Ah, a word in my office, Miss Dorson, if you don't mind," he said.

"Sorry, I'm busy," Daisy replied stiffly.

"It can wait. I need to have a word with you."

"And I said I'm busy. There's something urgent I need to

sort out with a client."

Greg sighed. "Okay, sort it out then come to my office... please."

Without replying, Daisy flounced off to her office and shut the door.

Stella had been watching the conversation with interest and smirked. Ha, all was not well between Daisy and the boss, good. Daisy needed taking down a peg or two, the way she swanned around all high and mighty. Stella wondered what had gone on between the pair. Little did she know, she was soon to find out.

Daisy didn't go to Greg's office, and she managed to avoid him all morning. At lunch time, she sneaked out before Greg could catch her, and went to the park. Simon was there on the bench they usually shared.

As she sat down, Gilbert came waddling out of the pond, a female duck close behind him.

"Oh look," Daisy said in delight, "he's brought his mate."

She bent down to the female, who nervously backed away. Gilbert turned and quacked at her as if he was saying "these two are okay, they feed me".

"Aww, that's so sweet. I wonder if they'll have babies?" Daisy looked questioningly at Simon.

"I expect so, it's about time for them to mate. When she disappears, that'll be when she's sitting on her eggs. So, did you have a good weekend?" he asked.

Daisy rolled her eyes. "Not really, but I just want to forget it. You?"

"Oh you know, so so, bit quiet."

Daisy laughed. "What are the pair of us like?"

Simon looked down at Daisy's left hand and nervously coughed. "Aherm, so, I've noticed you don't wear a wedding or engagement ring. Do you have a boyfriend?"

"Nope."

"Oh. Okay, s-o-o-o, would you like to go out sometime?"

Daisy looked at Simon; he was quite good-looking. Not her usual type, but they got on well. He made her laugh, never pressed her for information – he could have asked why she wanted to forget her bad weekend, but didn't – and he was so easy to get on with. Plus, he loved animals, which showed Daisy that he was a kind person. She'd not had much luck so far with men, maybe Simon would grow on her.

"It's okay, you don't have to, I'll understand," Simon was saying now.

"No, I mean, that's not why I haven't answered. Sorry I was thinking about something. Yes, I'd like to go out. When and where were you thinking of?"

Daisy expected him to name a pub somewhere, but he surprised her by suggesting a day out at the wildlife park on Saturday. She thought it was a great idea.

"We have all week to change our minds," he said looking at her with his head on one side.

He wasn't a confident man, and Daisy liked that. Better than being an arrogant pig who thought he could just kiss a girl. Damn. Until now, she'd managed to avoid thinking about Greg's kiss.

"I won't change my mind, but it's okay if you decide against it," she said.

"I won't either." Simon smiled.

They ate their lunch, fed Gilbert and his mate their crusts, then walked slowly back to their offices.

"Same time tomorrow?" Simon asked.

"Yes, of course," Daisy replied.

When she got back, Greg was waiting for her. "Daisy, can I have that word now?"

"Sorry, can't, I need to cover reception for Stella." It had worked out quite well that Stella needed to take her lunch much later because she had an appointment.

Greg tried to control his temper. He was the boss; she should be doing what he said. But he didn't want to make matters worse.

"Right, cover for Stella's lunch, then as soon as she gets back, I want you in my office. No excuses."

"Ooh, what have you done to upset the boss?" Stella asked when he'd gone.

Daisy couldn't tell her about going to Rialto's, so she said she'd made a mistake with a client and that Greg wasn't happy about it.

"Oops, well, you better go see him when I get back. Don't want to make it worse, do you?" Stella said sweetly, secretly delighted that Daisy was in trouble. So little Miss Perfect wasn't so perfect after all.

Daisy sat on reception, wishing time would stop. She hated confrontation, and was dreading talking to Greg. But she wasn't the one at fault, so why was she worried? That cheered her up, and by the time Stella got back, Daisy was almost looking forward to making Greg squirm.

She knocked at his door.

"Come in. Ah, Daisy…"

She was about to launch into an attack, but Greg held his hand up.

"Before you say anything, please let me apologise. I'm really sorry for kissing you." He whispered as he said 'kissing you', and looked around, as if the walls could hear him.

"It was totally unprofessional of me, and I shouldn't have done it. It must have been the alcohol."

"Oh, thanks a lot."

"No, I mean… I didn't mean it to sound like that. Some of it was your fault too."

"It was not my fault. What did I do?"

Greg ran his hand through his hair, he wasn't handling this well.

Daisy actually wanted to laugh. She'd never seen her usually calm and collected boss look so frazzled.

"You didn't do anything other than look totally gorgeous." He picked up his coffee and took a sip.

Daisy preened. "Thanks." But then she narrowed her eyes. "But me looking gorgeous shouldn't have bothered you."

Greg frowned. "Why not?"

"Because you're…"

Oh heck, she wasn't supposed to know he was gay, but she couldn't back out now. She might as well say it.

"Well, because you're, were, maybe…gay."

Greg had taken another sip of coffee, and now he literally

109

spat it out. "I'm WHAT?"

Daisy said in a quiet voice, "Gay, homosexual…"

"Yes, I know what the word gay means, Daisy. Good God, whatever gave you that idea?"

"Stella said…"

Oops, she hadn't mean to let that slip out. Actually by the thunderous look on Greg's face, Daisy decided a great big BOLLOCKS was a better word. Oops seemed so small and totally insignificant right now.

Greg got up and closed the blinds at his window, as if doing so would drown out his words. He paced around, then sat back down.

"Daisy, I want you to tell me word for word, what Stella said, and when."

Daisy had a feeling that all was not as it had been portrayed to her. She was standing up, but she now sat down opposite Greg and said, "It was when you'd given me the promotion. Do you remember? I was in your office and stupidly burst into tears, and Stella brought your coffee in? Well, I saw her give you a dirty look. After that, she caught me in the loo and asked why I was upset."

Daisy stopped talking. Greg had sat forward, elbows on his desk and steepled his fingers together. She gulped. This was awful; it felt like telling tales, but what choice did she have?

"Go on."

"She said she thought you and I were in a clinch, but then realised how stupid that was as you wouldn't be interested in me. I asked why, what was wrong with me and she said you were gay."

Greg's face grew dark and serious. "And how did she know I was gay?"

"One of the previous matchers had apparently seen you in a gay bar with a man, and you'd asked him not to say anything, but he told the whole office. Stella thought I ought to know in case I put my foot in it at some point."

"I bet she did. Anything else?"

"She asked me not to let on that I knew. She said you wanted to keep it quiet in case it affected the reputation of The

Love Shack. It might give the wrong impression – a gay man running the agency."

Greg took a deep breath and put one hand across his mouth as if to stop himself saying something he shouldn't.

"No wonder you were so upset at me kissing you," he said eventually.

"Well, you have to admit it's a mean thing to do. If you want to test out your sexuality, why choose me?"

"Because I happen to find you extremely attractive, utterly gorgeous, and I think I've wanted to kiss you from the moment you first walked into this agency and told me my matchers weren't doing a good job."

Daisy held her hand against her chest. She was shocked. She opened her mouth, but nothing came out.

She eventually found her voice and muttered, "But… but…"

"Daisy, I am NOT gay."

She took a few minutes to digest what he'd just said. "But what about the gay agency you know. And I heard you making a dinner date with Robin."

Greg frowned. "Robin?" Then he rolled his eyes and sighed. "Robyn, with a Y, is my sister. She was coming down from London for a few days, and I arranged to take her out for dinner. As for the agency… Daisy, I know every other agency for miles around. I make it my business to know who my competitors are. I check out their prices and what services they offer. We all do."

Daisy's eyes widened as she realised Stella had played her good and proper. She gasped and held both hands against her mouth before saying, "Greg, I am so sorry. I didn't know, I was just going by what Stella—"

"Right, I'll tell you this, but keep it to yourself. Stella tried it on with me. Not just once, but on several occasions. She more or less offered herself to me. I turned her down in no uncertain terms. She's a hard faced cow, not my type at all. I can only assume that she's jealous of you, so told you I was gay in revenge."

"Christ. What are you going to do?"

111

"Dismiss her, with immediate effect. I want her desk cleared as soon as I've spoken to her, and I'll escort her from the building."

"But don't you have to follow procedures to sack someone?"

"I'm doing so. She's already had a verbal and written warning; this is gross misconduct – spreading scandalous lies about not just a member of staff, but her boss. She deserves all she gets. I could have dismissed her before for sexual harassment, but I didn't. Right, I need someone here whilst I dismiss her. I can't risk her making any accusations, and I wouldn't put it past her. Under the circumstances, it may be better if another member of staff does it. What do you think?"

Daisy was livid with Stella for lying to her like that, so was quite happy to see her get her come-uppance.

"No, I'll stay. I wouldn't mind seeing her get what she deserves. She's been horrible to me from day one, really."

"Okay, but stand here beside me, and don't say a word. Right?"

Daisy nodded.

Greg picked up the phone and asked Stella into his office.

She came in all smiles, but the smile slipped when she saw Daisy standing beside Greg's chair.

"What's this? A special meeting?"

"Stella, I'm dismissing you with immediate effect. You will go and clear your desk from all personal belongings, and leave the premises."

"What? You can't do that. What reason do you have?"

Greg's eyes flicked to Daisy. "I think you know why, unless you want me to spell it out?"

"Oh, I see, teacher's pet been telling tales, has she? You rotten cow!" Stella lunged across the desk and Daisy moved back in fright.

"RIGHT, OUT NOW. And don't expect a reference. Daisy, you stay here, I'll get one of the others to help me escort her off the premises."

Seething with rage, Stella smashed open Greg's door and stomped across to reception. She started pulling stuff out of the desk and slamming it onto the counter.

Greg stood watching, then got out his phone and fiddled with it for a bit.

"If you damage anything, it's coming out of your final wages. Use that box to put your things in, and hurry up about it. I don't want you here any longer than necessary," he said.

"You're going to regret this, Mr Bigshot," Stella spat at him.

"Threatening me now, as well as sexual harassment? I'd be careful if I were you, Stella."

"Ha, it's your word against mine. You should have taken me up on my offers, Greg, you need a real woman, not a prissy little princess like her." Stella tossed her head in the direction of his office where they'd left Daisy.

Greg pressed a button on his phone.

"Thanks, Stella, I now have all I need. You do anything to either me, Daisy or this company, in any way, shape or form, and this," he pressed a button on his phone and played back the conversation they'd just had, "will find its way into the hands of the police. Do I make myself clear?"

Stella gave him a hard stare and nodded.

He phoned for one of the other matchers to come out and help him see her off the premises.

Stella picked up the box. "You don't need re-enforcements. I'm going. I didn't like this job anyway," was her parting shot as she stalked out of the doors without a backward glance.

Greg went back to his office and sank into his chair. "God, I could do with a drink. What time is it?" He looked at his watch. "Almost three, a couple of hours left yet. Daisy, you can go home now if you want. I think we could all do with finishing early, it's been a hell of a day."

Daisy agreed. "You can say that again. Thanks, but I'll stay. Greg, I'm really sorry for believing that you were gay, but it all seemed to fit at the time. And sorry for over-reacting when you…well, you know."

"Don't worry. I'm sorry for kissing you. Well, I'm not actually. Like I said I've wanted to do it for ages, but as your boss, I should have had some more restraint. Am I forgiven?"

Seeing his pleading face made Daisy's heart lurch. She couldn't stay mad at him now.

"You're forgiven. But can we have some honesty here? Much as I like you – and I do – you're my boss. I've always had this rule about not dating someone I work with. It can only lead to disaster and spoil our working relationship."

"Who said anything about dating? I'm quite happy with kissing and whatever else you might want me to do."

Daisy was shocked until she realised he was kidding her. "Hmm, I suppose you think that's amusing? I believed you for a moment. But no, we can't get involved, sorry."

"You're probably right. If we got involved, it might compromise our working relationship. Pity though." Greg grinned until he saw the serious look on Daisy's face. "Okay, my apologies again. I'm glad in a way that we've sorted things out. So I guess we can thank Stella for that."

"Talking about Stella, we need a new receptionist."

"Damn. I don't suppose you know anyone?"

Daisy shook her head.

"Okay, I'll place an ad. Frank will put one in the local paper for me. Do you want to help me interview people?" Greg cocked his head to one side.

"Sure. Male or female?"

"Either. As long as they are capable, and seem like they'd actually do some work and not sit around reading magazines, I don't mind."

"Okeydoke. It might be fun."

"Oh, and before I forget, you ran off without collecting your jacket." Greg got up and opened the door to the cupboard where he hung his spare shirt and kept the champagne and other bits and pieces. Here." He handed it to Daisy.

"Thanks. I actually rang the restaurant and they said you'd taken it. Getting it back meant having to talk to you, so I didn't bother." She smiled meekly.

"You silly girl. Go on, back to work if you're not going home."

"Okay. Want a coffee?"

"In the absence of something stronger, yes please. I'm

going to nip in and tell the others Stella doesn't work here anymore. Thanks, and sorry again. Friends?"

Daisy smiled. "Yes, friends. I'll get that coffee."

Chapter Thirteen

"So," Daisy said, waving her fork in the air as she and Kris ate dinner, "everything worked out for the best."

"See, I knew he wasn't gay." Kris pushed his food around his plate.

"Are you going to eat that or just play with it?"

Kris stabbed a piece of sausage with his fork and nibbled the end of it.

"I'm eating, look." He made exaggerated swallowing motions.

"Oh I give up with you, it's worse than getting a child to eat. If you want to end up with anorexia, that's your problem. If you're not going to eat it, give me that other sausage." Daisy leaned over and took a sausage off his plate.

"So, things go back to normal and everyone's happy?" Kris asked.

"Yep, except we need to find a new receptionist. Greg's placing an ad and I'll help with the interviews. I don't know what we're going to ask, but I'm going to go with my gut feeling. If I click with someone and they have the right qualifications, they're in. I didn't take to Stella at all. I tried being friendly, but I knew she disliked me."

Kris didn't understand how anyone could not like Daisy, she was so easy to get on with.

"And what about this Simon?"

"We're going out on Saturday to the wildlife park." Daisy beamed. She loved animals, it was the perfect place to take her. "It's a regular thing now, eating our lunch together in the park, and Gilbert – the duck – has been bringing a female duck along with him. She must be his mate. It's so cute."

"What's he like?" Kris asked. He'd eaten some of his mashed potato and beans, and got up to scrape the remainder in the bin.

"Small, green head, light brown and grey body with blue on the wings, and a funny bit on his beak that looks like an exclamation mark."

Kris turned to look at her. "What?"

Daisy laughed. "I take it you meant Simon, not Gilbert."

"Yes, you idiot." Kris laughed. "So, what is he like?"

Daisy sighed. "He's…nice."

"Hmm, that doesn't sound like it's going to be the romance of the year. 'Nice' sounds a bit bland."

"Well, he makes me laugh, he's kind, open and honest, not bad looking, but…"

"But there's no spark?"

"No. I like him, I really do, but I don't get that tingle if our hands accidentally brush like I did with Greg." Daisy sighed again. "Why does the man I do feel those things for have to be out of bounds?"

"He's only out of bounds because you make it so. He's told you how he feels about you; you're the one who put a stop to it."

"Yes, because of the circumstances. Nothing good ever comes out of work relationships and I love my job too much to risk losing it by getting involved with the boss."

"Isn't it worth trying, just to see how you get on?"

"No. When it ends – and it will do at some point – how could we carry on working together? Nope, much better to keep work and personal life separate. Besides, Simon might grow on me."

"Like a huge spot, you mean?"

"Oh shut up, you." Daisy whacked him with the tea towel, so he scooped up a big mound of soapsuds and threw it at her. She scooped some up and threw it back, then they chased each other round the kitchen, shrieking and laughing.

Later, as they watched TV, Daisy said, "I'm quite happy with my life as it is. I know I used to moan that I didn't have a boyfriend, but I don't need a relationship to make me complete." She looked up at Kris. "I'm perfectly content spending my evenings here with you, and I enjoy our nights out. As you keep saying, if and when I'm supposed to meet someone, I will."

Kris knew Daisy was putting on a front. Truth was, she'd like nothing more than to settle down with the love of her life… kids…the whole family thing.

He hugged her. "I'm happy too, sweetie and yes, que sera sera."

***

They had quite a few responses to the ad for a receptionist, but so far, none of them seemed right. There were a couple who'd do the job okay, but neither Daisy nor Greg had taken to them.

They'd just looked through the list to see who was left, and spotted one who'd written under marital status 'Newlywed', when Daisy suddenly smacked her forehead and exclaimed, "Duh, that reminds me, I was going to ask you something."

Greg gave her a slow, lazy smile. "You're not going to propose to me, are you?"

Even though she knew he was teasing, Daisy's heart somersaulted and she blushed.

"Of course not. But you know Marjorie and Fred – the elderly couple who are getting married?" Greg nodded, and she went on, "Well, they invited me and a plus one to their wedding. I was going to take Kris, but then I thought…" She left the sentence hanging.

"You wondered if you ought to ask me instead? I mean it is my agency, and if it hadn't been for my agency they wouldn't have met."

Daisy looked uncomfortable and Greg laughed. "I'm just kidding. No, it's okay, take Kris. You'll relax a bit more with him – you won't have to worry that he might kiss you."

Again that slow lazy smile, which made Daisy's insides do strange things. She knew he was teasing, but she wished he wouldn't, because it made her remember the feel of his lips against hers, and that started her wondering what it would be like to feel those lips in other places.

Greg was watching her, an amused look on his face.

Daisy was glad he couldn't read her mind. She pulled herself together. "I thought we'd moved on and weren't going to mention that again?" She picked up the interview folder and got to her feet.

She looked a bit annoyed, and Greg immediately felt bad. They had decided to put the whole episode behind them, but truth was, he couldn't forget the feel of her soft, warm lips. And he knew she'd enjoyed that kiss as much as he had. He'd tried to put her out of his mind, but it was hard when she looked so utterly gorgeous. Those green eyes, those long slim legs, that body. He mentally shook himself, and apologised.

"If my teasing upsets you, I won't do it again." He looked at his watch. "It's your lunch time, off you go. We have a couple more interviews this afternoon, let's hope someone suitable turns up, or at this rate I'll have to double your wages for doing both jobs."

When she didn't have any profiles to match, Daisy sat on reception. One of the other matchers also filled in, and even Greg had the odd turn. He quite liked sitting there and watching the goings on out in the street.

***

Simon was at their usual park bench and smiled in greeting as Daisy approached. It wasn't long before Gilbert came waddling out of the pond to greet them, and this time he was alone.

"Oh, no Mrs Gilbert today? I hope she's okay." Daisy opened her lunchbox, unwrapped her sandwich and took a bite.

Simon threw some duck food to Gilbert. "Maybe she's sitting on eggs?"

"Ooh, that would be wonderful. I wonder if they'll bring the ducklings to see us?"

"Maybe when they're a little older. I think it takes a couple of months before they're able to fledge."

119

"How long will she sit on the eggs?"

"About twenty-eight days, so if we don't see her for a month, we can pretty much guess she's on a nest. Or a fox has got her."

Daisy's hands flew to her face in horror. "Oh no."

"I'm sure foxes do prowl around here – anything for an easy meal – but I expect the ducks are pretty safe if they nest and roost in the banks of the water." Simon turned his face up to the sun, and relaxed back on the bench.

Daisy couldn't bear to think of their ducks being attacked by a fox. She'd grown so attached to Gilbert and his mate, so she made herself think of something else.

"I'm looking forward to our day out tomorrow."

Simon looked at her, and his brown eyes crinkled as he smiled. "Me too, it'll be nice."

And that was the problem. He was 'nice', but that was all. Her heart didn't contract when he looked at her, her insides didn't do funny things when she thought about him. She sighed. Maybe she was expecting too much. Maybe Simon was the right man for her and they'd grow to love each other – a slow burning love that would deepen with time. That way, it would last, rather than the heady, exciting feeling she got with Greg – everyone knew that the first excitement died down once you were used to each other, and then what were you left with?

They spent the rest of their lunch time chatting companionably and feeding Gilbert, who got so impatient he snatched the bag of food right out of Simon's hand and dropped it on the ground, then greedily pecked it all up, making them both laugh.

They walked back to their respective offices and arranged to meet at the entrance to the wildlife park at ten the following morning.

Daisy was humming as she entered the foyer, and Greg, who was sitting on reception, looked up.

"You sound happy, have a nice lunch?"

"Yes, thanks. I met Simon again. We're going out tomorrow."

"Who's Simon?" Greg asked trying to keep his face

impassive.

"Oh, haven't I told you about him? I'm sure I've mentioned him before. We spend our lunch times together. He's taking me to the wildlife park tomorrow."

Daisy didn't know why she'd said that. Simon wasn't taking her, she was meeting him there. It wasn't a date.

Greg frowned. He didn't like the sound of that. He wanted to be the one taking Daisy out and sharing lunches in the park. But he knew he couldn't muscle in, she'd made it quite obvious she didn't want to get involved, so he smiled and said, "I hope you have a nice time."

"Thanks. I'll sit on reception now."

As Daisy went behind the desk, the doors opened and a girl bounced into the foyer. She had long, copper-coloured, curly hair, which framed a small freckled face, and she looked about the same age as Daisy.

"Hi. I've come about the job. I know the deadline has passed, but I've been away and only just got back. I saw the job advertised in my mum's newspaper, she keeps them for me to read. She thinks I need to know what's going on." She rolled her eyes then smiled at them both and held out her hand to Greg. "I'm Jessica – Jess."

She had the loveliest smile. Daisy liked her immediately.

"Well…"

Greg started to talk but Daisy butted in. "Yes, the deadline has gone, but we're still interviewing, so if you'd like, we can have a chat now?" She shot Greg a pointed look.

"Okay," he said, understanding Daisy's look. "Come into the office."

He buzzed through to ask one of the other matchers to take over on reception and showed Jessica into his office.

Daisy knew they'd found their receptionist before they'd even asked Jess the main questions. She was bubbly and friendly, and when Greg asked her what she'd do when it was quiet, she gave the perfect answer.

"I'd make you both a drink, then tidy up, see what supplies we were low on, clean the desk and anything else I could find. I hate sitting around with nothing to do."

Daisy and Greg looked at each other, and Daisy nodded.

"The job's yours," Greg said dropping the interview folder into his bin.

Jess looked from one to the other in amazement. "You mean it? Really?"

"Yes, really." Daisy smiled. "We've done loads of interviews and not found anyone suitable yet, so, welcome to The Love Shack."

Jess squealed, jumped up and did a little jig on the spot, making Greg and Daisy laugh.

They didn't even know if she had the right experience or qualifications to do a reception job, but they found out she'd been working as a hotel receptionist and was fed up with the long hours. She'd just been away covering another hotel, which she hated doing. She wanted a job with steady hours, based in the same office.

"If you need me, I'll start Monday. I know I should give the hotel notice, but they've really taken advantage of me. I still have four weeks holiday owing as I worked through it to cover someone who left suddenly."

Jess realised how that might have sounded – like she was in the habit of leaving a job with no notice, so she rushed on, "I can assure you I haven't done that before. I'd never leave a job without working my notice, but the hotel have treated me pretty shoddily." She gulped, worried that she may have just talked herself back out of a job she hadn't even started.

Greg asked the name of the hotel and Jess told him. Greg knew of them. They had a reputation for treating their employees badly and always had a high staff turnover. No wonder Jess wanted to leave.

"Well, your contract must say that you have to give notice, but if you're owed holiday, they can take that in lieu of your notice. You'd better phone them as soon as you can to tell them you won't be in again. If you have any problems, let me know."

"Oh my word, thank you so much. I won't let you down, I promise."

Daisy asked Jess what she was doing for the rest of the afternoon.

"Nothing much. I wanted to get in here as soon as I could, but I don't have anything else planned."

"Well, if it's okay with you both," Daisy turned to Greg and raised her eyebrows in question, "how about you stay, and I'll train you – not that you'll need much, it's pretty straightforward and you've done reception work."

"Okay with me." Greg reached for the phone. "I better phone the other interviewees, stop them from coming in. Jess, use the phone on reception to call your hotel."

The girls went out to reception, Daisy got another chair for Jess to sit on and Jess made the call.

"Huh," she said as she hung up, "they didn't give a damn anyway. I don't know how I stuck that job for as long as I did."

She opened her handbag and took out two bars of chocolate. She handed one to Daisy. "I expect you're not allowed to eat here, but save that for later."

"Jess, I love you already." Daisy laughed. "You'll fit in well. We can eat it here as long as we keep it under the desk and are discreet. Okay, this is how we do things…"

Daisy spent the rest of the afternoon showing Jess the computer system, introducing her to the other members of staff and giving her a tour of the rest of the building. She found out that Jess loved animals, and was actually twenty-eight years old.

"Gosh, you look young for your age."

"Everyone says that. My mum and grandmother are young-looking too, so I guess we have good genes, or it's the chocolate. I love the stuff."

"Me too. Maltesers are my favourite."

"Ooh yes. I think my fav are those Belgian seashell ones, but I'll eat any chocolate really, except the really strong dark stuff. Want a cuppa?" Jess got up.

"Tea please – I only drink tea, but Greg likes coffee – hot, no sugar and strong. And I don't like strong dark chocolate either." Daisy grinned. "Looks like we have plenty in common."

Jess picked things up quickly and easily. With her friendly, bubbly character, Daisy knew she'd be an excellent addition to the agency, and she had a feeling she and Jess were going to be great friends.

Daisy told Kris about Jess that evening as he prepared dinner. "So, I think we'll get on brilliantly. What are you making?" Daisy peered into the drained pan of spaghetti that Kris was stirring a concoction of green stuff into.

"Spaghetti with pesto, then topping it with rocket, sundried tomatoes, pine nuts and parmesan shavings."

"That sounds delish. I don't know where you get your ideas from, but you're a fab cook."

"Thanks. So, it'll make working there even better now. Did the boss man like Jess too?"

"Yes, he seemed to. I think he's just glad to have a decent receptionist."

"What does she look like?" Kris had put the pesto spaghetti into bowls and was now adding the other ingredients.

"Tallish, gorgeous curly copper hair, and a pretty, freckled face. She has the loveliest smile too, it lights up her whole face."

"Hmm…" Kris waved the tongs at Daisy. "Careful, sweetie, you might have competition."

"For what?"

"Not what, babes, who."

That shocked Daisy. She hadn't had time to think about it, but yes, what if Greg went off her and switched his affections to Jess instead?

She shrugged. "If he chases Jess, that's up to him. I've made it quite clear I don't want to get involved. Jess is welcome to him."

"Ha, I know you too well. Despite your protestations, I know you'd love to settle down, do all that family stuff, and you fancy the boss man something rotten."

Daisy was about to object, but Kris said, "Okay, answer me this, If he wasn't your boss and you didn't work with him, would you go out with him?"

Daisy didn't need to think about it. She answered immediately. "Yes. But, like I've said numerous times, I do not mix business with pleasure. Nothing good can come of it. So if he goes after Jess, to use your terminology, 'que sera sera'. Now hurry up with that food, I'm starving."

Chapter Fourteen

When Daisy arrived at the wildlife park the following morning, Simon was waiting for her. They went to the entrance to get their tickets. Simon didn't offer to pay for her, so she got out her purse, but then he handed her a ticket and she realised that he'd bought two.

"Oh, you didn't have to pay for me. Here, let me give you the money back." Daisy fumbled in her purse.

"No need, my treat." Simon smiled at her.

He was such a kind man, and Daisy wished she felt more for him.

"Okay, I'll buy lunch then. Where shall we start? Ooh, the giraffes are over there, let's go see them."

They wandered around the park, looking at all the different animals, and Simon made her laugh by doing voices for them. When he did one for a penguin who kept opening and closing its beak, Daisy laughed so hard, her sides ached, and tears poured down her face. She realised she was actually having a great time.

As they walked down a slope to go and see the monkeys, Daisy slipped on some loose gravel and Simon caught her, then held her hand, and she let him. It didn't send any sparks of electricity through her, but it felt safe and comfortable.

They stopped for lunch in the park's restaurant and, despite Simon protesting, Daisy paid. For some reason she didn't want to be beholden to him. She was sure he'd be astounded if she'd voiced that thought, but paying for lunch made her feel better.

They had a great afternoon. They went on the train ride around the park and got a boat across the lake to see the seals and hippos. They stopped for ice creams, and bought some food to feed the deer. Daisy loved the Asiatic lions, although she jumped a mile when one ran at the fence with a roar. She was glad there was a barrier between them and the fence. Simon said the lions were probably agitated as it was close to their feeding time.

They'd seen the last of the animals – the timber wolves – and were back in the restaurant, having a drink.

"Thanks for today, I've had a really nice time," Daisy said. There was that word again, 'nice'.

Simon smiled. "Me too, thanks for coming."

He leaned towards her and Daisy panicked. Oh, no, he was going to kiss her. She didn't want him to kiss her.

She leaned down to pretend to pick up her bag, just as Simon leaned in, and they banged heads.

"Ouch." Daisy rubbed her head and Simon rubbed his, then they both laughed.

"That was rather disastrous. Sorry," he apologised, and blushed.

"It's okay." Daisy took a deep breath. She had to say something. She couldn't let him go on hoping.

"Simon…oh heck, look, I like you – I really do – and I've had the best time today. I haven't laughed so much for ages. The only other person who makes me laugh like that, is my flatmate Kris."

"But?"

"But…I don't like you in that way. I've had a great day out and I'd love to do it again, but as friends."

"You don't fancy me?"

"No."

She saw his face fall, but only fleetingly, he managed to hide it really well.

Daisy touched his hand, then withdrew, she couldn't give him the wrong impression. "You're a great guy, you've got a fab sense of humour, you're kind and caring."

"Just not boyfriend material," he said in a quiet voice.

"Yes, of course you are, you'd make a perfect boyfriend for someone, just not me. I'm sorry, but I have to be honest. It's not fair to let you think there's more to us than friendship."

Simon smiled and kissed Daisy on the cheek. "That's okay. I can't pretend I'm not gutted though, you've wounded my fragile heart."

He held his hand to his chest and pulled a sad face, and Daisy felt awful, but then he laughed. "Daisy, I'm half joking. Yes, I'd like us to be more than friends, but if you don't feel that way about me, I can't change your mind."

"Sorry."

"Nothing to say sorry for. Thanks for being honest and telling me. I hope we'll still meet up lunch times?"

"You bet, and I truly would like to go out with you again. I wasn't just saying that, I've had a fab time today."

"I'd like that too. Well, if it's not going to work out for us, maybe I ought to join The Love Shack. Don't suppose I could get mates rates?"

"Why don't you hang on a bit, someone else will come along."

"Until you turned up they hadn't. I'm not that interesting – a lawyer who loves animals – and maybe you've got someone on your books who'd be a perfect match for me?"

"Maybe. If you're serious, I'll ask Greg if you can have it cheaper. Why don't you call into the agency on Monday? We can have a quick chat, then go for lunch together after."

"Sounds like a plan."

After walking to the car park, Simon kissed Daisy goodbye – on the cheek again – and they got into their separate cars to drive home.

Daisy felt relieved, but was also a bit sad. What was wrong with her? Simon was a lovely guy, many women would be delighted to have him as a boyfriend. He was everything most women looked for – kind, caring, considerate, funny and an animal lover. But he's not Greg, said a little voice that she tried to ignore.

***

Monday morning, around mid-day, Jess buzzed through to tell Daisy there was someone asking for her. Daisy frowned, then wondered if it was Simon. Damn, she'd forgotten to ask Greg if Simon could have their service cheaper seeing as he was her friend.

"Jess, is it a guy called Simon?"

Jess whispered into the phone. "Yes, it's Simon. Where did you find him? He's gorgeous. He's sitting in the foyer, are you coming out?"

"Keep him there a few minutes longer, I need to speak to Greg."

"My pleasure."

Daisy hung up and dialled through to Greg, then her mind went into overdrive as it always did when she had an idea. Wait, Jess said Simon was gorgeous, she was an animal lover… Maybe Simon would think Jess was nice too? She was aware of Greg waiting on the other end. "Oh sorry, Greg. I have a friend in reception who's thinking of joining up, and I wondered if he could have a cheaper rate?"

"He? Who is it?."

Greg grinned at Daisy's answer. Simon, the guy she'd gone out with. So, if he was looking to join the agency, that meant things didn't go as expected between him and Daisy. Hell yeah! Greg punched the air. Simon could have the premium service free of charge as far as he was concerned, but that wasn't good for business. Greg coughed and answered. "He can have a twenty percent discount. Seeing as he's a friend of yours."

Greg emphasised the word friend and it wasn't lost on Daisy, but she didn't dwell on it, because her mind was still whirring away.

She went out to reception, and saw Jess gazing dreamily at Simon, who was reading a magazine. He looked up as Daisy approached, then looked across at Jess and smiled.

"Hi, Simon, would you like to come into our interview room for a moment?"

Just as they sat down, there was a knock at the door. Daisy called, "Yes?" the door opened, and Jess walked in.

"Can I get either of you a drink?"

"No thanks, Jess. Simon?"

"Oh, erm, a coffee, thanks."

Jess sashayed out, and Simon watched her leave, which wasn't unnoticed by Daisy.

"Right, I've spoken to the boss m... I mean, Mr Hanson, and we can do you a twenty percent discount," she told him.

Jess arrived with Simon's coffee, and Daisy was delighted to see him watch her again as she left.

"Jess is our new receptionist."

"She's pretty. All that gorgeous hair and cute freckles. A big improvement on the other sour faced woman who used to work here."

"Did you know Stella?"

"No. I came in once, but she was so scary looking, I walked out again."

Daisy laughed. "Nothing scary about our Jess."

Daisy studied Simon for a few seconds, then said. "Before I sign you up, do you really think Jess is pretty?"

Simon gave Daisy a look that she interpreted as are you blind?

"She's lovely. I bet she's married though, all the nice ones are...or just not interested." He looked pointedly at Daisy.

She raised her eyes and sighed. "I'll ignore that remark. I happen to know that Jess thinks you're pretty hot too."

Simon's eyes widened. "Really? I mean, how do you know?"

"Because she told me when she phoned to say you were here."

"Wow." Simon was stunned to think such a pretty girl thought he was hot.

"Look, I have an idea. It means you don't get to spend your lunch time with me today," Daisy saw Simon's face fall, "but, you get to spend it with Jess."

Greg would probably kill her as it was doing them out of money, but she still felt bad for letting Simon down, and wanted to play Cupid.

"Okay, follow me." She got up and went out to reception.

"Jess, this is Simon, Simon, this is Jess. Now, Simon and I usually have lunch together, but today, Jess, you're going to take my place."

"What? I can't." Jess looked at Simon tentatively, but he was smiling.

"Yes, you can," he said. "We usually sit in the park and feed the ducks."

"Aww, I love little duckies. I like all animals. I should have trained as a vet, except I couldn't bear to put an animal to sleep."

Simon was smiling broadly. "You like animals? Me too. I took Daisy to the wildlife park on Saturday and we had a great time."

"I love the wildlife park, I haven't been for years," Jess said.

"We should go together," Simon enthused, forgetting that Daisy was still there. He only had eyes for the girl behind reception.

Before Jess could answer, Daisy interrupted. "Off to lunch, you two. Simon, say hi to Gilbert for me."

Jess slid off her chair and grabbed her lunchbox, giving Daisy a grateful smile, and Simon rushed to hold open the door to let Jess through.

Daisy heard Jess ask, "Who on earth is Gilbert?" and Simon said, "wait and see."

She sat at reception, feeling pleased with herself, and hoping they'd hit it off. She couldn't bear it if Simon was let down again, and he'd probably blame her.

She buzzed through to Greg.

"Sorry, Greg, but my friend may not need our services after all. He's just taken Jess to lunch."

Greg was obviously confused, and Daisy said she'd tell him later as a potential client had just arrived.

Jess came back from her lunch date with a big smile on her face.

"That man is wonderful. I wish our lunch breaks were longer, I could have sat with him all day."

"So you liked him then?"

"Liked him? I think I've fallen in love already. I'm meeting him this evening, for dinner." Jess sighed, a dreamy look in her eyes.

131

"Did he say anything about me?" Daisy wanted to know if Jess knew she'd turned him down.

Jess grinned. "Yes. I know you spend your lunch times together, and Simon liked you, but you said you only see him as a friend."

"Oh."

Jess laughed. "Daisy, it's okay. I'm glad, because otherwise, I wouldn't be going out with him, so you did me a favour."

Daisy had a sudden thought. "I guess I won't see him anymore."

Jess frowned. "What do you mean?"

"You'll want to spend lunch times with him now."

"No, well, yes, I'd like to, but Simon said you should continue your lunch chats and we can see each other in the evenings."

"Really? Are you okay with that?"

"Of course. I know you're not interested in him as a boyfriend, so it's fine. Besides, I know who you really like."

Daisy cocked her head on one side. "Who?"

"Greg."

"Shh." Daisy held a finger against her lips. She was shocked. Were her feelings for Greg that obvious?

Oh, crap. Jess had only been there a day, well, two including Friday afternoon, but she could already see that Daisy liked Greg. She'd better control herself more. If Jess could tell, maybe it was obvious to everyone, Greg included.

Daisy shook her head. "I don't know what you're talking about."

Jess smiled. "You can't fool me, Daisy. I see the way you look at him whenever he's around, and, he likes you too."

"Rubbish. Did you see Gilbert?"

"Stop changing the subject." But Jess could tell Daisy didn't want to discuss it, so she talked about her time with Simon instead. "No, we didn't see Gilbert."

"Oh, I hope he's okay. Right, I'm going to lunch now, see you when I get back."

Daisy rushed to the park, worried about Gilbert and

praying he wasn't injured, or even worse, that he hadn't ended up as a fox's dinner.

But she'd literally just sat down on her usual bench, when a familiar bird came waddling out of the pond, with a loud quack.

"Gilbert! Aww, I'm glad you're okay."

Daisy was so pleased to see her feathered friend, that she broke up a whole sandwich and gave it to him. He waddled back to the pond to dip the bread in the water.

"I should get you some proper food. Hang on a mo." She walked to the little kiosk that sold duck food, and Gilbert followed her.

She went back to her bench to feed Gilbert and think about her morning. She was pleased that she'd got Jess and Simon together, but not pleased about her feelings for Greg being so obvious.

She should stop being so friendly, and behave more professionally. Maybe her friendliness was giving the wrong impression. Right, it was time to step back a bit. No more joking around, she'd be a professional business woman from now on.

She texted Kris. "Played Cupid to Simon & Jess, now feeding Gilbert in park. Hope your day's ok, D x"

A few moments later, she got a reply. "Well done, my day's good, new student started this morning, he's hot! Tell all tonight, K xx"

Daisy smiled. If Kris said someone was hot, then he must be special, as Kris was really particular. She wondered if they'd end up together. She sighed and looked at Gilbert. "Everyone seems to have a partner except me. Even you found a mate. Pretty bad when my duck friend gets a mate before I do. Gilbert, where am I going wrong? Why can't I find someone to love?"

A wave of sadness engulfed her, and her eyes brimmed with tears, which she quickly wiped away. What would people think – she was sitting on a bench, talking to a duck, and crying. She pulled herself together. Daisy's bubbly nature meant she was never down for long, and whenever she had an odd bout of self-pity, she soon talked herself out of it.

She shook out the last of the duck food and stood up. "Right, I'm going back to work, nice to see you again, Gilbert, see you tomorrow – same time, same place."

She looked around to see if anyone was watching her talk to the duck. They'd think she was crazy. At least she'd have Simon to chat with tomorrow.

Chapter Fifteen

When Daisy arrived at the agency the following morning, Jess was talking to an older well-dressed man and she heard Jess say, "Ah here she is now."

"Daisy, this gentleman would like to take out our premium service. I said you'd be in soon and could interview him."

Daisy was surprised he was there so early, it was only eight fifty, and they didn't usually open up until nine. But she put on a big smile and held out her hand. "Daisy Dorson, senior consultant. Pleased to make your acquaintance, Mr…?"

"Harrington, Otto."

"Mr Harrington. If you'd like to follow me to the interview room, I can take some details. Would you like a coffee?"

Mr Harrington looked at his watch and frowned. "I'm sorry, I really don't have a lot of time for coffee, or the interview right now, but if I sign up quickly, could we do the interview another time?"

"Of course. When were you thinking?"

"I don't suppose you do evenings, do you? Sorry, but I'm too busy during the day, I'm already late for a meeting."

"Yes, I can do an evening. The office is closed, but we could arrange to conduct it at a venue of your choice."

"How about my home, this evening?"

Daisy glanced at Jess, whose eyes widened, and Jess shook her head, but Daisy knew they sometimes interviewed clients in their homes. However, she wasn't too happy about going to a strange man's house on her own.

"We can certainly interview you at home, but if that's what you'd prefer, then it'll be the agency owner Mr Hanson who'll conduct it. I'm sure you'll appreciate that we can't expect a woman to go to a strange man's house alone."

Mr Harrington looked a bit bemused. "I'm not going to attack you – I'm not an axe murderer or anything."

Daisy smiled sweetly. "It's as much for your protection as it is ours. Imagine if a female came to interview you, then later went to the police claiming you'd attacked her – even if you hadn't. We try to protect both staff and clients at all times."

Mr Harrington rubbed his chin thoughtfully. "Hmm, yes, I quite see what you mean." He looked at his watch again. "Well, why don't the two of you come this evening. Here's my card, phone me if it's okay, but I really have to go. Can we sign up this evening too? I don't have time to do it now."

Daisy took the card. "Yes, of course, I'll phone you later to finalise the arrangements."

And with that, the man hurried out of the doors to whatever meeting he was late for.

"Whoa, no way would I go to his house alone. He wasn't bad for an old guy though, nice clothes and he was wearing a really posh watch, I think it was a Breitling."

"How do you know that?"

"He looked at it several times, and I have a thing about jewellery, not that I can afford anything expensive, but I'd love a decent watch."

Daisy, who wasn't the least bit interested in watches, shook her head in amazement. "As long as it tells the time, I don't care what make it is."

"I need to educate you on the finer things in life, Daisy dear," Jess said and they both giggled.

"Why were we open so early? We don't usually unlock the doors until nine."

"I got here about five minutes before you, and he was waiting outside. I could see he was impatient, looking at his watch, so I let him in."

"Hmm, if it happens again, make them wait. We have to sort things out before we open up. Is Greg in?"

Jess nodded.

Daisy knocked on Greg's door and he answered with his usual, "Come in."

Daisy entered and sat opposite him.

"Morning, Daisy, nice to see you." His gaze travelled to her legs, then back up to her face. "What can I do for you?"

She told him about Mr Harrington, and that he'd suggested they both go to interview him. "But it doesn't need both of us, surely?"

"No, it doesn't, but he may feel more at ease with you there as well, seeing as he's now made contact with you. He hasn't met me yet."

Daisy bit her bottom lip. Greg knew that was usually a sign that she felt uneasy.

"You don't have to do it, I'll go on my own if it bothers you that much." He raised his eyebrows questioningly.

Daisy felt flustered. It wasn't the interview that bothered her. She didn't want to spend time with Greg outside of work. But, it was work business, just in a different location, surely that would be all right?

"It's okay, I'll do it. What time shall we meet there?"

"Meet? Don't be daft, I'll pick you up. What's the point of us both driving?"

"NO. I mean, no, it's okay, I'd rather drive," Daisy said.

"Don't want to risk being alone with me, huh?" Greg winked at her.

Damnit, why could he see right through her? Was she that transparent?

Daisy snapped at him. "Yes, if you must know. I want to maintain a strictly business relationship, so that means not being alone with you outside of work. And can you please stop all the teasing and flirting. Winking at me, the lingering looks, and that…that smile of yours."

Greg held his hands up. "Hey, back off. Okay, if that's really the way you want it – purely professional from now on. Tell your Harrington bloke we'll meet him at seven thirty. That should give you enough time to grab something to eat beforehand."

Greg wasn't happy. He'd wanted to suggest they go for dinner somewhere before going to Harrington's house, any opportunity to spend some extra time with her, but fat chance of that now. And what did she mean by 'that smile of yours'? What smile?

Daisy went back to her office feeling miserable. Yet again, she felt like the bad guy, when all she was trying to do was the right thing.

When she went out to get a cup of tea mid morning, Jess ran over and handed her a bar of chocolate.

"To cheer you up. What's wrong? You came out of Greg's office earlier looking really unhappy, and he's got the grumps too."

"It's nothing, but thanks for the chocolate."

"You're welcome. If you want to talk, you can trust me."

Daisy squeezed Jess's arm, "Thanks, Jess, but I'll be okay, honest. Greg and I are going to Mr Harrington's tonight. Oh, how did you get on with Simon last night? Sorry, I should have asked you earlier."

Jess's eyes shone and she beamed. "We had a great time. We didn't stop talking, we've got so much in common, and when he kissed me at the end of the night – oh my word, if he's that good a kisser, I can't wait to get him into bed."

"Jess!"

Jess laughed. "Don't worry, I'm not going to shag him anytime soon, that's not my style. I know a lot of girls have one night stands and 'friends with benefits', but I'm not like that. Never have been, which is probably why I'm still single at the age of twenty-eight. I think guys expect a girl to jump into bed – or wherever else – on the first date nowadays. Well, not all guys obviously, Simon doesn't."

Daisy smiled. "I'm really pleased you hit it off. When you said he was gorgeous, and I saw the way he looked at you, I knew you'd be great together."

Daisy felt a bit sad. Greg looked at her the same way, but he wouldn't after her outburst earlier. It wasn't even him she was annoyed at, it was herself. She didn't want to be alone with him because despite her adamant rule about not mixing business with pleasure, she just couldn't trust herself to not reach out and touch his hair, or his handsome face, and if he did try to kiss her again, she knew that even if her mind protested, her treacherous body wouldn't, so it was best all round that she'd put a stop to his flirting. "But, you'll miss it," a devilish little voice told her.

***

She met up with Simon at lunch time, and he was pleased to see Gilbert greet them.

"I'm glad he's okay. When he didn't appear yesterday, I was a bit concerned."

"Didn't Jess tell you? I spent my lunch break with him. He even followed me to the kiosk when I went to buy him some food."

"Aha, that proves my theory that he recognises people, and it's not just about food. He was obviously waiting for you."

Daisy sniffed. "At least someone loves me, even if it is just a duck."

Simon looked concerned. "Hey, Daisy Doolittle, you okay?"

Daisy smiled. "Yes, I'm just being silly. So, tell me about your evening with Jess."

Simon was just as smitten with Jessica as she was with him, and he said it was almost as if they were destined to meet.

"That's what Kris always says, that things are meant to be." Daisy bent down to feed Gilbert.

"Mm, just think about it. If you hadn't turned me down, and Jess hadn't gone in for the job – even though the deadline had passed – we'd never have got together, so I do think fate helped us out."

"Erm, excuse me, I think I may have had a hand in it too." Daisy poked him in the ribs. "After all, it was me who told you Jess thought you were hot."

Simon had to agree. "True, but if you hadn't said anything, I think we'd have got there on our own eventually. I'm seeing her again tonight. This is going to sound stupid – especially coming from a guy – but I think I love her already."

Daisy smiled and Simon said, "What?"

"I'll let you into a secret. Jess said the same thing this

139

morning."

"Really?"

"Really."

Simon grinned, a big soppy look on his face. Daisy hoped things stayed good for them, it was nice to see him happy. Bloody hell, she was surrounded by loved-up people, and spent her days playing Cupid, but her own love life was non-existent.

"It doesn't have to be," said that little voice again, "it's only your own rules that makes it so."

Whilst Simon finished his lunch, Daisy texted Kris. "Gotta go interview a client at his house tonight, so need to grab quick eats when I get in. D x"

"You're not going to a strange man's house alone – want me to come? K xx"

Aww, bless him. She'd amend her earlier statement about only a duck loving her, Kris did too.

"No need, the boss man's coming. D x"

"Interesting. K xx"

"No, just work. Catch you later. D x"

Daisy put her phone away and looked at Simon. He still had that daft expression on his face. She made a decision.

"Simon, you don't want to spend your lunch times with me when you could be with Jess, why don't you change it so you can spend it with her instead?"

"But then you and I won't get to see each other."

"I know, but now Jess is in your life, you'd rather be with her. And we can see each other now and then, maybe you could both come out with Kris and me one night? He goes to this club and we have a right laugh."

Simon didn't need telling twice, Daisy could see he wanted to spend as much time with Jess as possible.

"That's sorted, I'll tell Jess when I get back to work."

"Thanks, Daisy Doolittle, you're a great girl you know. Aw, I won't see Gilbert anymore. Tell Jess what happens with him, and she can keep me updated."

Daisy laughed. "Of course I will. Right, better get back."

They walked together, and when she was outside the agency, Daisy said, "I'm so pleased for you, Simon, take care, and I hope to see you soon for a night out."

Simon waved to Jess through the door as Daisy went in, and Jess blew him a kiss.

Daisy felt she ought to apologise to Greg. She loved her job, and now Stella had gone and Jess was around, it was perfect. She didn't want an atmosphere to spoil things.

However, she wasn't brave enough to do it in person, so she emailed him from the safety of her office.

"Sorry about earlier, didn't mean to snap at you. D"

She half expected Greg to leave her to stew, but she should have known he wasn't the sort of man who played games, and he answered right away.

"Don't worry about it. I was going to invite you for dinner before we interviewed this client, but I guess the answer would be no? G"

"Sorry, what I said still stands, professional only. D"

Greg sent back a sad face icon and an 'okay' and that was it.

Well, she'd apologised, but still let him know where he stood, and she felt a bit better. She sighed, and got on with matching some new profiles that had just flashed up.

Chapter Sixteen

There was a plate of macaroni cheese waiting for Daisy when she got in. Kris often arrived home before her, so he usually cooked dinner.

"I didn't do garlic bread seeing as you're interviewing someone. Don't want you breathing garlic breath all over him."

Daisy laughed. "Thanks for this, Kris." She put a forkful into her mouth. "Mmm, oh that's so good. You're a star. What are you going to do this evening?"

"Well, seeing as you're going out, I decided I would too."

"On a week night? Blimey that's not like you."

"Well, you sometimes need to ring the changes, sweetie, otherwise you become a BYF."

Daisy frowned. "A BYF? What's that?"

"A boring young fart."

Daisy laughed out loud. "I think the saying is 'boring old fart', isn't it?"

"Yes, but I adapted it to fit us. Now, ask me where I'm going."

"Okay, where are you going?"

"Out for a quiet drink with…the new student I mentioned." Kris clapped his hands in delight.

"Ooh, get you. So he's gay then?"

"Ob-vi-ously, darling, I wouldn't be going for a drink with a straight guy, would I?"

"You might do, just as friends."

"I don't do friends with straight guys – only girls."

"Kris. That's…erm, there must be a term for it… straightist."

"No, it isn't. It doesn't work being friends with straight

142

guys, they get all funny and think you're going to try to convert them. Well, the ones I've met do anyway."

"Stop generalising. What about the straight drama students? You get on with them."

"Yes, at the drama school. I wouldn't socialise with them. Anyway I was telling you about Josh." He pouted, wanting to talk about his date.

"That's his name, is it? What's he like?"

"He's funny and good-looking – well, I think so – and clever and talented, and we were paired together in a class and got chatting."

Kris was dancing around the kitchen as he talked. He could never keep still for long.

"When I got your text lunch time, I read it and moaned that I'd be home alone tonight, so he asked if I wanted to go for a drink, and I said yes."

"That's great. Well, I shouldn't be too long, the interview will only take about an hour, so I'll catch up on the soaps when I get back. Make sure you've got your key in case I'm in bed when you get home."

"Sweetie, I'm going for a quiet drink, not to the club. I won't be late."

"Hmm, we'll see. Have you eaten? If you're going to be drinking, you should eat."

"You're not my mother, Baby D, thank heavens. I'm not going to drink a lot. Josh and I both have classes tomorrow. It's just a 'getting to know you away from work' drink."

"Okay, have a fab time. I'd better go."

She grabbed her bag and keys, kissed Kris, and headed out the door.

She knew the area where Mr Harrington lived was upmarket, but if Daisy could whistle – she couldn't, she'd never been able to – she'd have given a long one on seeing his house.

It was massive; with a huge driveway and electronically controlled gates.

Greg's car was already there.

She pressed the button on the wall, announcing her arrival, and the gates swung open.

"Christ on a bike," Daisy muttered. She'd never seen anything so palatial. She wondered what he did for a living – if he even worked. He must be minted to have a house like this. She wondered why he needed a dating agency.

Mr Harrington opened the huge front door, and, taking her arm, guided her into the hallway.

Daisy tried not to look around, tried to act as if seeing a house like this wasn't new to her, but she had to stop her jaw from dropping. It was the epitome of money, but not in a trashy way. Mr Harrington had good taste and the hallway wasn't overly cluttered, but tastefully decorated with a few obviously expensive, modern ornaments and paintings.

She didn't have chance to look around any further, because he guided her into what she assumed was the living room, where Greg was seated on a huge squashy leather sofa.

"Now, what can I get you to drink, young lady?" Mr Harrington asked. "I have wine, spirits and champagne."

Daisy couldn't resist the champagne.

"I knew you'd have that." Greg grinned at her. "It's Daisy's favourite alcoholic drink," he informed Mr Harrington.

Daisy's heart beat a little faster. Fancy Greg still remembering that.

"A girl after my own heart. You obviously have good taste," Mr Harrington said as he handed her a glass of sparkling bubbles.

"Thank you, Mr Harrington."

"Oh, we can dispense with such formality, call me Otto."

Daisy smiled. "Thanks, Otto."

Whilst he poured himself a drink, Daisy studied him. He must have been in his early fifties and wasn't unattractive. Slightly greying hair, but plenty of it, and he obviously kept himself in good shape.

He turned and caught her staring and she blushed.

"I bet you're wondering why a man like me, who obviously has money, wants to join your dating agency?"

Daisy stuttered. "I…I wasn't thinking that at all." She blushed again. "Well, maybe I was."

Otto laughed. "Honest too. If only you were a few years

older."

Daisy smiled. She liked him.

"To answer you, so far I've discovered that the women I've dated are only with me for my money. They attach themselves to me like leeches as soon as they know I'm rich."

Greg raised his eyebrows at Otto's forthright attitude.

"Oka-a-ay," Daisy said. "How do they know or find out you're rich?"

"I guess the places I frequent are the sort of places where you need to have money. Fancy restaurants and hotels." Otto laughed. "I'm hardly your 'night down the local pub' man, am I?"

"Maybe you ought to be?" Daisy said.

Otto sat down. "I'm not with you."

"Well," Daisy leaned forward, eager to tell him what she thought, "maybe if you went somewhere less exclusive, and it wasn't so obvious you were rich, you'd meet a woman who liked you for yourself, not your money."

Otto nodded. "A simplistic view, my dear. I can't not be myself. I'm used to my lifestyle. I like eating in good restaurants and staying in the best hotels. I couldn't stay in one of those twenty-nine pound a night rooms."

Greg spoke up. "No, but I understand where Daisy's coming from. Okay, what if we sign you up – we'll do the premium service, which is more discreet. You won't be on our website, and we'll hand-pick a match for you. We can omit certain facts such as where you live, and just put in your interests, hobbies and tastes in music etc. Then we'll match you up with someone with similar interests. You'll meet in a mutually agreed venue – nowhere too posh."

Daisy joined in, "Yes, and if you don't dress too obviously – don't flash your watch around etc, she won't know you're loaded. Then if you like each other, you can let her know about your status later on."

Otto looked at the two people sitting in front of him and smiled.

"Okay, let's do it. It'll probably do me good to come down a bit, be in touch with ordinary folk."

Daisy laughed. "You never know, you might even enjoy eating fish and chips out of paper on a bench somewhere. It's the little things that are so nice." She stopped speaking, then continued, "Can I say something?"

Otto nodded.

"Money wouldn't always impress me. Oh, it'd be nice to be treated occasionally, but anyone can buy gifts and take you to fancy restaurants. What would impress me, was a man who went to the trouble to find out what I'd really like to do."

"Such as?" Otto asked.

"Well, I love trees and being out in the fresh air. So...oh, I don't know, if a man surprised me with a simple picnic in my favourite beauty spot for instance, that would mean more to me than being taken to a fancy restaurant."

She could feel Greg's eyes on her, but wouldn't look at him. Instead she finished the last drop of champagne in her glass.

Otto looked thoughtful. "Excellent, you've really made me think, young lady. Thank you for that. Now, would you like another drink or shall we get down to business?"

"We'll get down to business as we're both driving," Greg said, and he got out the paperwork he needed to fill in.

For the next forty-five minutes, Daisy asked questions – with the odd interjection from Greg – and he filled in the forms. Otto made them coffee and tea, and once they'd finished chatting and drank their drinks, he gave Greg a cheque for a year's premium service.

"Wouldn't you rather sign up for six months? What if we find you a match within a month, you'll have paid all that money," Daisy said. Even if the guy was loaded, she didn't want him to waste money.

Greg interrupted. "Usually the money is non-refundable, but I'm sure we could come to some arrangement if you were to meet someone quickly."

"No need. If that happens, it proves how good you are at your jobs and worth every penny, so don't worry about it. Use the money to give this young lady a bonus or something."

Daisy blushed. "That won't be necessary, Greg pays me a

reasonable salary."

"I really do wish you were a few years older," Otto said. "You haven't got an elder sister, have you?"

Daisy laughed. "Yes, but she's married and lives in Australia."

"Pity."

When Daisy and Greg left, Otto stood at his huge front door to wave them off.

Daisy turned to say, "Thanks for the champagne" and as she did, Otto warned, "Mind the step."

Too late. Daisy tumbled down the step leading to the gravelled driveway, badly twisting her ankle.

Greg rushed to her aid.

She brushed him off and tried to stand.

"Ouch. Shit, that hurts." Tears welled in her eyes at the incredible pain. She couldn't put any pressure on her foot and her ankle hurt like hell. She sat on the step, feeling shaky.

"Want me to call an ambulance?" Otto said, mobile phone in his hand.

"No, that won't be necessary. If I can just get to my car, I'll drive home." Daisy winced.

"Daisy, don't be stupid, you won't be able to drive," Greg said as he inspected her rapidly swelling ankle.

"Well, can we just try?"

Greg helped her to her feet and as soon as she tried to walk, she collapsed against him, tears springing to her eyes.

He swept her up into his arms as if she weighed nothing more than a bag of flour.

"Put me down. What do you think you're doing?"

"Daisy, stop protesting, how else do you think you're going to get to your car?"

"Can I do anything?" Otto asked as he paced up and down, a concerned look on his face. "Why don't you bring her back inside and we'll call the doctor?"

"I'll be fine if I can just get home. Thanks, Otto, sorry for being a nuisance," Daisy said.

She felt really stupid. "I'm so bloody clumsy," she berated herself. And what she didn't want to admit, was that she enjoyed being held in Greg's arms.

Greg placed her in the front seat of her car, knowing full well she wouldn't be able to drive. If her ankle hurt that much, she wouldn't be able to press down on the pedals.

"Okay, see if you can drive."

As soon as Daisy moved her foot, she cried out in pain. Greg raised his eyebrows at her.

"Okay, okay, you're right, I won't be able to drive."

Greg turned to Otto. "Is it okay if I leave my car here and collect it early in the morning? I'll drive Daisy home and get a taxi out for my car tomorrow."

"Why don't I follow you and bring you back for your car?"

"That's a kind offer, Otto, but I may be a while. I want to stay with Daisy and sort her ankle out."

Whilst the men discussed the logistics of getting Daisy home and Greg's car back, she sat there feeling weak and shaky, her ankle hurting like hell. She wanted to yell at them to just get her home, but knew that was unfair, they were only trying to help.

Otto said he'd collect Greg early in the morning. He felt responsible. If they hadn't gone to interview him, Daisy wouldn't have hurt herself. So, with that sorted out, Greg reached into the car and lifted Daisy into his arms again. He went round and placed her gently on the passenger seat, and, saying goodbye to Otto, got in the drivers' seat.

"Will Kris be home to sort you out?" Greg asked as he drove.

"No, he's out tonight. Just get me indoors and I'll be okay."

"Daisy, I don't think you will, that ankle seems pretty bad to me. You'll probably need to go to A&E."

Daisy felt even more foolish. "I'm really sorry, Greg, I'm so clumsy."

She winced again as she moved and Greg could tell she was in a lot of pain. He hated seeing her hurt, and wished he could make her better.

When they reached Daisy's flat, she gave Greg her keys, which he held in his mouth, then he lifted her into his arms again. He carried her up to the front door, Daisy took the keys from him, and opened it. Greg kicked it shut behind him, and carried her into the living room.

Daisy's heart and insides were doing all sorts of crazy things. She tried to pretend it was because of the pain, but it wasn't. She liked being in his arms, and suddenly, more than anything, she wished he'd kiss her again. She wouldn't stop him this time.

Greg must have picked up on her thoughts, because he looked down at her as she looked up at him. He glanced at her lips and Daisy gasped. Oh, bugger the rules. Rules are made to be broken. She gave a small, almost imperceptible nod. Greg smiled and lowered his head. He kissed her, and Daisy floated on a cloud.

It was the sweetest kiss, and she didn't want it to stop.

He pulled away. "I'm sorry, Daisy, but I have to put you down."

He gently placed her lengthways on the sofa and put a cushion behind her. Then he knelt down in front of her. His eyes questioned hers and she reached down, put her hand behind his head, and pulled him towards her for another kiss.

When it ended, Greg groaned. "Daisy, I've been wanting to do that for so long."

"I've wanted you to as well."

"So why all the aggro?"

Daisy sighed. "Because I've always had a rule with myself to not mix business with pleasure. It can only end badly. I love my job and don't want to jeopardise it."

"Have you ever had a work relationship?"

"No."

"So, how do you know it'll go badly?"

"I've heard it enough times and read about it."

Greg rubbed his chin. "So, you've read in some sensational women's magazine about someone who had a disastrous liaison with a colleague, and that means every work relationship is doomed?"

Put like that, Daisy had to admit it sounded daft. She tried to defend herself. "Not just that, the psychologists say you shouldn't mix business with pleasure." She folded her arms in that defiant gesture she often made.

Greg laughed. "Well, my rule is to never dismiss something until you've tried it. So," he cocked his head on one side, "want to give it a go?"

Daisy moved and winced. "Ouch."

Greg was filled with concern. "Okay, let's have a look."

He pulled up the leg on her jeans. Her ankle was swollen, and already turning black.

"It's either badly sprained, or even possibly broken. Daisy, we have to get you to the hospital to have it x-rayed."

"Can't you just put some frozen peas on it to reduce the swelling?"

"No, that won't help if it's broken. Come on, I'll drive you."

Luckily, the accident and emergency department wasn't too busy, so Daisy was seen within fifteen minutes. Whilst she was having an x-ray, Greg pondered over recent events. He couldn't believe that she'd finally given in and allowed him to kiss her, not once, but twice – the second time initiated by Daisy herself. He then worried that it may have been because she was hurt and feeling vulnerable. Would she go back to her usual 'professional only' rule once she'd come to her senses?

"Don't pressure her, take it easy and at her pace," he told himself. Having finally broken through Daisy's barrier, he didn't want to mess things up.

A porter wheeled Daisy back to where Greg was waiting.

"So, what's the verdict?"

"It's a bad sprain, nothing broken, but the ligaments are torn, which is why it hurts so much. They're going to strap it up and I have to use crutches for a couple of weeks, and keep my leg raised as much as I can."

"That's two weeks off work for you then," Greg said.

"It certainly isn't. I'll still be able to do my job, I'll just have to hobble around on crutches, and put my leg up on a chair." Daisy was adamant.

"And how are you going to get to work?"

"Oh." She hadn't thought of that. "I'd ask Kris to bring me, but it's in the wrong direction for him." She bit on her bottom lip. "I'll get taxis."

"Don't be daft, that'll cost you a fortune. If you really insist on working, I'll collect you and take you home." Greg grinned at her. "Besides, that'll give me an excuse to carry you in my arms again."

"Ah, but I'll have crutches."

"Oh, bummer." Greg pulled a sad face.

With a twinkle in her eyes, Daisy said, "So, you'll just have to settle for kissing me better, and I think I'm going to need a lot of kisses for an injury this bad."

Greg raised his eyebrows and leaned towards her with a grin. "The sooner we start your kissing treatment, the better then."

Chapter Seventeen

Jess was full of concern the following day when she arrived for work, and saw Daisy trying to hobble on her crutches to get herself a cup of tea.

"Oh my gosh, what happened to you?"

Daisy told her what had happened, omitting the bit about Greg and herself now being an item. She wanted to keep it quiet, not wishing to become the object of office gossip. She knew Jess wasn't a gossip, and could be trusted to keep things to herself, but it was early days, and Daisy didn't want anyone to know yet.

However, when she told Jess that Greg had carried her to the car, and then into her house, Jess smiled, a knowing kind of smile.

"What?" Daisy asked, feigning all innocence.

"Daisy Dorson, if you were any more transparent, I'd be able to see that table behind you."

"I'm not with you."

"If a picture paints a thousand words, your face speaks volumes."

"Stop talking in idioms – or is it metaphors?" Daisy tried her hardest to keep her face impassive, but didn't succeed.

"Okay, spill. I want to know what else went on. I know you two fancy each other something rotten, it's so obvious," Jess said.

Daisy caved in. "Okay, but you better not breathe a word to anyone, and I mean anyone. Don't even let Greg know I told you." She sighed dreamily. "He kissed me."

Jess squealed and Daisy hushed her up.

"Sorry, but this is the best news. So, go on, I want all the details."

Daisy told her about the kiss, and that she'd kissed him too. And, that he'd stayed with her until Kris got back.

"He was so sweet. Really caring. Treating me as if I was a piece of fragile china. And there was a lot of kissing." Daisy grinned, and sighed again. "Now, if I could just master these ruddy crutches, things would be perfect. Well, perfect would be not having a sprained ankle, but you know what I mean."

Jess made Daisy's tea for her. "I'm really pleased for you, but anyone could see how much you like each other, so it was only a matter of time before you caved in. Come on, I'll carry your tea to your office for you. Don't want you having any more accidents. I've finally met someone even more clumsy than me." Jess laughed.

Daisy hoped her ankle would heal quickly. It was most inconvenient. Trying to do even the most ordinary things took her twice as long. As a person who didn't have good balance anyway – she often fell over or bumped into things – mastering crutches was a real challenge.

Kris had gone berserk when he'd got home the previous night, and found Daisy laid up on the sofa, Greg beside her and the crutches on the floor.

"I should never have gone out," he'd wailed dramatically.

"Kris, calm down, what good would you staying in have done? I'd have still fallen over, you wouldn't have been there to stop me."

"No, but I could have taken you to the hospital, and been with you. Why didn't you phone me?" He was almost in tears. Ever since Daisy's other accident, when she'd helped the police, Kris had been paranoid about her getting hurt again.

"I wasn't on my own. Greg helped me. It's nice that you're so concerned, but stop worrying, I'm okay, really."

Greg had kissed Daisy on the cheek, said he'd collect her in the morning, and made himself scarce.

Daisy had patted the sofa beside her, and when Kris sat down she'd hugged him. He'd taken a few minutes to calm down, but then had been a brilliant nurse for the rest of the night. He'd even taken her breakfast in bed that morning, and helped her put her black trousers on, before heading off to his drama school.

Daisy texted him now, to say she was okay, then emailed Greg.

"I'd like to go to the park lunch time, fancy coming with me? I might need some help getting there, you can meet Gilbert. D x – note the kiss at the end."

Greg replied within seconds. "Yes, I'll come – you're not safe out on your own. I'll claim that kiss later. G x"

Daisy read it and her heart somersaulted, as it did every time she thought about him. Funny how things happened. Maybe she was destined to be with Greg, but her stupid rule was keeping them apart, so fate had intervened.

The sequence of events couldn't just be coincidence. Mr Harrington had turned up when he was already late for a meeting, meaning that he wanted to be interviewed at home. Greg could have gone by himself, so, had fate stepped in and made her go as well? Then, had fate also made her fall down the steps so that Greg would carry her?

If none of that had happened, she'd still be sitting here clinging to her stubborn rule about not mixing business and pleasure.

Or, maybe she had a guardian angel. Jess said everyone had one, and they worked in mysterious ways. Maybe hers had got fed up with Daisy's obstinacy, and given her a helping hand.

She looked up at the ceiling and whispered "Thank you." Good job she was in her own office, anyone watching her would think she was bonkers. That made her chuckle, and for some reason, she couldn't stop, and sat at her desk giggling her head off, tears pouring down her cheeks.

At lunch time, her usual seven-minute walk to the park took quite a bit longer as she tried to manage the crutches on the pavement and across the road. Greg thought it would have been a lot quicker if he'd just carried her, but she had to learn to cope by herself, so he walked slowly beside her.

When they got to her bench, Greg sat beside he, and pulled her into his arms for a kiss.

"I've wanted to do that all morning."

"Me too. I didn't quite get that one, can you do it again please."

He kissed her again and Daisy swore she heard angels singing. She'd been kissed before, lots of times, but never had they made her heart beat faster and her insides feel like jelly with such a feeling of…well, she couldn't describe it, just happiness bubbling up inside her.

They were disturbed by an indignant quacking, and broke apart to see Gilbert standing in front of them.

"Gilbert!"

The duck waddled forward a bit more, and pecked at Daisy's trousers. She reached down, and he actually let her stroke his soft head.

"Greg this is Gilbert. Gilbert this is Greg."

Greg laughed and held his hand out to the duck, who pecked at it.

"Ouch. That wasn't very friendly."

Daisy laughed. "He just wants food."

"He didn't peck you, he let you stroke him."

"Yes, but he's known me for months. We've built up a friendship. Oh blast, I forgot to buy his duck food."

"I'll get it – he might decide to befriend me if I feed him."

Greg walked up to the small kiosk and bought a bag of duck food.

They sat together on the bench, feeding Gilbert, eating their sandwiches, and chatting.

"So," Greg said, crumpling up the duck food bag, "have you told anyone about us yet?"

Daisy blushed. "No."

She just couldn't lie though, so she admitted that she'd told Jess.

"Only because she'd guessed. She said it was obvious we fancied each other rotten. I've made her swear not to tell anyone else though. I don't want people at work knowing. It may cause problems."

"Such as?" Greg asked.

"I don't know, jealousy, being accused of favouritism, that sort of thing."

"I don't think any of them would think that. If it's obvious to Jess that we like each other, don't you think it's obvious to everyone else?"

"So, how do we deal with it?" Daisy finished her sandwich and closed her lunchbox.

"Why don't we just take things easy, and if we become serious, then maybe I'll tell them. But to be honest, our personal lives are nobody else's business. What about Kris?"

Daisy sighed. "I haven't told him yet. I'll do it tonight."

Greg looked at his watch. "Okay, we better head back seeing as it'll take you ages to get there. It'd be quicker if I carried you."

"Don't you dare," Daisy said and that was a challenge Greg couldn't resist. He swept her up into his arms.

"What about my crutches?" she squealed.

A man and his wife were passing by so the man gathered up the crutches, and with a smile, gave them to Daisy.

"Thank you."

Greg went to walk off, but Daisy protested.

"What's the matter?" Greg stopped, wondering what was wrong.

"I haven't said goodbye to Gilbert."

"You're crazy, do you know that?" Greg swung her around so she could say goodbye to the duck. He was astonished when Gilbert quacked, then headed off to the pond.

"Did he just quack goodbye? Please tell me that was just a coincidence."

"Maybe, but he often does it. I like to think he's saying goodbye."

Greg laughed. "I can see life with you is going to be very interesting."

He carried Daisy until they were around the corner from the office, then he put her down on the ground.

"Better not let the staff see me carrying you. They're probably already wondering why we went to lunch together."

"The only one who will have noticed is Jess, and she knows. The others are in the office. You can only see the street if you're out in the foyer."

"True. Now, before we go in…" Greg dipped his head and kissed Daisy, a long lingering kiss.

"Mm, cheese and pickle," he joked.

Daisy was horrified. "Do I really taste of cheese and pickle?"

"Relax, I was kidding. I saw what you had in your sandwiches."

"Oh." She laughed and smacked him. "You really worried me then."

"Daisy, nothing would put me off you. I'd even kiss you after you'd eaten a curry."

"I'll put that to the test one day. Now, come on, we'd better get in."

Daisy had been worried about Kris's reaction to her and Greg, but he was really pleased.

"About time, girlfriend. You've been mooching over that man for weeks…no…months. Ever since you started there, in fact."

"I so have not."

"Sweetie, yes you have, and you know it."

Daisy grinned; Kris was right, as usual.

"So, how are you and the boss man going to work things?" he asked as he washed the dinner dishes.

"What do you mean?"

"When are you going to see each other? That kind of thing?"

"We've talked about it – it was naughty really, we spent most of the afternoon emailing each other – and we're going to take things easy. We'll spend our lunch times together, but only see each other at weekends, and a couple of evenings, maybe Fridays and Sundays."

Kris thought about it. "Seems like a good idea. Hey, so that means we can still go to the club on Saturdays?"

"Too right. I'm not ready to give up my Saturday nights out with my best friend just yet, and I like our evenings in too."

Kris didn't want Daisy putting her love life on hold for him though.

"Baby D, you don't have to stay in with me every evening. If you want to go out with Greg, I'll invite Josh round."

"Really? You two getting on well then?"

"He's a dreamboat. We spend our lunch times together – hey, we're a bit like you and the boss man. But I wouldn't mind seeing him on the occasional evening too. We can't exactly snog at work, can we?"

Daisy laughed. She was relieved Kris understood. That's what had worried her the most. She and Kris were so used to their nightly routine, she was concerned he'd be upset if it all changed.

She wanted to spend as much time as possible with Greg, but she didn't want to rush into things, and she loved Kris to bits and wanted to spend time with him too. She just had to try to get the balance right.

"I've decided that you may be on to something with this destiny business." Daisy went on to explain how everything seemed to conspire to get her and Greg together.

"See, what did I tell you. It's all in the hands of fate – or our guardian angels." Kris washed up the last of their dishes and put it on the drainer. "Hey, maybe we ought to have our tarot cards read, see what's in store for us? Apparently there's a really good reader in Merrilies bookshop in Bewford."

"No thanks," Daisy said. "I don't want to know. As you keep saying, que sera, sera. I'll just let it happen. Besides, don't you think that whatever she tells you, might influence you – even subconsciously?"

"Hmm, maybe you're right. Okay, we'll just let fate do whatever it's going to do, and hang on for the ride."

Chapter Eighteen

Daisy was glad to be rid of her crutches when she went back to the hospital to see if her ankle had healed. She was afraid to put all her weight on her foot though, scared it might give out, but when the nurse helped her back from x-ray, Greg was there to hold her as she tested it.

Gingerly, she put her foot down, anticipating a shot of pain through her ankle, and was delighted to find it was okay.

"Yay, thank heavens for that. I can finally get back to normal."

It had been a challenging couple of weeks, and Daisy had hated feeling like an invalid, with everyone doing things for her.

"Right, no excuses from now on, back to work properly; you've been slacking a bit these last two weeks," Greg teased.

"Ha, carry on like that, and you might need to find another senior consultant."

Greg laughed, but then his face softened. "I could never replace you, and I don't just mean at work. I can't imagine my life without you in it now. I look forward to work every day – not that I didn't before – but it's extra nice with you there. I love our lunchtimes together and I look forward to the evenings when we see each other." He bent down and kissed her.

Daisy hated to admit it, but she felt the same. Being with Greg was like having the missing half of herself back again. She hadn't realised it was missing until she'd got together with Greg, it was the strangest feeling, but at the same time, the most magical.

As well as spending lunch times together, they sent little email messages back and forth during the day, although Greg sometimes got a bit naughty with his.

Daisy had read a particularly steamy message, and had a shocking thought. What if he sent it to the wrong person by mistake? The notion horrified her, but made her giggle as well. She could just imagine Greg's embarrassment as he pressed 'send' then realised it had gone to someone else, he'd certainly have some explaining to do.

They'd settled into a good routine at work. Daisy knew her job inside out, and was an excellent matcher – she was thorough, methodical and also choosy – making sure she picked the best match possible, and she had some great ideas for ways to enhance the business. She was a real asset – in more ways than one.

***

Daisy was at her computer one morning, when Jess buzzed through with a phone call.

"It's from a lady called Marjorie."

"Ah, put her through. Marjorie, how lovely to hear from you, the wedding's soon isn't it, I'm so looking forward to it…" Daisy broke off as Marjorie started to cry.

Her heart beating rapidly in her chest, she was afraid to ask what had happened. She hoped Fred hadn't changed his mind and called the wedding off.

"Marjorie, what on earth's wrong?"

Daisy listened, then gasped, and her eyes filled with tears. "I am so sorry. Can I do anything? Would you like me to come round? No, okay. Can you tell me what happened?"

She listened some more, trying not to cry.

"I'm so sorry, Marjorie. Let me know if I can do anything. Yes, I understand. Thanks for telling me."

Daisy replaced the receiver, got up and ran out into the loo, where she burst into tears.

Jess had seen her go, and not being able to leave reception, she buzzed through to Greg.

Greg hurried into the toilets, to find Daisy sobbing her heart out. "Oh, Greg." She turned and wept into his chest, as he

160

held her.

When she'd pulled herself together a bit, he led her out, and sat her in the foyer whilst he made her a cup of tea.

Jess rushed over, her face full of concern. "What the heck's happened?"

Daisy wiped her eyes on a tissue and hiccoughed on a sob. "Marjorie is a dear old lady who I matched up with an elderly man called Fred. They came in to tell us they were getting married, and invite me to the wedding."

"Oh, don't say he's changed his mind and dumped her?" Jess said.

Daisy shook her head. "No, worse than that. He died a couple of weeks ago."

Jess held her hand to her mouth. "Oh no. Oh, poor woman. Do you know what happened?"

"Marjorie woke up one morning, to find him dead beside her. They'd only moved in together a couple of months ago. They were getting married in three weeks' time." Daisy cried all over again.

Jess didn't know what to say to comfort her, and then the reception phone rang so she had to go and answer it.

"Come into the office, darling." Greg carried Daisy's tea, led her into his office and sat her down.

Daisy sniffed and wiped her eyes. "Greg, it's so sad. They'd just found each other, and then this happens. Why is life so cruel?" Tears welled up and spilled over. "They didn't even have chance to get married. Why couldn't they at least have had a bit of time together as a married couple?" She gulped and hiccoughed again.

"Drink some tea, Daisy."

She took a shaky sip and Greg leant down in front of her and took her hands. "Look, honey, if it wasn't for you, they wouldn't have found each other. So, they had a happy few months together."

"But that wasn't enough. It's so unfair! They were looking forward to a lovely wedding, and instead Marjorie had to go to his funeral." Daisy bent her head and cried her heart out.

Greg felt helpless. He hated seeing her in so much distress.

All he could do was hold her while she cried.

When her body stopped shaking, he said, "Do you want to go home? Why don't you take the rest of the day off?"

Daisy shook her head. "No, I'll just sit at home thinking about poor Fred, and poor Marjorie. Do you know, she apologised for not telling me sooner, and not inviting me to the funeral. She said she just had too much to think about. But when she went through the wedding list, she remembered me, and had to phone to let me know. I wish there was something we could do for her."

Greg had been thinking, and he now said, "Remember when they came in and I took photos of them for the newspaper?"

Daisy nodded.

"Well," Greg went on, "I emailed them to Fred, but I don't know if he'd have got round to printing them. What if we print a nice one of them together, and frame it for her?"

Daisy smiled. "That would be a lovely thing to do. I don't think they'd have printed any, I remember Fred saying it was a pity he didn't have a printer."

"Okay that's what we'll do. I'll phone her later and offer my condolences. Are you sure you don't want to go home?"

"Yes, I'll be fine. And you're right; at least they had some time together. It makes you think that you should spend as much time as you can with the people you love though."

She realised what she'd said, and Greg realised the implication of it too. They looked at each other.

"Daisy, I know it's not exactly the right time, but, well, I wanted to ask you something."

Daisy waited, her green eyes watching him.

He knelt down again. "You're right – about spending time with the people we lo— care about. I know we see each other every day at work, and have our weekend arrangement, but I want more."

"We see each other evenings too."

"Yes, but only Fridays and Sundays. I want to see you on all the days that have a Y in them."

Daisy frowned, then smiled as she realised that was every

day.

"You mean it?"

Greg kissed her, and stroked her hair. "Yes. I want to be with you every second of every minute of every day."

"Oh, Greg, I want that too, but didn't tell you because I didn't want you to think I was rushing things. There's nothing worse than a needy woman."

"Daisy, you dope. You're not needy; far from it. I like caring for you. I want you to need me. And I felt the same. I didn't want to pressure you into more than you were happy with. I know we agreed to take things easy, but…"

"Hearing news like what happened to poor Fred and Marjorie makes you realise what's important, doesn't it?" Daisy sniffed.

"Yes. It really does." Greg stroked her hair back, and gently touched her tear-stained face.

"Okay, we'll chat about it later. But I have one condition," Daisy said.

"Oh?"

"I still get my Saturday nights out with Kris." Her lovely face suddenly fell again. "I hope he'll be okay about this new arrangement."

"I'm sure he will." Greg groaned as he got up and his knee creaked. "He's got to accept that you'll leave one day."

That thought made Daisy a little sad, but she knew that whatever happened, Kris would always be in her life.

"Okay, I better do some work. We can chat about it lunch time." She kissed Greg, went into the ladies to tidy up her face, and went back to her office. She couldn't help thinking about poor Marjorie though, and cried all over again when she saw a photo of dear Fred as she went through his profile. She couldn't bring herself to delete it, so put his file into archived items. They kept old client records, just in case they wanted to sign on again.

When they went to the park at lunch time, Greg bought some duck food, and as he sat down, Gilbert came waddling out of the pond, followed by Mrs Gilbert, and… Daisy squealed with delight. Toddling beside their mother, were five little ducklings.

"Oh, Greg, look at them. Hello, you little darlings."

Daisy slowly leaned over, and Mrs Gilbert kept a beady eye on her as she reached down to one of the babies. It scurried away from her.

"Here, try some food. Offer it to Gilbert first, then his mate, then the ducklings might take some," Greg said.

He poured some food into Daisy's hand. She held it out and Gilbert pecked it up. Then Mrs Gilbert took some, and she turned and quacked at her babies as if to say, "It's okay, you can tuck in."

One by one, they crept over, and tentatively pecked at the food in Daisy's hand, before scuttling off again.

She took a photo of them on her new phone, then sat back and sighed.

"Life is strange. We hear about death in the morning, then we come here and see new life."

Greg squeezed her arm. "That happens every day, all over the world, darling. Someone dies and another one is born."

"I know. At times I love this world, but at others, I hate it."

Greg changed the subject before Daisy got upset again. "So, fancy a drink after work tonight?"

"I'm not sure, I think I'd rather stay in. I don't go out on work nights, and to be honest, I'm not in the mood for a night out."

"Okay. How about I cook dinner for you at mine instead, with a bottle of wine?"

"Do I get dessert?"

"Only if you're a good girl, and eat all your dinner up." Greg grabbed her and nuzzled her neck.

Daisy squealed and laughed. "What sort of dessert?" she asked with a naughty gleam in her eyes.

"The sort where we need to get undressed, and then I do this." Greg kissed her. "And then, I…" He whispered in her ear and she gasped.

"Sound good?"

"Does it! Can I have second helpings?"

"You, my darling, can have seconds and thirds."

An excited feeling fluttered in Daisy's stomach, and other regions, at the thought of what Greg was going to do to her that evening. She crossed her legs to try to stop her body's reaction.

"I'd better text Kris, and let him know I won't be home until late."

"No. Text him to say you won't be home until tomorrow evening."

Daisy raised her eyebrows. "Are you asking me to spend the night?"

Up until now, she hadn't spent the night with Greg. This was certainly moving their relationship on to another level. But the thought of spending the evening in his arms, and the whole night with him, was very appealing.

"I am," Greg answered. "A whole night of scrumptious dessert; I can't wait." He kissed her neck and his hot breath sent shudders through her, causing her body to react in ways only Greg could make it.

They were interrupted by a quacking. Gilbert was back, on his own this time, looking expectantly at the bag that was still on Greg's lap.

Daisy laughed out loud. "Saved by the duck. Here you are." She emptied out the rest of the food and watched her feathered friend gobble it up. Then she reached out and stroked his soft head.

Greg checked his watch. "Right, better get back to work. Don't forget to text Kris, he'll worry if you're not home."

Daisy texted him when she was back at the office, and he replied soon after.

"No probs, Josh asked me to his as well, so I can go now. K xx"

Daisy smiled, and replied. "Excellent. Have a great night, don't do anything I wouldn't, see you tomorrow D x"

Then she went out to reception.

"Jess, whilst I remember, what's Simon's mobile number again?"

Jess didn't even take out her phone, she just recited the number, then asked, "Why do you want it?"

"You know his number off by heart?" Daisy laughed. "You

must be in love. I want to send him a photo of Gilbert's babies."

"Gilbert's got babies? Aww, let me see." Jess huddled over Daisy's phone, and both girls awed and ahhed at the photo of the ducklings.

"They are so sweet. Simon will be made up to see them. He often asks how Gilbert is, and you – Daisy Doolittle he calls you."

Daisy smiled. "Hey, we haven't had a night out together for ages. We should arrange something soon." She sent the photo to Simon's phone.

"That'll be great. Are you okay now? I felt so sorry for you earlier."

Daisy sighed and gave a small smile. "Yeah, I'm okay, I was just so upset to think they didn't even get married. Poor Marjorie, instead of looking forward to her wedding, she's now had to go to a funeral." Daisy's bottom lip trembled as she tried not to cry again.

"It certainly makes you stop and think about things. It did us. In fact…" She stopped talking, not sure whether to tell Jess what she and Greg had discussed.

"Out with it. You can't start something, then stop. Come on, you know you can trust me," Jess said.

Daisy lowered her voice. "Okay. Greg and I had a chat. He told me he wants to spend every minute with me, so I'm staying over at his place tonight."

Jess's eyes widened. "Ooh, a night of passion, eh? Don't do anything I wouldn't." She grinned.

"Ha, that leaves me plenty to do then. I'm a bit nervous, I haven't stayed over before."

Jess was amazed. "You haven't stayed the night with Greg yet?"

"No. I was kind of saving it."

"Aww, you're so sweet. Bloody hell, I stayed over at Simon's the week after we started seeing each other."

"Jess. You're just a hussy." Daisy laughed.

"Yeah and then some. Simon loves it."

Daisy looked around. "Shh, keep your voice down."

Jess laughed. "You are so prim and proper sometimes."

Daisy frowned. "You say that as if it's a bad thing."

"No, I'm just teasing you. I think it's nice. It's what makes you, you – being so particular about certain things. Don't ever change; you're lovely as you are."

Daisy smiled, pleased at the compliment, even if it was kind of back handed.

Her phone bleeped and she looked at it. "It's a message from Simon. He says, "Aww they are so cute, I want to see them." The trouble is, he doesn't see Gilbert now he lunches with you."

"Well, we can swop one day, you go with Simon and I'll have lunch here when you get back."

"You sure?"

"Yes, it'll make him happy seeing the ducklings, and you can have a good old natter."

"Okay, thanks, Jess." Daisy sighed. "Must go get some work done."

She went back to her desk, feeling happier than she had that morning. Then she had a bit of a panic. She couldn't stay at Greg's, she didn't have any clean underwear, make-up or face cleaning stuff, and she couldn't arrive at work tomorrow in the same clothes. What had seemed like a great idea at the time, now seemed a bit of an issue.

She emailed Greg. "Can't stay over, what about my work clothes? And I'll need make-up, cleaning stuff and, erm, underwear. D x"

Greg replied within seconds. "You most def won't need any underwear – I'll have it off as soon as you step through my door. G x"

Daisy blushed and looked around as if scared someone might be reading over her shoulder.

"Stop it – one of these days you'll send a naughty email to the wrong person. But what am I going to do? D x"

"Relax, I'll drop you home first so you can put a few things together. Now do some work! G x"

Daisy smiled. Ah, problem solved.

Chapter Nineteen

It was moving from summer into autumn, and they'd had a real influx of clients, many recommended by Otto Harrington. Although he hadn't found 'the one' yet, he'd had a few interesting dates and was so pleased with the agency's service, he'd spread the word at his golf club, and other places.

Greg and Daisy had worked on a new advert, which Frank had placed in the paper for them at a reduced rate, and it had obviously worked, as the agency had never been so busy.

Greg had thought about doing a TV advert, until he saw the cost. It was a huge amount of money, and as Daisy had pointed out, why spend out when we don't really need to? Word of mouth, and the newspaper, had done a good enough job.

Greg didn't want to say anything to Daisy until he'd considered it properly, but he was thinking of opening another agency, out of town, to attract even more clients. He liked the idea of branching out, and he thought Daisy was more than capable of running an office on her own, but he needed to think more seriously about it. So for the time being, he was keeping things to himself.

He'd also been thinking about Daisy's birthday in a couple of weeks' time on September 13th. She would be twenty-five, so he wanted to do something special for her. Maybe he'd take her to Rialto's again, she'd loved it last time.

He decided to mention it lunch time as they sat in the park feeding Gilbert, his mate and the ducklings, who were growing up fast.

"So, you'll be a quarter of a century soon."

Daisy's eyes widened. "Christ on a bike, that sounds so old!"

Greg sputtered crumbs out of his mouth as he laughed at the look on Daisy's face, and the expression she'd used. He wiped them off his trousers.

"Where on earth did you hear that?"

"What?"

"The expression you just used."

Daisy thought for a bit. "I have no idea. I've been saying it for, well, as long as I can remember. I must have read it somewhere." She munched her sandwich, then said, "It's rather daft actually, they didn't have bicycles in those days – did they?"

Greg threw the last of the duck food on the ground, and watched the birds race to peck it up, before waddling back to the pond.

"No. I think the first bicycle of sorts was invented in the late eighteenth century, or it may have been early nineteenth, so no, they didn't have bikes when Jesus was alive."

"Oh, well, it's a stupid saying then."

"Yes, but funny. Especially when you say it."

Daisy grinned. "So, you were saying, about me being twenty-five soon?"

"Yes. Well, I was wondering what to do to celebrate. I thought you'd like to go to Rialto's again?"

Daisy's eyes gleamed. "Ooh, yeah." Then she pushed out her bottom lip and made a sad face. "Aww, but I want to spend my birthday with Kris as well."

She cuddled up to Greg, looked up at him with her green eyes, and fluttered her eyelashes as she said, "Darli-i-i-ng…"

Greg laughed, knowing the things women did when they were after something. "What are you creeping for?"

Daisy gasped and acted shocked. "Moi, creeping?" She laughed. "Okay, well, you know how much Kris would love to go to Rialto's? I can't go again without him, he was so jealous last time…"

Greg sighed. "So…you want Kris to come as well?"

Daisy bobbed around on the bench, getting excited. "Please can he come too? I know it's expensive, but it's not like we do it every day, and as you said, it is a special occasion."

Greg was planning to invite Kris, and Jess, anyway, to make it a bit of a party, but he wasn't going to let Daisy know that. He wanted to see how much she'd plead. He pretended to think about it, and frowned.

Daisy snuggled up more and kissed his neck. "Pretty please, I'll make it worth your while."

That's what he wanted to hear. He tried to stop himself grinning. "If you put it like that, then okay, but I want extra rations."

Daisy squealed and threw her arms around him. "Ooh, you're a star! Have I told you what a brilliant boyfriend you are?"

"No, not yet, but you can start now."

Daisy kissed him over and over, and in between she said, "You…are…the…best, best…boyfriend…ever."

Greg laughed and held Daisy away. "In that case, Jess might as well come too."

Daisy whooped, then stopped and looked at him. "You were going to invite them both anyway, weren't you?"

Greg grinned.

Daisy slapped him. "Fancy making me go through that, Gregory Hanson, you beast." She slapped him again and Greg caught her hands, held them behind her back, and kissed her, a long lingering kiss.

When she came up for air, she tenderly stroked Greg's face. "Thank you, you're so generous. This is going to be the best birthday ever."

"That's okay, you're worth it. Seeing as it's turning into a bit of a party, we might as well invite Jess's boyfriend – you know him well, don't you?"

"Simon? Yes, he's the man I used to spend my lunch times with."

"Hmm, the one you went on a date with. When you told me that, I was so jealous, I wanted to punch him. I was really pleased when you said it hadn't worked out."

Daisy was quiet for a bit. "That's because I only had eyes for one bloke. He was all I could think about, even though I tried my hardest not to. It was getting impossible. Every time he was near me, I got all nervous and excited, and if we accidentally touched, I felt…well—'

Greg interrupted. "Like a jolt of electricity had hit you? And whenever he looked at you, you just wanted to melt. You found yourself thinking about him all the time. You just wanted him to take you in his arms and kiss you?"

Daisy's eyes met Greg's, and she nodded. "Yes, that's exactly how it felt."

Greg nodded as well. "Me too."

"Really?"

"Yes. I think I fell in love with you the moment you came into my office, all bolshie and ready for a fight. Those beautiful green eyes, full of fire."

Love. He just said the L word. Daisy's heart hammered. He probably didn't mean it like that, it was just a figure of speech.

Greg noticed that Daisy had gone quiet. He tilted her face towards him. "What's up, Daisy?"

She gulped. Oh heck. The big declaration. This would either make or break their relationship, but she had to tell him, she'd wanted to say it for ages.

"You said… I've been wanting to tell you…" She ran a hand through her hair, not quite sure whether to say it or not. What if it ruined things? They were so happy at the moment, she'd be devastated if this blew it.

Greg held her hands. "I know what you're trying to say, but if you're not brave enough, how about I go first?"

Daisy's eyes widened as she looked at him.

Greg's heart filled with love as his beautiful Daisy, with those wonderful, innocent green eyes, stared up at him. She was so sweet, kind and caring, she wouldn't hurt a fly, and he wanted to wrap her in his arms and protect her for the rest of their lives.

"I love you, Daisy Dorson. And just in case you didn't hear that, I. LOVE. YOU."

He kissed the tip of her nose and then kissed her mouth, a soft tender kiss. As he held her, he felt her shaking in his arms, and pulled away to look at her.

She was crying.

"Hey, silly thing, I didn't mean to make you cry."

She sniffed and smiled. "It's okay, they're happy tears. Oh, Greg, I love you too. I've wanted to tell you for so long, but was afraid it would ruin things, scare you off." She sniffed again.

Greg held her. "Never. You're stuck with me now. And I'm glad you love me too, it would have been a bit awkward if that wasn't what you were going to say."

Daisy laughed, and being the mad girl she was, she started singing. "I'm sticking with you, cos I'm made out of glue."

Greg laughed, then looked at his watch. "Oops, come on, Crazy Daisy, we'd better get back to work."

Daisy stood up and looked around. The world was already great, but it had suddenly got a whole lot better.

Holding hands, they walked back to the agency.

Chapter Twenty

Jess was so excited about going to Rialto's, but when Daisy told Kris that evening, he actually screamed, and ran around the kitchen. Then he sat on a chair, stunned.

"Oh my God, I can't believe it. The boss man is really taking me too?"

Daisy laughed, pleased with his excitement. "Yep. You, me, Jess and Simon."

"Stars, moon and the whole universe! I'm going to Rialto's. Baby D, I can now die happy."

"Ha ha ha, you idiot."

"I take back everything bad I ever said about the boss man. He's ace. Oh Lordy, what am I going to wear?" Kris shrieked, ran into his bedroom, opened the wardrobe and started flinging clothes onto the bed.

Daisy followed, and stood in the doorway, watching him.

"Erm, Kris, I hate to tell you this, but we aren't going this evening. We have two weeks to go yet."

"Only two weeks to put together the most important outfit I'll ever wear? I'll have to go shopping, I can't wear any of this trash."

He picked up a luminous pink and green spattered shirt between his finger and thumb, as if it was covered in something disgusting, then dropped it back on the bed with a disdainful look.

Daisy rolled her eyes. "Kris, it's just a restaurant."

"Yes, but lots of celebrities go there, so surely agents must go as well. What if I'm spotted? I have to look my absolute best. People have lost auditions because of the way they were dressed."

"I don't think so."

"They so have."

"Okay, who? Name me one person who lost an audition because of their clothes."

Kris peered down his nose at her and flounced back to the wardrobe.

"Ha, see you can't."

"Well, Josh told me that a friend of his friend got rejected for turning up at an audition in ripped jeans."

Daisy raised her eyebrows and folded her arms. She didn't believe a word of it.

"Okay, tell you what, I'd like a new outfit too, so how about we have a shopping spree on Saturday? We can help each other choose something nice," she said.

Kris clapped his hands in glee. "You're on. We can make a day of it. Get to the shops early, have lunch and do some more shopping, then go to the club in the evening."

"Sounds like a plan."

***

At work the following day, Jess buzzed through to Daisy. "I have a rather impatient client here."

"I'm on my way out."

Daisy greeted the woman in reception. "Daisy Dorson, senior consultant, how can I help you?"

"How soon can you find me a man?" the woman asked. She was in her early thirties, expensively dressed, with her blonde hair in a chignon, and she had an upper class accent.

"It doesn't quite work like that, Miss?"

"Forsythe, Victoria."

"Miss Forsythe. Why don't we go to an interview room and have a chat? We can discuss your requirements. Would you like a drink? Coffee, tea?"

"Any Earl Grey?"

"Yes. Jess, would you kindly bring us two cups of Earl Grey, thanks."

Once Jess had taken the drinks in, Daisy set about the

interview.

"Now, I hope you'll appreciate that it may take some time to pair you with a suitable partner, we are meticulous, and like to choose someone we think will be a perfect match."

Victoria sipped her tea, then sat back. "Sorry about the impatience. My father is trying to marry me off to the son of one of his friends, and I've told him I already have a boyfriend."

"Ah. And I assume, that was a fib?"

"Yes. Daddy thinks that because I'm thirty-three, I ought to be married by now, with a horde of children round my feet. He's threatening to disinherit me if I'm not married by the time I'm thirty-five."

"Oh dear."

Victoria rolled her eyes. "It gets worse. He says I can't just marry anyone. It has to be someone rich, which is why he's trying to pair me up with this son of his friend. The man's filthy rich, but his son is a dreadful bore. All he talks about is his horses."

Daisy tried not to laugh, but she could understand Victoria's predicament.

"I'd hate to have to marry someone my father chose. When I marry, it'll be to a man I love, and I won't care if he's rich or poor,"

"Exactly. I want to marry someone I'll love too – although I have to agree somewhat with Daddy, he has to have a bit of money. I'm used to a certain lifestyle."

"Okay, let's take some details, and I'll explain the two services we offer."

As Daisy went through the forms, she wondered what age Victoria would prefer. If she didn't mind an older man, maybe Otto would be suitable. He was rich, interesting and a nice guy. If they had the same interests, it could be a good match.

"Victoria, what age range would you be happy with?"

"I don't want anyone younger than me, or even the same age, they tend to be so immature. So, I guess, oh I don't know, late thirties to mid fifties?"

Otto was fifty-two, so he fitted in, just. Daisy could have

recommended the one-off service they'd thought up a while ago, for people they already had a potential match for, but Daisy wasn't sure yet that Otto would be suitable, and if not, she'd need to do some work finding someone else, so she kept quiet.

Victoria signed up to the premium service – she liked the fact that it was discreet, and said that people who took that option must be the wealthier types. She was right, they usually were.

Daisy couldn't wait to get back to her computer and see what interests Otto had. Please let them be the same as Victoria's, she silently prayed.

Daisy scrolled through the profiles on her screen – Hs. Harrington, Otto. Okay. She almost held her breath as she read his profile. Interests: tennis, she checked Victoria's; yep she liked tennis – playing and watching. Daisy wondered if Otto played, maybe that was how he stayed in shape. Otto liked the theatre and Victoria liked musicals. Well, you had to go to the theatre to watch a musical, so that was two things. Good food and wine was another they both put down. Otto had put boating, but there was no mention of boats on Victoria's forms. But, Daisy decided, most rich people liked boats. And even if Victoria didn't, that small detail surely wouldn't put her off?

She decided they'd be a good match for each other, but now wondered whether to set them up right away. Should she wait a few days before getting in touch so it looked like she'd been working on it? Daisy hated it when a client – who hadn't taken out the one-off service – parted with their cash and she found a match straight away. It had happened a few times. She remembered Marjorie and Frederick, then tried not to, as it still upset her to think about them.

She phoned Greg. "It's me."

"Hi, me. I've just been sitting here thinking about you."

"Oh?"

"Yes. Want to stop over tonight?"

"Love to. I'll text Kris and let him know."

"I don't want him coming too."

"Ha ha. Erm, bit of a dilemma. A client has just joined and she'd be a good match for Otto. Do I contact them both now, or leave it a few days?"

"As soon as you can. Why wouldn't you?"

Daisy sighed. "Because I didn't offer her the one-off service, and I hate taking money from someone when I already have a match in mind for them. It feels wrong."

"Daisy, we're running a business, not a charity. If we find a match immediately, we're doing a good job. What about other times when it takes ages?"

"Well, that's okay, it means they're getting their money's worth."

Greg thought back to his recent idea of Daisy running her own branch. Hmm maybe she wasn't quite ready yet. She was too soft. She needed to toughen up if she was going to run a company.

"Okay, one day won't hurt. Phone them both tomorrow morning though."

"Thanks, darling, speak later." Daisy didn't mind using endearments openly now as all the staff knew she and Greg were an item.

She hung up, and then remembered that, actually, Victoria had asked how soon they could find her a man, so she was only doing what the client requested.

She texted Kris to let him know she'd be at Greg's that night.

"Okeydoke, I'll invite Josh over. Have fun. K xx"

"You too. See you tomorrow, can you make your macaroni cheese please? I'll bring salad and dessert. D x"

She looked forward to the evening ahead. She wouldn't even need to stop off on the way home, as she'd bought some new – sexy – knickers to leave at Greg's, along with a washbag of essentials, and some spare clothes.

She wondered if he'd ask her to move in at some point, and felt a bit panicky at the prospect. She played the scenario through in her head. Greg asking her, and how she'd react. She was shocked to realise that she didn't know what her answer would be.

She loved Greg, and couldn't imagine her life without him, but moving in would be another huge leap on from their relationship as it was at the moment. And there was Kris to think of.

She tutted and shook her head. "Stop fantasising, he hasn't asked, and isn't likely to, either."

Chapter Twenty-One

When Daisy arrived home the following evening, Kris was cooking macaroni cheese, but she could see from his red-rimmed eyes that he'd been crying.

She dropped her bag on the floor and ran to him.

"Kris, darling, what's wrong?"

He sniffed, then threw his arms around her, and sobbed.

She led him to a chair and sat him down, then opened the fridge and got out a bottle of white wine. She poured two large glasses, and handed one to Kris.

He took a huge gulp, then stood up to finish cooking. Daisy pressed him back in the chair.

"Stay there, I'll finish it. Want to talk?"

Kris wiped his eyes, and took another gulp of his wine. "Josh and I broke up."

"Oh, Kris, I'm so sorry. What happened?"

"We were both auditioning for the Christmas play – they always start auditions early – anyway, we were both up for the lead role, but I was due to audition before Josh." Kris took another gulp of his wine. "I was in the dressing room, getting ready, when I heard a noise. When I went to have a look, I couldn't open the door. Someone had locked it."

Daisy's eyes widened and she shook her head.

Kris looked at her sadly. "Yep. Josh locked me in so I couldn't attend my audition."

Daisy was shocked. "No. Maybe it wasn't him?"

"It was, someone saw him sneaking away, and when they played back the CCTV, there he was, locking the door and walking off."

"That's a terrible thing to do, especially to your boyfriend.

Oh, Kris." Daisy held him as he started to cry again.

"Hang on a minute," Daisy frowned. "Why have the dressing rooms got locks on the outside?"

Kris sniffed and blew his nose. "They don't have usually, but this was a small office which had been turned into a dressing room, and it locks from both sides."

"Well, they better do something about that to prevent it happening again." Daisy hugged Kris as tears trickled down his cheeks.

He took a deep breath and told her the whole sorry story. How Josh had been so jealous that Kris might get the role, he'd come up with a plan to prevent him being able to attend the audition, in the hope of getting it himself. What Josh hadn't banked on, was that Kris would make sure they investigated the sabotage, and he'd get found out.

"Well, I hope he didn't get the role." Daisy was so angry at what Josh had done to her lovely BFF.

"No, he didn't, and they've suspended him until they decide whether they want to let him remain at the drama school. He wasn't even sorry. He said all was fair in auditions and acting roles."

"So, you've lost your boyfriend, and your chance at the starring role? Aww, you poor thing."

Kris sniffed again and smiled thinly. "Actually, there is one bit of good news. Now they know it wasn't my fault that I didn't attend the audition, they're letting me do it tomorrow."

"Oh, well, that's good at least. Sorry about Josh though, what an absolute pig. You're better off without someone like that."

"I know. The sad thing is, I was pleased he was up for the role too, and would have been proud of him if he'd got it. I wouldn't have been jealous. I guess his career is more important to him than his friendships, or love life."

Daisy felt so sorry for Kris. He was one of the kindest people she knew, and wouldn't dream of treating anyone so badly. She was upset and angry that someone could do that to him.

"Right, you go to that audition tomorrow, and give it your

all. If you don't get it, you'll know you tried your hardest. If you do, it'll be a poke in the eye for that sneaky bastard. He won't get far in life behaving like that. Then, on Saturday, we'll go shopping, and I'll treat you to lunch."

"Thanks, sweetie. I'll be okay. I'm more angry than anything else. I trusted him, and it hurts that he abused that. Shows how shallow he is, I guess." Kris finished his wine and topped his glass up.

"Yep, he'll make a lot of enemies and end up a sad lonely man, whilst you'll find someone to love you, and be eternally happy."

"Hope so. Now, let me finish the macaroni cheese. What did you get for dessert?"

"Apple crumble and double cream."

"Yum, my favourite."

For once, Kris ate all his dinner and a huge helping of the crumble. Daisy guessed he was comfort eating, and although she felt sorry for him, she was glad to see him eat a proper meal.

They had a good reason to have a slap up lunch on Saturday, Kris had got the role he'd auditioned for. He was like a little kid at Disneyland, so happy and pleased with himself.

"See, so it's not all bad," Daisy told him. "Have you heard from Josh?"

"Who?" Kris waved his hand at her as if he was waving the name away. "I haven't given him a moment's thought, sweetie."

Daisy knew he was fibbing and putting on a brave front, but good for him.

"I know you better than that, Kris, but it's good that you're pretending he doesn't matter. Let him see that you're getting on without him. Ha, I bet he's so jealous that you've got the part."

"I don't think he's even heard. Nobody knows when he's coming back – if he comes back. Quite frankly, darling, I don't care if I never see him again. There's plenty more where he came from. Now, how about this shirt, and…" Kris shrieked as he saw a pair of skinny leather trousers. "I have SO got to try those bad boys on." He grabbed the trousers and literally ran to the changing room, then stopped, ran back to Daisy and snatched the shirt she'd been holding for him. "Back in a mo, mwaah." He blew a kiss at her.

After a few minutes, he emerged from the changing room, and Daisy had to admit he looked great. The trousers fitted him like a second skin, and the blue paisley style shirt went well. "You look fab. What do you think?"

Kris twirled around in front of her, then turned back to admire himself in the mirror. "I love it. I haven't seen the price tag yet though. Have a look for me."

He turned around, Daisy pulled the price tag out of the back of the shirt, and told him the cost. He then looked at the price of the trousers and gasped. "Oh, well, I'll have to look for something else. But I do love this outfit." He pursed his lips and looked like a sad little boy.

"Okay, tell you what," Daisy smiled. "You buy the trousers, and I'll treat you to the shirt."

Kris looked at her, his eyes shining. "Really?"

"Yes. Can't have you showing me up on my birthday, can we? You've gotta look almost as fabulous as I will. Get them off, and we'll pay for them. Then you can help me find something suitable."

After searching around several shops, stopping for tea and cake, and more shopping, Daisy found a dress she loved. Deep midnight blue, with three quarter length sleeves, a sequinned V neckline, and a hem which came to just above her knee, it suited her slim figure. The dress was so well-made, it swirled around her legs as she moved.

Kris had found some great ankle boots to go with his trousers, which he really couldn't afford, but Daisy went halves with him. She then found some dark blue strappy sandals, which matched the dress perfectly.

"Okay, I've had enough shopping to last me a month, and spent an absolute fortune," she said as she collapsed into a chair outside the mall café they'd stopped at.

"Me too. Thank you so much, sweetie, we are going to look abs fab walking into Rialto's, I can't wait."

"Me neither, only ten days to go. I'm going to be so old,"

Daisy wailed.

"Baby D, you'll be twenty-five, that's hardly old."

"A quarter of a century."

"Oh, put like that, it sounds ancient."

Daisy slapped Kris. "Just for that, you can get the drinks."

Whilst she waited for Kris to be served, Daisy looked around the mall. She liked people watching. She liked imagining how the couples had got together. As she glanced around, she saw two people she recognised. It was Otto and Victoria, together.

As she watched them, Victoria glanced in her direction, and waved. Daisy waved back, then moved her bags off the chairs as they approached.

"Fancy seeing you here," Otto said. "How are you, little Daisy?"

"I'm good, thanks. Just been shopping with my friend Kris – he's getting us a drink."

"I could do with a large cappuccino. Mind if we join you?" Victoria asked.

Daisy smiled. "Not at all, sit down."

"I'll get them." Otto disappeared into the queue.

"What are you doing out shopping with Otto?" Daisy asked.

Victoria told her that on their first date, while having dinner, Otto had asked her what she'd like as a birthday present.

"Christ, that was a bit quick!" Daisy raised her eyebrows.

Victoria laughed. "Yes. I was rather surprised, as we'd only just met. But it turned out that it's his sister's birthday soon, and he didn't know what to get her. So he thought he'd ask what I'd like, and get that. I offered to come shopping with him and help him choose something."

Daisy smiled. "Ah, I see. He wanted a woman's opinion."

"Yes."

"So, how are you getting on?"

"Good, actually. I know he's quite a bit older than me, but I like that. He's mature, intelligent, kind, witty, not to mention stinking rich."

"Victoria!"

"Well, he is. I like him, he makes me laugh."

Daisy was delighted. "I really hope it works out."

"It'll make my father happy if it does, and it's keeping him off my back at the moment, so, we'll see. What have you been shopping for?" Victoria nodded at all the bags.

Daisy told her about her forthcoming birthday, and evening out at Rialto's.

"Ooh, let me see the dress."

Daisy took it out of the bag.

"Daisy, that's fabulous. You'll look gorgeous in it."

As Daisy put the dress away, Kris came back with their drinks.

"Here you go. Hey, Vicky, fancy seeing you here."

Daisy looked from one to the other in surprise. "Erm, sorry, I'm obviously missing something. You two know each other?"

"Yes," they both answered together. Victoria let Kris explain.

"Vicky's one of the tutors at the drama school."

"No. Really? But…" Daisy was going to say, "you never mentioned that on your profile," but managed to stop herself just in time. Client confidentiality meant she couldn't discuss clients with anyone else.

Now Kris was confused. "So, how do you two know each other?"

Daisy was flummoxed. "Oh, erm…"

"It's okay, Daisy." Victoria turned to Kris and whispered, "I joined the agency Daisy works for."

The penny dropped. "Ah, I see. And the man with you, who's he?"

"That's Otto. Daisy matched us up, I'm helping him choose a birthday present for his sister."

Satisfied with the answers, Kris sat down and sipped his drink.

"Daisy, I'm sorry I didn't mention being a drama tutor. It's not a full-time job, I only do two or three days a week. And to be honest, it's not something I want people to know."

"Why not, I think it's great," Daisy said. "You must be really talented."

184

"She is," Kris joined in. "I don't know why you didn't become an actor, Vicky, you're a brilliant teacher."

Victoria sighed. "I just wasn't cut out for it. My nerves used to get the better of me every time I went for an audition. I even started taking medication, to calm me, beforehand. But after a while that stopped working. Then one day, I helped one of the other girls learn her lines, and showed her how to portray the character, and enjoyed it. I realised I'd be better at teaching people to act, rather than acting myself."

"Well, don't hide your job, you should be proud of what you do," Daisy said.

"I know. It's just that people have this preconception of you when they know you teach drama. They think you're all 'lovey' and up yourself. So I just don't tell them. Ah, here's Otto. He knows, so you don't have to change the subject."

They chatted for a bit, and when Otto heard that they were going to Rialto's for Daisy's birthday, he asked who was footing the bill.

Daisy laughed. "Not us. There's no way I could afford for myself to eat there, let alone five of us. Greg's putting it through the company."

"That's generous of him. Not all bosses would do that for their employees."

Daisy blushed.

"She's not just an employee though," Kris said.

"Ah, I see. I didn't realise you two were an item." Otto raised his eyebrows.

"We weren't when we came to see you, it just kind of happened after," Daisy explained.

Otto laughed. "When he carried you to the car, I bet. Good for you."

Daisy filled Victoria in on what had happened the night they'd gone to interview Otto.

"It was obviously meant to be," Victoria said. "I do think there's no such thing as coincidence, certain things are meant to happen."

"Me too. I'm always telling you that, aren't I?" Kris turned to Daisy all excited that someone else held the same beliefs as him.

"Yes, you are. Right, we better get going, we're off out tonight, and we have to eat first."

"You have to eat, you mean," Kris said.

"Yes, mainly me. Kris doesn't eat enough to keep a bird alive." Daisy frowned at him.

"Vicky, will you tell her that us actors have to keep our bodies in shape." Kris nodded at Victoria, hoping she'd back him up.

"I think this is a discussion for another time, but quick answer, yes, you need to stay in shape, BUT, you need plenty of fuel to keep going. Especially with the work you're doing, Kris – dancing, acting, you're on the go all the time. You should eat, but the right sort of food."

Kris was surprised. Everyone he knew existed on coffee and salad. "Yeah, you say that, I bet you don't eat, though."

Otto laughed, a deep booming laugh. "Victoria, not eat? Pah. You should have seen what she put away when we dined out the other night."

Kris was even more surprised now.

"Come and see me next week, and I'll give you a diet requirement sheet. I promise you, if you eat the food on that, you'll keep that nice slim body of yours, but most importantly, you won't faint from lack of food."

Daisy picked up on Victoria's last words, 'faint from lack of food'.

She looked at Kris, worry etched on her face. "Oh, Kris, please tell me you haven't passed out from not eating."

"Yes, he has, twice now. I've asked if he's eating properly, and he said yes." Victoria gave Kris a pointed look.

"What? He isn't at all." Daisy turned to Kris, her face flushed with anger. "Right, that's it, you'll bloody eat a proper meal every night from now on, even if I have to force feed you myself."

Victoria winced and made an 'oops' face. "Sorry, didn't mean to drop you in it, but Daisy's right, Kris, you need to start fuelling your body properly. I'll give you that diet sheet soon."

"Email it to me, would you. The sooner I can get him

eating properly the better." Daisy glared at Kris, and shook her head.

Otto put his arm around Kris's thin shoulders. "Looks like you're in for it, mate. With two women on your case, you don't stand a chance."

They all laughed, which broke the atmosphere a bit, and then Otto said, "Before you go, I was asking who footed the bill earlier, for a reason. Rialto's was one of my projects years ago, I'm friendly with the owners. I'll make sure you get a substantial discount."

Daisy knew Otto used to be a property developer, that's how he'd made his fortune. "Otto, that's so kind, but you don't have to do that."

"I know I don't have to, but I'd like to. It's my birthday gift to you, so have a wonderful time."

She was overwhelmed with his kindness. Victoria was right, he was a lovely man. Daisy leaned over and kissed Otto on the cheek. "Thank you, that's really generous."

He waved her thanks away. "It's nothing. Hope to see you again soon, and make sure you eat, young man." He wagged his finger at Kris.

As they left, Daisy said, "Kris, why didn't you tell me you'd fainted? I thought we were close and told each other everything?"

Kris sighed. "Because I knew you'd be upset with me."

"Of course I'm upset with you. How would you feel if I was making myself ill? You were worried enough when I had my accidents, and they weren't self inflicted."

Kris knew she had a valid point. "I'm sorry. But you don't realise what sort of life I'm in. It's not just about talent; you have to look your best too."

"I understand that, but if you end up really ill, there won't be any auditions. You'll have to give up acting, full stop. Look, we'll get this diet sheet from Victoria, and see how you go on that. Please, for me? I'd be devastated if anything happened to you – same as you would if something happened to me. Deal?"

Kris hugged her and smiled. "Deal. Now let's get home, try our outfits on again, and marvel at how fabulous we look."

Chapter Twenty-Two

Greg said Daisy could have the day off for her birthday. It was a Friday, which was usually a quiet day at work, but she said she'd rather be working than sit at home alone.

"Well, have a lie in, and come in at ten instead of nine."

Daisy was happy with that. A nice lie in, a quiet day at work, and a fabulous evening to look forward to with her best friends and the man she loved – perfect.

Greg had a reason for wanting Daisy to arrive at work later. He'd planned a small surprise. She'd told him that she'd never really celebrated her birthdays. Apart from the cards from her family, and a present from Kris, it was just another day, so Greg wanted to make it as special as possible.

When she arrived at work, Jess wasn't on reception, and no-one else was about, so she went into her office and sat at her computer.

About ten minutes later, her phone buzzed. It was Greg, calling her into his office.

When she opened the door, Greg and Jess shouted "Happy birthday!" and Jess pulled party poppers, showering the streamers all over Daisy. She laughed in delight.

Greg gave her a bottle, tied up with a huge silver bow. It was Moet champagne.

"Wow, thanks, you know how much I love champagne."

Then he brought a cake up from under his desk, and lit the candles. The door opened, the other employees came in, and everyone sang to her.

"Make a wish before you blow the candles out," Jess said.

So Daisy closed her eyes, wished, then blew them out in one go.

After saying happy birthday again, the other employees went back to their desks. Jess stayed, and handed Daisy an envelope, and a small, beautifully wrapped present.

"Oh, Jess, you shouldn't have, thank you."

"Open it now," Jess said, excited to see if Daisy liked it.

Daisy sat on the edge of Greg's desk and opened the card – a soppy one with teddies and flowers – then carefully unwrapped the present. Inside was a pair of gorgeous silver drop earrings, with a beautiful indigo coloured gem in the centre.

Daisy gasped. "These are beautiful, thank you so much."

Jess smiled. "They're sapphires – your birth stone. I'm glad you like them."

"I love them. They'll go perfectly with my dress. You shouldn't have gone to so much expense though, they must have cost a fortune."

Jess shrugged. "You're worth it. You've been a good friend to me since I started here, and you got me and Simon together. Nothing can ever repay that."

"Aww, you're a good friend too. Thank you." Daisy hugged her.

"I'd better get back to reception, see you later."

With Jess gone, Greg took Daisy into his arms, and kissed her for a long time. When he released her, he said, "Happy birthday, Crazy Daisy."

Daisy smiled. "Thank you. This has already been the best birthday I've had for years."

"And there's more to come. Here's my present."

Greg handed her a box, tied with gold ribbon.

For a moment, Daisy's heart skipped a beat. Was he going to propose? But the box was too big to be a ring, so she quickly quashed that thought. She slid the ribbon off, opened the lid, and just stared.

"Erm, say something, do you like it?"

Daisy looked up at Greg, and down at the box again. "Oh, Greg, it's the most beautiful thing I've ever seen," she said, close to tears.

"Shall I put it on for you?"

Daisy lifted the necklace out of the box. It was a small, silver coloured, heart shaped locket, with silver angel wings covering the front. The wings opened out to reveal the interior of the locket. Engraved in small script on the inside of the left wing was, 'Guardian of my heart', and on the right, 'Love always, Greg'. The middle of the locket was free to put a tiny photograph.

Greg put it around Daisy's neck, and closed the clasp.

"I hope it's okay? I had it specially made. It's white gold. Jess told me you prefer silver coloured jewellery, so I thought white gold would be better."

Daisy turned and wrapped her arms around him. "I love it, truly. It's the best gift I've ever received. And I love you." She wiped away the tears that had spilled onto her cheeks.

"Hey, I didn't mean to make you cry."

Daisy laughed. "Sorry, but it's the nicest thing anyone's ever done for me. Thank you so much for making this a special day."

"It's not over yet. I was going to take you out for lunch, where would you like to go?"

Daisy thought for a bit.

"This is going to sound daft, but can we just go to the park as usual? I like seeing the ducks, and sitting in the fresh air. Besides, I don't want to eat too much as we have our meal out tonight."

Greg smiled. "Anything you want. It's your day. Did you bring a sandwich?"

Daisy looked puzzled. "Oh darn, no, I didn't. That's because I had a lie in this morning and didn't stick to my usual routine."

"I'll order us one to be delivered. What do you fancy?"

"Ooh, I don't know... Yes, I do, pastrami, cheese and salad."

"Consider it done. What about this cake?"

"I'll cut it up, and we can all have a slice with our drinks later. Is that okay? I'll never eat a whole cake to myself. I'll take some home for Kris too."

"Yep, that's fine."

Daisy kissed him. "Thank you for being a wonderful boyfriend. I really love my present." She headed for the door. "I'm going to show Jess, then I'll get back to work."

Jess agreed that Daisy's necklace was beautiful.

"I've had two wonderful presents today, and I'm going to wear them both to my party tonight. I can't wait," Daisy jumped up and down with excitement.

"Me neither. We've never been to Rialto's, even Simon's quite excited."

"And it won't cost as much as Greg thought. He phoned Otto to say thanks and invited him and Victoria to join us, but they declined. Otto said we didn't want them there, but I wouldn't have minded."

"Me neither, but we don't really know him, so it's probably better with just us."

"Yeah, probably. Right, better do some work. There's cake to have with your coffee later, please eat some. I can't eat it all, I'll get fat."

Jess looked Daisy up and down, and snorted, "Yeah right. And I'll grow horns out of the top of my head."

They giggled, and Daisy went back to her office.

At four o'clock, Greg told Daisy and Jess they could go home; he knew they'd want to get ready for the evening ahead. He sat on reception, and at half past four, he decided to close up. He knew the other employees would be pleased to leave early, and he wanted to have plenty of time to get ready too.

He was glad Daisy liked her present. It had taken him ages to decide what to get. He knew Jess was buying earrings, he didn't want to get a ring – he'd save that for another occasion – so eventually decided on a necklace, but wasn't sure what sort. He wanted it to be unique, and something that would show how much he loved her. Then he remembered hearing Daisy say something about guardian angels, and mentioned it to the jeweller, who came up with the locket idea. Thank heavens she'd liked it, it had cost him a fortune. But his Crazy Daisy was worth it.

Daisy and Kris were having a fabulous time getting ready. Daisy had opened the champagne, and they'd already had two glasses. She was feeling pleasantly tipsy as she danced around to the music Kris had put on.

"I shouldn't drink champagne on an empty stomach, but I'll be okay once I get some food inside me." She waved her empty glass at Kris. "Top me up, and I hope you ate something for lunch."

Kris refilled their glasses, draining the bottle. "All gone. Yes, I did. I had some pesto pasta. Victoria said pasta is great to eat, as long as you don't have a humungous portion, and it's not smothered in creamy sauces."

"Well done. Have we run out of champagne? Oh, that's rubbish. I'm going for a bath, and using my new present."

Kris knew how much Daisy liked a certain expensive perfume, so had bought her a set containing a handbag sized perfume atomiser, bubble bath, and body cream.

Whilst she was relaxing in the bath, with a facemask on, Kris knocked on the door.

"Come in."

Kris often sat chatting to Daisy when she was lying in the bath, or sat on her bed whilst she was changing.

He entered, with a bottle, and their glasses. "Here you go, birthday girl."

Daisy sat up. "More bubbly? Yay, you're a star."

"It's only cava, I can't afford champagne."

"I don't care, it almost tastes the same."

They clinked glasses.

"Cheers, happy quarter of a century."

Daisy groaned. "Ugh, don't say that, I sound so old."

"You're as young as the fella you're feeling," Kris grinned and sipped his drink.

"Kris, I'm shocked."

"No, you're not. You better get that face mask off, babe, your skin's going red underneath." He pointed to her face.

Daisy shrieked and grabbed a flannel. She wiped around

her face.

"Is it all off?"

"Yes."

"Is my face red? Hand me the mirror."

She gazed at herself. "Phew, it's okay, it's probably from the heat."

"From all the booze, more like." Kris grinned.

Daisy threw the wet flannel at him.

"Okay, I'm getting out now. Are you having a bath or a shower?"

"Shower, I think, it's quicker. I don't know how you can lie around in hot water like that. It's not good for your skin, sweetie."

"It's relaxing. You're all warm and cosy, and can just let your mind drift. I could fall asleep in the bath." Daisy lay back and closed her eyes.

"You better not, you'll drown. I'm going for that shower. When I'm out, we can finish this cava."

By the time the taxi dropped them at Rialto's, an hour later, both Daisy and Kris were tipsy and giggly.

Greg's eyes shone when he saw how gorgeous Daisy looked. He was waiting outside, and the sight of her almost took his breath away.

"Greg, this is Kris; Kris, this is Greg." Daisy made the introductions.

"Duh, we have met before you know," Kris laughed.

They'd met in the hospital, and their paths crossed when Greg picked up or dropped Daisy off after an evening out, but they'd never chatted for any length of time.

"Thank you so much, Mr Boss Man for inviting me," Kris gushed, slurring his words slightly.

Daisy giggled and shushed him. "Tonight, he's Greg. He's only 'the boss man' when we're chatting on our own." She held her finger against her lips and giggled again. Kris looked apologetic.

Greg laughed. "Come on, let's get you both inside. Jess and Simon are already in there, having a drink."

As Kris went ahead, Greg held Daisy back. "You look beautiful tonight, really amazing." He kissed her tenderly, but released her as he felt his body responding. "We'd better join the others."

They sat at the small bar, chatting. Kris looked around to see if he could spot any celebrities, and his eyes almost popped out of his head as he recognised two of the presenters from the motor show, Top Gear.

"Look," he hissed excitedly, trying to keep his voice down, "it's Jeremy, and that little guy."

"Kris, stop staring." Daisy nudged him.

"Sorry."

A waiter handed them menus so they could place their order before going to their table. They tried to choose something, but it was quite difficult as there was so much tempting food on offer, and they were distracted every time someone entered the restaurant, because Kris would look round to see if it was anyone famous. His antics had them all in stitches.

A handsome waiter, carrying a tray, approached them.

"My name is Romeo, and I'm to be your waiter for evening, please to follow me at your table," he said with a heavy Italian accent.

They waited whilst he put their drinks on the tray, then followed him to a table near the windows.

"Omg, he's gorgeous," Kris whispered to Daisy. "I wonder if he's single."

"He might not even be gay," Daisy muttered back, but she suspected he was. He was like an Italian version of Kris – flamboyant, with exaggerated gestures.

Greg pulled a chair out for Daisy to sit down, and Simon did the same for Jess. Kris was about to pull his own out, when Romeo rushed over.

"Allow me, please." He pulled the chair out, and Kris sat down.

Then he placed napkins in their laps, and asked if they'd like a jug of water.

"I think that would be a good idea," Greg said. He thought

194

Daisy and Kris needed something to dilute the alcohol they'd already consumed.

When Romeo had gone, Kris pretended to swoon. "He pulled out my chair for me, how sweet. I think I'm in love."

"He is rather good looking," Jess said.

"Yes, but I expect he's taken, all the nice ones usually are," Kris sniffed.

Their starters arrived, but before they tucked in, Greg said, "Can you all raise your glasses – to Daisy, happy birthday."

"Happy birthday, Daisy," they chorused and clinked glasses, then got on with the serious business of eating.

Halfway through their main course, Kris looked around for Romeo, to order another drink.

"I can't see Romeo, I wonder where he's gone."

Quick as a flash, Jess said, "Romeo, Romeo, wherefore art though Romeo?"

Everyone burst into laughter, which drew several looks from nearby diners.

"Ah," Greg said, "but do you know that it doesn't actually mean, where is he, but why"

Jess looked puzzled.

"Juliet was asking why he was a Montague, and not a Capulet. They weren't allowed to be lovers because they were from feuding families, so she was asking him to deny his name, so they could be together."

Kris held his hand against his chest. "How wonderfully tragic." Then he grinned and said to Daisy, "Hmm, intelligent as well as handsome, you want to hang on to this man."

Daisy smiled. "I intend to."

Greg squeezed her hand under the table.

"Well, you learn something new every day," Jess said. "I haven't read much Shakespeare. Romeo and Juliet's the only play I kind of know."

"I knew, but I've studied Shakespeare. Where's our Romeo, ah there he is." Kris beckoned the waiter over.

He ordered two bottles of wine for the table. "Can you add these on a separate bill please. I'll pay for them at the end."

"Kris, no, this evening is on me. I don't want you to pay

for anything," Greg objected.

"But I'd like to chip in."

Simon joined the conversation. "How about you and I go halves on the drinks for tonight, Kris?"

Kris was about to agree, but Greg held his hand up. "Look, lads, it's a kind offer, but things are in order." He lowered his voice, "We're getting a substantial discount anyway, from a mutual acquaintance."

Romeo was waiting for them to sort things out, and Kris said, "Sorry, Romeo, all on one bill."

"Bene." Romeo leaned down and spoke quietly to Kris, "But you still come see me at end, anyway?"

Kris pointed at himself. "Me?"

"Si. If you like?" Romeo picked up their empty glasses and walked away.

Kris's eyes widened. "Why does he want to see me?"

"I should think," Jess said, "that he's probably going to ask for your number or something."

Kris shrieked, then looking around said, "Oops, sorry." He leaned in and lowered his voice. "That hot waiter wants to see me at the end of the night? I can't believe it."

Daisy laughed. "My birthday may be your lucky night." She placed her cutlery onto her empty plate. "That was delicious, but I'm full now."

"So you don't want pudding?" Greg asked.

Daisy patted her tummy. "I'm sure I can fit one in somewhere."

"Me too. That was the nicest food I've ever eaten. This place is amazing," Jess said. She got up and put her napkin on her chair, "Just nipping to the ladies."

Daisy got up too. "I'll come with you."

Greg watched them leave, and smiled as a couple of men eyed them up as they walked past. That was Daisy. Beautiful, funny, amazing, and all his.

He caught the eye of the maitre d', and nodded. The man nodded back, knowing what Greg was referring to.

When the girls sat back down at their table, a waiter approached with a spectacular looking concoction. It was a wide sundae glass, filled with sponge pieces, mousse, chocolate sauce, chocolate balls and cream, and coming out of the top, were white and dark chocolate streamers, and a big fizzing sparkler.

The waiter placed it in front of Daisy. The other waiters all gathered around the table and sang happy birthday, twice. First in Italian, then in English. The other diners clapped when they'd finished.

Daisy blushed, but laughed with delight. "Look at this dessert. What on earth is it?"

"It's new, especially for you, but the maitre d' said they might keep it, and alter it slightly to make it more Italian."

Daisy waited for the sparkler to stop, then took it out and plunged her spoon in. "Wow, it's got Maltesers in it. And look at these streamers, they are actually made from curled slivers of chocolate, how clever. Oh, Greg, this is wonderful, thank you so much." She sat back. "I'll wait for you guys to order yours, though. Let's have another drink."

They chatted and drank whilst waiting for the other desserts, and then the table once again became quiet whilst they ate.

When they'd finished, Romeo appeared, and asked if they'd like coffees.

Greg looked at them all. "Anyone want coffee?"

"I don't. I'd like another drink. I don't want this evening to end, it's been wonderful," Daisy said.

"Same here, wish it could carry on all night," Jess agreed.

"We could go on to a club?" Kris suggested.

"Phew, I don't know if I've got the energy to go clubbing, especially on such a full stomach." Daisy rubbed her tummy.

"Why don't we carry on back at my place?" Simon said.

Greg asked where he lived.

"It's only small though," Simon apologised.

Greg made an offer he'd probably regret in the morning. "My house is bigger, come back to mine. I've got plenty of space, and you can sleep over. Jess, Simon I assume you'll want the spare room, so Kris, you'll have to slum it on the sofa or floor."

"Not a problem, as long as you've got enough drink."

Greg rolled his eyes. "I'm sure there's plenty for us all."

When he went to pay the bill, he was shocked to find there wasn't one. "But, there must be some mistake; we were a table of five – the birthday group."

He was assured that no, there wasn't a mistake, the bill had been taken care of. He knew who'd done that, Otto Harrington. That was more than generous. Greg wasn't sure he was happy about having the whole bill paid for. He'd have to phone Otto to thank him again, and persuade him to accept half the total.

Whilst the others went outside to phone for a taxi, Kris stood waiting to catch Romeo. He took a deep breath as the waiter came out of the kitchen.

"You wanted to see me?" Kris asked.

Romeo took him to one side. "Si. You want to go out some time?"

Kris couldn't believe his luck. "Yes, I'd love to. Where would you like to go? For a meal? For a drink? I often go to this place." He mentioned the name of his favourite club.

Romeo nodded. "Si, I know this, I go sometimes. I give you my number."

He tore off a sheet from his notepad, wrote his mobile number, and gave it to Kris. "You give me yours too, in case you lose mine?"

Kris told him the number. Romeo wrote it down, tore off the sheet and put it in his trouser pocket.

"Now I must work, but I call you soon. Ciao."

Kris ran outside to the others, waving the piece of paper around excitedly.

"He gave me his number, and asked for mine. This has been the best evening for, oh simply ever."

Daisy laughed, then grabbed his arm as the taxi pulled up. "Come on, you, let's get back to Greg's and we can carry on the party."

Chapter Twenty-Three

When she was back at work, Daisy phoned Otto to say thank you for footing the bill for her party. Greg had told her Otto wouldn't accept any money from him, no matter how much he tried to argue.

Otto said it was his present to them all, for Daisy's birthday, and for finding Victoria.

"Well, thank you, it was kind of you," Daisy said. "And," she continued, "I thought you weren't going to let your dates know you were financially well off? Victoria knew that day we met you out shopping."

"If she'd been an ordinary girl," Otto replied, "I wouldn't have told her. But it was obvious from the start that Vicky enjoys the same lifestyle as I do. We eat in the same restaurants, visit the same places. She's pretty well off herself, you know; has a rich father, so at least I know she's not after my money."

"Hmm, true I guess. Keep in touch, Otto; drop in if you're in the area, Victoria too, I'd like to see you both. Thanks again," Daisy said.

"No problem. You're worth it, young lady. I'm just pleased I signed up with your agency. Vicky's a super girl. I know there's a bit of an age gap, but she keeps me young, and she says I'm good for her too – I make her laugh, and I'm wise and understanding." Otto laughed, his deep booming voice echoing down the phone. "I think she likes it because I'm of an age where I cherish a woman – chivalry and all that – which you don't get from young men nowadays. Anyway, yes, we'll pop in whenever we're around. Bye, Daisy."

Daisy hung up feeling all happy and pleased with life. She'd successfully matched another couple, she'd had the best birthday ever, had the best job in the world, and most of all, was in love with the most wonderful man.

She went out to get a cup of tea, and called across to Jess. "Want a cuppa?"

"Coffee please."

She made their drinks and took Jess's over.

Jess sighed. "I still can't get over what a great evening we had. I think I'll remember it forever."

Daisy smiled at the memory. "It was rather fab, wasn't it?"

"And, you've got the best boyfriend in the world – apart from mine of course. Fancy getting up and cooking us all breakfast."

Daisy laughed. "He said he knew we'd have the hangovers from hell, and a big fry up was just what we needed."

"It worked too. I woke up feeling like death, but was okay once I'd eaten."

"Yeah, same here. Even Kris ate a huge plateful, and that's unusual for him."

Jess sipped her coffee. "Talking of Kris, has he gone out with Romeo yet?"

Daisy rolled her eyes. "Yes. Romeo had an evening off, so Kris took him to the club, and I stayed with Greg. Kris is full of it – his new Italian lover. That's all I'll hear for weeks now."

Jess laughed. "Aww, bless him. He's so sweet. At least he's happy though."

"Until it goes wrong, then he'll be in the depths of despair again. Yes, Kris is sweet, I love him to bits, but he can be a bit OTT at times."

"Well, he is a drama student, Daisy," Jess said, and laughed, which made Daisy laugh too, and then, for some unknown reason, both girls ended up in a fit of giggles.

They were interrupted by the doors opening. Daisy looked across to see Marjorie approaching. She put her tea down, and rushed to greet the old lady.

"Marjorie. It's lovely to see you. How are you?"

"Not too bad, my love. Can we have a chat?"

"Of course, come into the interview room."

Daisy looked back at Jess, who raised her eyebrows in

question, and Daisy shrugged. She didn't know what Marjorie wanted, but she'd soon find out.

"Can I get you a drink?"

"No, my dear, don't worry."

"Okay, what can I do for you?"

"I'd like to sign up again."

Daisy was surprised. It was only a few months ago that Marjorie was going to marry Fred, and then he'd died, was she really ready to move on?

"I can see what you must be thinking," Marjorie said. "How can I start dating again when the man I was going to marry has recently died?"

"Well, yes, I was wondering."

"The thing is, I don't have a lot of time like you youngsters, and what little time I do have left, I don't want to spend on my own. Fred was a wonderful man, and we'd have been happy if we'd got married. But we didn't, he's not here, and I think he'd want me to be happy with someone else, not stuck on my own, feeling lonely."

Daisy's eyes welled. "Oh, Marjorie."

She got up, sat next to the old lady and hugged her. Marjorie got out a tissue.

"Now look what you've done, started me off too." She sniffed and blew her nose.

Daisy sat back in her own chair. "I'm sorry, Marjorie, but it breaks my heart to think of poor Fred, and you."

"No point getting upset anymore; it happened. Now, do you have anyone else on your books who's my age? I'll sign up for six months, like last time. Do I have to go through all the questions again?"

"No, of course not, I still have your file."

"Good. Can I pay you with a debit card?"

Daisy raised her eyebrows. The first time Marjorie had come in, she'd brought a bag full of money.

"Ha, that surprised you, didn't it?" Marjorie chuckled. "Fred taught me a lot of things, one of them, to trust banks. He came with me whilst I opened my own bank account. I even do my banking online. I'm a surfer."

For a moment, Daisy wondered what Marjorie was on about. Surfing? At her age? Then the penny dropped. "Oh, you mean a silver surfer." It was a term for older people who used the internet.

"Yes, that's it. Sounds good doesn't it."

Daisy laughed. "Well, look at you, Mrs Modern. You'll be getting a mobile phone next."

"Already got one – we can swap numbers if you like. I enjoy sending texts."

Daisy avoided answering that. She wasn't sure she wanted Marjorie having her personal phone number, she could end up being called at all odd times.

Instead she said, "Let's process your payment, and when you're gone, I'll start looking for matches. It's lovely to see you again, Marjorie, I hope we can find you someone else."

They went out to reception, Jess processed the payment, and they waved Marjorie off.

"That's the lady who was going to get married, but the poor man died before they tied the knot," Daisy explained.

"Aww, bless her. She's a keen old bird, ready to sign up again?"

"Yes, I was a bit shocked to be honest, but I suppose like she says, at her age, you can't hang about."

"True, and good on her for wanting to find love, better than sitting in misery at home alone."

Daisy smiled. "That's exactly what she said. I'm going to tell Greg. See you later."

"The only problem," Daisy said, as she sat opposite Greg, "is that we don't have one single elderly man on our books, and I'm not sure we will have in the next six months."

Greg frowned. "Hmm, I guess Fred was a one-off. I wonder why elderly people don't sign up as much as younger ones?"

"Maybe they think they're past it, and possibly the cost puts them off. Don't forget not all old people have money, many of them struggle on their pensions."

Greg thought about that. "I'm not sure what we can do

about it though."

"We-e-ell," Daisy said, "I've got an idea. Why don't we have a half price offer for people over seventy? That should get us some older clients. You could place an ad in the newspaper, and I could make up some posters or leaflets, and we could leave them at the old people's centre, and ask the bookshop and library if they'll take some. What do you think?"

"Daisy, you're a star. It's a great suggestion. I'll ask Frank about placing an ad, you work on the posters and leaflets. Email me your finished template before you print any off."

Daisy leaned across the desk, "See, I do have my uses."

Greg leaned across to meet her and they kissed. His eyes twinkled. "You, my darling, have many uses. I know what my favourite one is." He grinned and raised his eyebrows.

"I'm going, before this conversation goes any further. See you lunch time."

***

Initially, Daisy thought her plan wasn't going to work, because they only had a couple of older people join the agency, but as Christmas approached, they suddenly got an influx of clients. Daisy, and the other matchers, were kept busy sorting out all the profiles.

"I guess Christmas can be a pretty lonely time of year if you're on your own, whatever age," Jess said when Daisy went to cover her on reception one lunch time.

"Yes. It's heart-breaking to think of people being lonely."

Daisy looked sad, and Jess hated seeing her upset.

"Well, hopefully you'll match a few people up. Even if it doesn't come to anything, maybe they'll have some company for Christmas. Have you found anyone for Marjorie yet?"

"No, but she's still got three months membership left. With any luck, someone will come along. What are you two doing for Christmas?"

"We're spending Christmas Eve with my parents, Christmas Day on our own, and Boxing Day with Simon's parents," Jess said.

"Urgh, the dreaded in-laws." Daisy laughed.

"They're okay, actually. His dad's a hoot, and his mum always fusses around me. What about you?"

"I'm spending it all with Greg. With my sister in Oz, and my parents down in Devon, I have the perfect excuse."

"What about Greg's family?"

His father's taking his mum away for Christmas. She's always wanted to spend Christmas in the snow, so he's taking her to Switzerland this year. A romantic Christmas, on their own."

Jess whistled. "Wow, lucky lady. I bet that'll be brilliant."

"Yes, she's so excited. But it means Greg and I get to spend the whole holiday by ourselves."

"What's Kris going to do?"

"He's spending some of it with Romeo – when he's not working – and for the first time in a few years, he's going to his mother's. She's having a small gathering of family and friends, and invited Kris."

"That'll be nice."

Daisy wrinkled her nose. "I'm not sure. Kris is quite nervous about it. His father died when Kris was young, and he hasn't got on with his mother for years, ever since he came out. Apparently she got all upset – going on about how she'd never have grandchildren etc, and asked him to leave."

Jess tutted. "That's stupid. He's still her son, it doesn't change who he is."

"I know. We've had this conversation so many times. They've had some contact since, but it's always a bit strained. Maybe inviting him to this family get together is her way of offering an olive branch. We'll have to see. I've told him if it all goes horribly wrong, to phone me, and he can come to ours. Greg said he doesn't mind."

"Ah, he's such a nice man."

"Isn't he?" Daisy smiled. "So's Simon. Aren't we both the luckiest girls?"

***

The week before Christmas, Jess put a call through to Daisy from George, an elderly man she'd recently set up a date for.

Daisy was shocked when he announced he and Mary were going to get married, the first Saturday of February, the following year.

"George, I don't know what to say. Isn't it all a bit sudden? You only went on one date."

Daisy wondered if the old gentleman was losing the plot, but when he explained the circumstances, her eyes widened in disbelief.

"That's amazing. What are the chances of that? I'm absolutely thrilled for you both. Yes, of course I'll come to the reception, Thank you."

She hung up, and sat back in her chair, shaking her head in disbelief. She must text Kris, he'd love to hear this. Now she really did believe in fate. That couldn't have been serendipity, or coincidence.

She ran into Greg's office. "You'll never guess what?"

"I'm the most gorgeous bloke you've ever met, and you want to shag me, right now, over the desk?"

"Greg, shh." Daisy laughed.

Greg laughed too. He loved seeing her beautiful green eyes widen with shock when he said things like that to her. It had become a bit of a game between them. He'd whisper in her ear, or mutter suggestive comments only she could hear, in the most inappropriate situations, and watch her try to keep a straight face.

She flopped down into the chair opposite him. "Two of our clients are getting married after just one date."

Now it was Greg's turn to be shocked. "You're kidding?"

"Nope. It's true, he's just phoned me. But, listen to this. Mary, the lady George is marrying, was his girlfriend almost fifty years ago. They'd lived up in Yorkshire at the time, and were going to get engaged, but George was offered a job in a different area, and Mary wasn't ready to leave her family and friends, so, even though it broke their hearts, they decided to part. They kept in contact for a while by letter, but then the letters stopped and they lost touch."

Daisy paused for breath, then went on excitedly, "George got married and moved to the Cotswolds, Mary stayed in Yorkshire, married and had children. Her husband died two years ago, and her daughter persuaded her to move down here to be near them. Mary felt a bit lonely, and didn't really know how to meet people, so joined our agency when we offered that discount for older people. By sheer coincidence – but I believe it was fate – I matched her up with George. How amazing is that?"

Greg had been listening to this incredible story, and could hardly believe it. "Wow, even for an unromantic bloke like me, that's some story."

"You're not unromantic and you know it. What about this beautiful necklace you got me? That's the loveliest thing I've ever been given."

"Tsk, I only got you that so I'd stay in your good books," Greg said, but the look in his eyes told Daisy how much of a romantic he was, and how much he loved her.

"Yeah, yeah, fibber. You're a pushover for a love story, same as I am."

"Don't you go letting people know, I have a reputation to keep up, Crazy Daisy."

Daisy gave a blissful sigh. "I love my job. There's nothing better than helping people find love. I'm like a modern day Cupid."

"Mmm, the sexiest Cupid I've ever seen."

"You're not so bad yourself. Right, I'm going to tell Jess, then get on with some work. It's a fab story though."

"I agree and we can't let a story like this go unheard, I bet Frank would love it for the paper."

"Yes, probably, and if we get a mention, it'll be good publicity for us too."

"We can't do anything without the clients' consent, so I'll leave that to you. Give them a call and ask if they'd fancy telling their story to the local paper."

"Okay. They may not want people knowing they joined the agency though. I'll ask them."

Greg knew if anyone could persuade them, Daisy could.

***

"Oh, that's the most romantic thing I've ever heard," Jess said when Daisy told her. "They've probably never forgotten each other all these years, how sweet."

"I know, lovely, isn't it? I'm going to phone George back, and ask if he'd mind telling his story to the paper."

Daisy started to leave, but Jess stopped her by saying, "Oh, by the way, we're thinking of having a New Year's Eve party. We can't be bothered to go out, it's so horribly expensive. Simon said he'd move things out of the lounge, so there'll be more room. You, Greg and Kris are all invited, if you like?"

"To be honest, I haven't even thought about New Year's Eve. But it would be lovely to get together, wouldn't it? Can I let you know?"

"Of course. It's not a definite yet, just something we thought of instead of going out."

***

George and Mary were quite happy to tell their story, and the newspaper wanted to run it, but the editor decided he'd make a whole page feature, to coincide with their wedding. Greg agreed it was probably better to print it then. With Valentine's Day in February, seeing the feature may make more people join The Love Shack in the hope of finding a partner for the most romantic day of the year.

Chapter Twenty-Four

Greg was talking to Daisy in her office on the morning of 23rd December – the last working day until they opened again on 2nd January – when the phone on her desk rang. It was Jess, saying Otto wanted to speak to her.

"Put him through, thanks, Jess. Otto, hi, how can I help? Ooh, sounds good, I'll check with Greg and get back to you if that's okay? Jess and Simon too? That's great, thanks."

She hung up and met Greg's questioning gaze.

"That was Otto."

"Yes, I gathered that."

Daisy laughed. "Ha, silly me, sorry. He's throwing a New Year's Eve party and has invited us all."

"All?"

"You, me, Kris, Jess and Simon. He said we don't need to worry about getting home as he's laying on taxis for everyone, or we can crash at his place, he's got enough room. Can we go? He's good fun, and I like Victoria. It'll save Simon doing it." Daisy lowered her voice and whispered. "I'd like to spend it with Jess and Simon, but his place isn't really big enough for a party. We'll all be squashed in."

"How come Otto's invited Jess? Do they know each other?"

"He's popped in a couple of times for a quick chat when he's been in the area, so they've met."

"I see." Greg thought about it.

"Please can we go? Pretty please with a cherry on top," Daisy wheedled, and Greg laughed, never able to deny her anything. "Okay. Go and see what Jess says before you call Otto back."

"Ooh, you're the best," Daisy squealed, and went out to reception.

"Wow. I've wanted to see his house ever since you told me about it," Jess said. She clapped her hands. "I'm so excited. It'll save us having a party at Simon's." She pulled an 'ugh' face.

Daisy grimaced too. "Sorry, Jess. We want to celebrate New Year's Eve with you both, but I have to admit, I wasn't too keen on spending it at Simon's. His place is only small, we'd be squashed in like sardines."

"Yeah, and it'd be hot and stuffy, with sweaty bodies everywhere." Jess grinned. "It's okay, I felt the same and told Simon so. We just couldn't think what else to do. We want to spend it with you guys too, you're our best friends."

Daisy hugged her. "Well, this way, we get to celebrate it in style. Wait till you see Otto's house, it's fab."

***

On Christmas Eve, Greg got up early, leaving Daisy in bed. He took her up a cup of tea and some toast.

"Now, you stay here," he said as he kissed her, "I have to nip out quickly to get something."

"What?"

"It's one of your presents, if you must know. Well, it's for both of us. I can't say any more than that."

"I want to know what it is now."

Greg laughed and ruffled her hair. "You're like a little girl at times. Well, you can open it when I come back, as we can't keep it wrapped up all day and night."

Daisy rubbed her eyes. "I do think it's lovely of you to let us all have Christmas Eve off."

Greg gave a rueful smile. "When I first started the agency, I opened on Christmas Eve, but, nobody came in, and I realised that people were just too busy preparing for Christmas, so I decided to close the following year, and have done ever since."

"So, it was nothing to do with being a generous boss, and letting people have time off?"

Greg laughed. "Sorry to disappoint you. It was more to do

with not wanting to waste money on lighting, heating, and paying wages when there was nothing to do."

"Makes sense I suppose. And no need to apologise, you could never disappoint me."

"Good, enjoy your breakfast, be back in a bit."

With that, Greg left, whistling as he went.

Daisy stretched, sat up and ate her toast. She tried to think what sort of present you couldn't keep wrapped up, and decided it must be food or something perishable. She drank her tea, then had a shower, and just as she was drying her hair, Greg came back.

"Daisy?"

"I'm upstairs, drying my hair."

"Okay, come down as soon as you can, will you?"

Daisy finished drying her hair, put her dressing gown on, and hurried downstairs.

There was a large box on the floor in the living room, with a bow on top.

"Here you are, come and open it," Greg said.

Daisy was just about to remove the bow, when the box moved. She jumped back in fright.

"Christ on a bike! What the hell is that?"

Greg laughed. "Open it and see."

"No, I'm too scared now, you open it."

"Darling, I wouldn't get you anything that would hurt you, would I?"

"No..."

"Well then, trust me. Open it."

Daisy sat on the floor beside the box and took the bow off. The box moved again, making her jump. She looked up at Greg, and he nodded her to continue.

She lifted the flap on top of the box and squealed in delight as she saw the prettiest kitten.

"Oh, you little darling," she said as she lifted the animal out, and held it up to look at.

It gave a tiny meow, its little voice all squeaky. It was a beautiful soft grey coloured kitten, with darker stripes in its fur, and blue eyes.

Daisy's eyes filled with tears at the sight of the tiny creature.

"Oh, Greg," she breathed, "it's gorgeous."

"It's a she."

"A little girl? Hello poppet," Daisy said and she cradled the kitten against her chest.

"Greg, she's absolutely beautiful. Where did you get her?"

"Frank asked me a while ago if I knew anyone who'd like a kitten as his cat was pregnant. I knew you'd love one. I like cats too, so said I'd get one for you, but she'll live here."

"She's lovely, thank you. How old is she?"

"Just six weeks. Frank said I could collect her today. She's litter trained, they learn from their mother. I've got plenty of kitten food for her and a nice little basket to sleep in. She just needs some toys, and a name."

Daisy was holding one of the kitten's tiny paws. "Look at the underneath of her paws, they're all soft and pink. Hey, I know what we can call her, Rosie."

"Rosie it is. She can't go outside until she's had her injections, which we can sort out in a few weeks. We just need to give her time to settle in."

Daisy gently rubbed her face against the kitten's soft fur, and it mewed.

"Aww, it's probably quite traumatic being taken away from her mother, poor little mite. She's in a strange place, with strange people, it must be scary."

Daisy cuddled the kitten again as it cried, and murmured gently to it.

"If you put her in her basket, she'll learn that it's where she sleeps," Greg said.

"Can she sleep in our room, in case she gets frightened? We can't leave her on her own at night, in the dark, she's only a baby."

Greg rolled his eyes. He knew Daisy was a big softy. But he actually felt quite sorry for the little creature too.

"Yes, but not on our bed. We'll put her basket on the floor beside you."

"Thanks, darling. She's the best present ever."

"You said that about your necklace, and you haven't seen your other presents yet," Greg said in consternation.

"I love my necklace, it is the best thing I've ever been given, but Rosie is as good too." Daisy smiled. "All your presents to me are wonderful."

She stood up, the kitten in her arms. "I need to get dressed, can I take her up with me?"

"I don't think she's mastered stairs yet, so if you do, close the bedroom door, or leave her here with me."

Daisy realised she couldn't be selfish and hog the kitten to herself, so she gave her to Greg. He sat on the sofa and Rosie climbed up to his chest, where she promptly fell asleep.

"Aww, I have to take a photo and send it to Jess and Kris."

Daisy got her phone and took several photos, then spent a couple of moments 'ahhing' over them, before sending them to her friends.

"Can we print this one out, it's so sweet?" She showed Greg the one she meant.

"Yes, now go get dressed. And we'll decide what to do for the rest of our first Christmas Eve together."

Chapter Twenty-Five

Daisy spent a glorious Christmas with Greg and their new pet, doing nothing much. Some days, they didn't even get dressed. They just lounged around, eating nice food, watching corny old movies on the TV, and playing with Rosie, who seemed to have settled in well.

Despite Greg saying the kitten wasn't to sleep on their bed, she did.

That first night, they carried her upstairs in her own little basket and Daisy placed it on the floor on her side of the bed. But when they switched their bedside light off to go to sleep, the kitten cried and scrabbled up on to their bed.

Daisy had picked Rosie up and put her back in her basket, but as soon as she lay down, Rosie scrambled up again. She quietly sneaked along the bed and tucked herself under Greg's chin, making Daisy giggle.

She was about to sit up and remove the kitten, but Greg said, "It's okay, leave her. She probably just needs reassurance. She must be missing her mother."

Daisy had smiled in the darkness. So much for Greg's willpower.

The kitten had slept on their bed every night since.

Daisy had phoned Kris on Christmas Day and they'd had a nice long chat, ending with Kris wishing her and Greg a happy Christmas from him and Romeo. But since he'd left to drive to his mother's, she hadn't heard from him. She assumed things were going okay, otherwise he'd have flounced out and come home. She didn't want to bother him too much – he probably had a lot to deal with being at his mother's. She knew he'd contact her when he was ready.

As well as the kitten, Greg had been extremely generous with his gifts to Daisy. He'd bought her perfume, a beautiful cashmere sweater, that matched the green of her eyes, and an iPad Air.

She'd felt a little upset because she hadn't spent as much on Greg, but he'd held her close and told her that the cost wasn't important. He loved all the gifts she'd got him because she'd put some thought into them, which was true.

She knew Greg was into fast cars so had got him tickets for a day at a race track, driving a Ferrari – something he'd never done, but had always wanted to. She'd also got him a personalised leather golf tee holder, and a pair of lovely silver cufflinks. He was the only person Daisy knew who wore cufflinks – but she loved the fact that he took pride and care over his appearance.

***

Daisy was sitting on the sofa, with Rosie on her lap, when her iPad started making a noise. She looked up at Greg, who laughed and said, "Pick it up and open it."

Daisy opened the iPad and saw a small picture of Jess, and an icon 'slide to accept' which she did, and a full screen version of Jess appeared.

The girls then spent the next twenty minutes excitedly chatting about what they'd got for Christmas. Simon had bought Jess an iPad Air too.

Greg leaned in to join the conversation. "I'm not sure this was such a great idea, Si." He laughed. "We'll never get them off it now."

Simon appeared and laughingly agreed.

The girls chatted a bit more, Daisy showed Rosie off, and then Greg invited Simon and Jess over for drinks that evening.

Just as Daisy closed the iPad, her mobile went off. It was a text from Kris.

"Home this afternoon, hope to see you later. K xx"

Daisy texted back, inviting him to Greg's for drinks and nibbles.

"Will be there. Looking forward to coming home, have missed you. K xx"

Tears sprang to Daisy's eyes. She'd missed Kris too.

They were both wrapped up in their new lives now – Daisy with Greg, and Kris with Romeo. It was sad in a way, because the old life they'd shared had disappeared. Daisy thought back to the days before Greg, and her heart contracted. She must make more effort to spend time with Kris. She had fond memories of their nights in together, watching soppy films, while sharing a box of chocolates, and the fun they had at his favourite club, where they'd dance the night away. Although they still shared the flat, neither of them were there much. She was usually at Greg's, and Kris was at Romeo's or at the club. Even their regular Saturday nights out together had tailed off.

Daisy didn't want to lose touch with her best friend, so she decided to arrange to spend one night a week together – either at the club, or just chilling together at home.

"Greg, I need to get some more clothes, and Kris is coming back this afternoon. Do you mind if I go home, so I'm there when he gets back?"

Aware that Daisy probably wanted some time alone with Kris, Greg said, "I have to get some drink and food for tonight, so why don't I drop you home, go off and do that, then pick you both up later?"

Daisy knew Greg would understand, and loved him for it. She kissed him. "Thank you, darling. Oh, what are we going to do with Rosie whilst we have our little party?"

"Ah, hadn't thought of that. Hmm. Okay, tell you what, we'll put her litter tray, food and water in our bedroom, and keep her in there for the evening. Just make sure no-one goes in there. If they want to see her, we can get her, then take her back up again after."

"Good idea. Kris hasn't seen her properly yet; he'll love her."

***

Daisy was back at the flat, doing some washing, when Kris

arrived home. She ran to greet him, and threw her arms around him as he came in the door.

"Hi, Baby D, had a good Christmas?" Kris hugged her in return. He held onto her for a long while, and Daisy knew something wasn't quite right. She knew Kris so well that she could interpret his behaviour, and the way he clung on to her, meant he was upset about something, and needed her comfort.

"Yes, it's been lovely. Kris what's wrong?" Daisy searched his face and saw the strain in his eyes. "Come and sit down. Let me get you a drink, and you can tell me all about it."

Kris nodded and his eyes filled with tears.

"Oh, darling." Daisy hugged him again. "Right, go sit. Do you want coffee, tea, or something stronger?"

Kris sniffed his tears back. "I'd love a glass of wine, or whatever alcohol we have."

"Have you eaten?"

"Yes, Mum made me a cooked breakfast. She didn't want me travelling on an empty stomach."

He sat on the sofa and Daisy went into the kitchen. If his mother made him a breakfast, things must be okay between them, so it wasn't that. What else could it be? She hoped Romeo hadn't dumped him.

She took their wine in, and sat beside her friend. "Right, what's happened?"

Kris took a large gulp of his drink before speaking.

"It's my mum. The reason she invited me for Christmas, was because she wanted to see me and say sorry. She feels really bad about rejecting me because I'm gay." He sighed.

"Well, that's good, isn't it?" Daisy said. "Hey, maybe you'll become close again; it's never too late."

Kris burst into tears.

Daisy put down her glass, and held him whilst he cried, her face full of concern.

When he'd stopped crying, Kris said, "She's ill, Daisy. That's why she wanted to see me and throw the party for all the people she cares about. She's got cancer. She wanted to make up with me before it was too late."

"Oh, Kris. I am so sorry." Daisy felt like crying herself.

Poor Kris.

"How bad is it? I mean, is she going to…"

Kris sighed. "We don't know. She's had one session of chemotherapy, she has to have several more, with rest periods in between. She's trying to be optimistic and hope it cures it, but until she's had more sessions and tests, we won't know."

"Oh, that's crap. I really am sorry. I wondered why I hadn't heard much from you."

Kris took a deep breath, let it out and then smiled. "One good thing came out of it. We had a real heart to heart. I cried, she cried, and we talked some more. I think what's upset her most is all the wasted years. She feels really sad and guilty for rejecting me. She said she knows it was wrong, and she wishes with all her heart she could turn back the clock."

Daisy didn't say anything, she just held Kris's hand and let him talk.

"When I was crying, she held me and said I looked just like I did when I was a little boy. She kept stroking my forehead, and saying, 'my lovely boy'. I think she's suffering an awful lot of guilt."

Daisy had to speak out this time. "So she should do. Sorry, Kris, but she chose to turn her back on you, just because you're gay, and not what she wanted you to be."

"I know. She knows it too, and is suffering for it."

Daisy couldn't help wondering, if his mother hadn't been diagnosed with cancer, would she still have contacted Kris, and apologised for her treatment of him? But she didn't want to go into that now.

"Anyway, we're trying to put it behind us, and start anew, with whatever time she may have left. It's been a funny few days, sad, but lovely too. Spending time with her, chatting and doing stuff we should have done years ago."

Daisy hugged him. "I'm really glad. And you never know, the chemo may cure her and she could have years left yet. She's not old is she?"

"Fifty-one, so no, she's not that old." Kris tried to brighten up. "So, sweetie, tell me, what did the boss man get you for Christmas?"

"Ooh, I got perfume, a lovely sweater, a kitten and an iPad —"

Kris shrieked. "An iPad? I got one too. My mum bought it for me. She's well cool, you know; she's more into technology than I am. She also gave me five hundred pounds. She said she has a lot of Christmases and birthdays to make up for."

"Hey, that's three of us who got iPads, Jess got one too. Do you know how to message and FaceTime on it?"

"Facewhat?"

"Here, let me show you, go get yours."

They spent most of the afternoon chatting, playing with their new gadgets, eating and drinking. They FaceTimed with Jess, and Greg, who held Rosie up for Kris to see.

When Kris went to get another bottle of wine, Daisy watched him go. She'd really missed his company. How could she have ever got so involved that she stopped spending time with him? Then she thought about his mother. If his mum died, he'd have nobody, except Daisy. Tears stung the back of her eyes and she swallowed a few times to try to get rid of them. She'd been such a selfish cow. Kris needed her, and she hadn't been there for him. She loved him, he was her best ever friend in the whole world, he deserved better.

The alcohol was making her maudlin, but she knew there was some truth in her thoughts.

When Kris came back, she said, "I've been thinking. We don't spend enough time together. I miss this," Daisy swept her arm around the room, "chilling with you over a drink, chatting and laughing. We should make a pact to spend one evening a week together. Either a Saturday at the club, or a week night, just chilling at home. What do you think?"

Kris smiled. "I'd love to. I've missed you so much, but didn't want to say anything because I know how happy you are with the boss man."

Daisy hit him with a cushion.

"Hey, what's that for?" Kris whacked her back with his cushion.

"Because you should have told me I was being a selfish cow. You don't usually hold back on what you think." She hit him again.

"Ow." He hit her back. "Well, I was going to, but then I met Romeo, so have been a bit distracted myself."

He hit her over the head.

"Ouch. Right, you, this is war."

She kneeled up on the sofa and hit Kris with the cushion. He knelt up and hit her back and then they both whacked each other over and over, shrieking like lunatics, until Daisy fell off the sofa and collapsed on the floor in giggles.

Kris sat down beside her. "That was the best cushion fight I've ever had. You're right, we really must make more effort to see each other, we have so much fun."

They were both trying to get their breath back, when the doorbell went.

"You get it, you're fitter than I am," Daisy gasped.

It was Greg, ready to collect them for the party back at his place.

He walked into the lounge, saw Daisy on the floor out of breath, her hair all dishevelled, and Kris looking just as messy and said, "What on earth have you two been up to? Just as well I know Kris is gay, otherwise I'd be rather suspicious."

Daisy laughed and held up her cushion. "We just had a cushion fight. I was winning."

"Yes, until you fell off the sofa," Kris pointed out.

Greg shook his head. "You two are like a couple of kids. I think you've already had plenty of alcohol, by the look of things, maybe you shouldn't come to the party?"

Daisy looked at her watch. "Is it that time already? Oops. Hang on a bit whilst I get ready."

"Me too," Kris said, and the pair of them disappeared upstairs to get changed, leaving Greg to wait for them.

Chapter Twenty-Six

They enjoyed their little get together at Greg's, but the New Year's Eve party at Otto's was one of the best any of them had ever been to.

"Apart from your birthday party at Rialto's, that was totes amazeballs," Kris said.

He'd been a little miffed at Romeo having to work New Year's Eve, but his annoyance soon disappeared when he'd arrived at the party, and seen all the food, drink and guests.

"Stars and moon, just look at this place," he'd whispered when they'd first arrived.

Otto had been the perfect host, greeting them all, making sure they had a glass of champagne to start the evening off, and telling them to help themselves to food.

"He's obviously got the caterers in. I don't think Otto made all this food," Jess said as she looked at the array of dishes on offer.

"Nor Victoria. I can't imagine her cooking anything, let alone cuisine like this."

Just as Daisy said that, Victoria approached them. She looked gorgeous in a sparkly gold jumpsuit.

"Hi, girls, glad you could make it." She beamed at them.

"Thanks for the invite. You and Otto are still an item then?" Daisy asked.

"Yes, still going strong. I really like him, he's a genuinely nice guy."

Daisy smiled. "I'm so pleased. Anything else? The sound of wedding bells looming?"

Victoria laughed. "Not yet, we're both happy as we are for the moment. But, you never know, maybe in the future. Put it this way, if he asks me, I'll say yes."

"Ooh, that would be fab. I can imagine the sort of wedding you'd have though, it'd be very grand."

"No, it would not," Victoria said indignantly. "Just because I have money, and am posh," she made quote marks as she said the word posh, "I wouldn't want my wedding to be a huge exhibition. No thanks. I want to go away and get married quietly, in a nice hotel or something."

Daisy laughed. "You better tell Otto that, as I have a feeling he'd want a huge affair. He'd probably take a notice out in The Times."

"We'd have to talk about it if, and when, the matter arose. Now I'd better circulate. Have a nice time, girls; help yourselves to food will you, there's tons of it. There's even more to come yet, it's all in the kitchen. I think Otto went a bit over the top."

"That's exactly what I mean," Daisy laughed.

Victoria rolled her eyes, and with a little wave, she disappeared into the crowd of guests.

Although they were plied with plenty of alcohol – Daisy had never drank so much champagne – they were also eating the delicious food on offer, so none of them got outrageously drunk. Instead, they danced, chatted, mixed with other guests, and had a wonderful time.

Just before midnight, Otto and Victoria directed everyone out into the massive garden – the word 'garden' was a bit of an understatement; it was more like the grounds of a stately home – where, as 12 o'clock struck, a fantastic firework display went off.

Daisy loved fireworks. She always had done, and she 'oohed' and 'ahhed' at them like a little kid.

Greg stood behind her and pulled her close. He loved her. Her childlike delight made him want to protect her and keep her from all the harm in the world. He loved her pure innocence, and naivety. That didn't mean she was stupid, far from it. Daisy was clever and bright, but she saw the world differently. Whilst many people looked, but didn't really see what was around them, Daisy seemed to have a natural ability to notice what others missed. She found deep joy in simple things, like a sunset or a rainbow. She cared about small creatures such as Gilbert. To many people, he was just a duck from the local pond, but to Daisy, he was more than that. It was a quality that made her so loveable.

"Promise me you'll never change," Greg whispered into her hair.

She turned to look up at him, her eyes shining with the reflection of the fireworks, and in that moment, Greg knew he wanted to spend the rest of his life loving and protecting her.

He'd never properly thought about their future together. He just assumed they'd carry on as they were. But now, at this moment, he knew he wanted more. He wanted to grow old with her, watch her stomach swell as she grew their child inside her – the whole shebang. He tightened his arms around her, and rested his chin on the top of her head. He wouldn't say anything yet. He wanted to do it properly. He had plenty of time to plan something special that she'd always remember.

***

Daisy was actually relieved when the festive season was over, and things were back to normal.

"I don't think I've ever eaten or drank so much in my life. It was lovely, but, phew, too much. I've put on eight pounds over Christmas," she moaned to Jess on Monday morning, when they were back at work.

"I know how you feel, I've put on weight too," Jess complained. "I was thinking of going to the Zumba class that's starting up in my local church hall, but don't want to walk in there by myself."

"When is it?"

"Tuesday evenings, at seven pm."

Daisy thought for a moment. "I'll come with you. I need to do something to get this weight off."

"Really?"

"Yes. It'll be fun. If we're rubbish, we'll just stand at the back and pretend we know what we're doing."

Jess laughed. "Okay, I think the first one is tomorrow, shall we go to that?"

"Yeah, why not."

***

"Ruddy hell, I didn't realise it would be this hard." Daisy puffed as she tried desperately to keep up with the dance teacher who was showing them the Zumba moves.

Jess had a fit of the giggles, and couldn't stop. When she'd managed to compose herself, and catch her breath, she said, "This is the most hilarious thing I've ever done. You look so funny trying to concentrate."

She laughed again, then swore as she got a move wrong and tripped over her own feet.

"I don't think this is quite the right exercise for us. How long does it last?" Daisy panted.

"An hour," Jess replied.

"An hour? How long have we been going?"

Jess looked at her watch. "About fifteen minutes."

"What? You're kidding. Jess, I won't last another forty-five minutes. I'll be dead before that."

Jess looked at Daisy's sweating red face, and laughed so hard she had tears rolling down her cheeks.

"Jess, it's not funny. Stop it." Daisy giggled now.

Both girls had stopped doing the moves, and were doubled over, helpless with laughter.

The class instructor glared in their direction. "If you're not going to take it seriously girls, then maybe you ought to leave?"

"Fine by me," Daisy said and, followed by Jess, she left the hall. She drove them to a pub she'd passed on her way to Jess's.

"That was so hard. My co-ordination's not good at the best of times, but that was almost impossible," Jess said as they sat with glasses of orange juice and plates of chips.

"I couldn't have lasted another forty minutes. It would have killed me. I'm going to ache enough tomorrow as it is." Daisy laughed. "We are so unfit."

Jess agreed. "The only exercise I get, is in bed with

Simon."

"Euww, too much information, thanks. But yeah, same here. I wish I was as fit as Kris, he puts me to shame."

"But he's running around acting and dancing all day, so he should be."

"I suppose. What else can we do? I'm not paying to join a gym." Daisy thought for a moment. "Hey, why don't we take up running?"

"Hmm, maybe. Ooh, I don't feel well. I think I'm going to…"

Jess got up and ran for the ladies lavatory. Daisy had to stay where she was because their bags and food were there.

Jess came back several moments later, looking rather pale.

"Ruddy hell, Jess, are you okay?"

"I don't know. I suddenly felt really sick. Ugh, that was horrible."

"You don't look too good." Daisy looked down at her plate, then pushed it away and whispered, "Maybe the food is off. Have you been here before?"

Jess shook her head. "Let's just finish our orange juices and go."

They quickly finished their drinks, and left.

"I'll drive you home, maybe you ought to go to bed? Don't worry about coming in to work tomorrow if you still feel ill. I'll tell Greg."

"Thanks." Jess grinned. "I'm probably allergic to exercise."

Daisy laughed. "You and me both. Text me in the morning if you're still feeling sick."

She dropped Jess off, and drove home, hoping her friend would be okay.

***

When Daisy arrived at work the following morning, Jess was already there, making herself a drink.

"Morning. You okay?" Daisy asked.

Jess smiled. "Yep. Fine again. It must have been that

Zumba, you know."

Daisy laughed.

"I'm serious. I'm perfectly okay now. I was okay once I'd got indoors and had a cup of coffee. I even ate a slice of toast. I suddenly fancied Marmite on toast. I haven't had that for ages. I found a jar in the cupboard."

Daisy shuddered. "Ugh, I hate Marmite. How can you eat that stuff? I'm glad you're better. I still need to do something about losing weight though. What about running?"

Jess considered it. "Yeah, not a bad idea, but it means you'll have to come to me, or I'll have to come to you every night."

"Every night?"

"Yes. There's no point going running just once a week, that won't do anything."

Daisy laughed. But we were going to do Zumba once a week."

"I know, but that was an hour long. We won't run for an hour."

"True. I probably won't be able to run for longer than ten minutes," Daisy said.

"We can start off fast walking, and build up to it. It's a pity we have our lunches at different times, we could run together in our lunch break, around the park," Jess said.

"Maybe we can. I know Greg has sat on reception a couple of times, maybe he'll sit in for you, and we can take our lunch together. Twenty minutes run, ten minutes to eat our sandwiches?"

"That's not a bad idea." Jess was quite enthusiastic. "Go and ask him. He'll say yes to you, he can't refuse you anything."

Daisy laughed. "I'll take him in a coffee and ask him then."

Greg agreed, so the girls decided they'd start their running regime the following day.

Daisy sat in the park at lunch time with Greg as usual, and tore off her crusts for Gilbert, who was waddling impatiently in front of her. His mate was pecking duck food from Greg's hand. Their offspring were no longer with them, having fledged a long while ago.

"So, this will be our last lunch time together, you'll be running around here with Jess tomorrow."

Daisy sighed, then smiled. "Well, running's a bit optimistic. Walking, to start off with. I'd like to get rid of this weight. All my clothes are too tight."

Greg squeezed her. "I quite like the extra padding on you, gives me something to feel."

Daisy laughed and pushed his hands away. "Stop it. I don't like it. It makes me feel uncomfortable. Besides, I'd like to get in shape for the summer, so I can wear my nice skirts and dresses."

"You never know," Greg said, "someone might take you on holiday, so you may need a new costume." He liked the idea of seeing Daisy in a bikini.

She turned to Greg. "You're taking me on holiday? Really? Where? When?"

"Steady on," Greg laughed. "I said 'might'. Not 'will'. It's something I've just thought of."

"Oh, that would be wonderful. I've never been on holiday overseas before. I've stayed in this country. The Lake District, Scotland, that sort of thing."

"If you could go anywhere, where would you like to go?" Greg asked.

"Italy," Daisy said. "I'd love to see the Coliseum, and some of the wonderful Italian architecture and sculptures."

She had a sudden thought, and frowned. "That means we'll have to fly, won't we? I've never flown before. I'm not sure I want to either."

Greg laughed and ruffled her hair. "Don't start worrying about something that may not happen, Crazy Daisy. If – and it's a big if – I take you to Italy, we can drive there. I like driving, and that way, we can take as much luggage as we want."

Daisy bounced up and down in her seat, and Greg knew he'd take her to Italy. He loved pleasing her and seeing her all excited.

He didn't know where the idea had come from, but it seemed like a good one. Strolling through one of the most romantic countries in the world, with Daisy by his side, was a lovely thought. And, if things went how he intended, it could be an addition to the other plan he'd had. But he was keeping that one to himself until the time was right.

When Daisy and Greg arrived back at work, Jess was returning from the ladies' loo. She looked pale and wan again.

Greg made himself scarce, and let Daisy find out what was wrong.

"I've been sick again. I just suddenly felt really queasy." Jess sat down in her chair.

"You must have a virus or something." Daisy's eyes widened. "Or…"

"Or what?" Jess asked, then she gasped. "No, I can't be."

"But, you said you suddenly fancied Marmite on toast. Oh heck, Jess, I think you might be pregnant."

Jess went even paler than she already was.

"I can't be. I'm on the pill."

"Have your periods stopped?"

"It's hard to tell because of the type of pill I'm on. Sometimes I hardly bleed at all. But I've taken my pill regularly and never missed one."

"Well, although they're ninety-nine percent effective, there's always that one percent who still get pregnant. It's your lunch time now, go get a test from the chemist," Daisy told her.

"I'm afraid to."

"Jess, you've got to find out, you can't leave it. At least you'll know. I'm here, you won't be alone."

"Okay."

Jess picked up her bag and lunchbox, and walked out of the door.

She came back ten minutes later.

"You've still got twenty minutes of your lunch time left," Daisy said.

"I know, but I'm not hungry, and I'm too wound up now to do anything. Let's get this over and done with."

She disappeared into the loo, and came back several minutes later.

227

"Now I have to wait for five minutes. Oh I can't bear this, Daisy, What the hell am I going to do if it's positive?"

Daisy could see how frightened her friend was. "We'll deal with that when we know the outcome. I'll help you, Jess. I mean that. Whatever you decide, I'll be with you."

She held her friend's hand.

Five minutes were up, but Jess was afraid to look.

"I can't, you look for me."

"Oh, give it here." Daisy took the test from Jess and looked down at it. She let her breath out, not realising she'd been holding it. "It's okay, Jess, it's negative."

"What?" Jess grabbed the test from Daisy, and stared at it.

"Oh, thank you, Lord." She burst into tears.

Daisy had never seen Jess cry before. She put her arm around her. "Would it really have been so bad if it had been positive?" she asked.

Jess looked at her as if she'd gone mad. "Are you kidding? It would have been terrible. I'm not ready for a child. I'm not sure I ever want kids."

Daisy was shocked. How could anyone never want kids?

"Oh, don't look at me like that. I'm not like you, Daisy. You'd suit the whole family thing. I don't think it's for me, though. I love Simon, and want to spend the rest of my life with him, but I can't see kids figuring in that anywhere. I guess I'm just not maternal."

"But you like animals," Daisy said in her simplistic way.

"Yes, I love them. I'd have hordes of animals around me, but not children."

Daisy pondered on this for a moment, and then asked, "Does Simon know? Does he want children?"

Jess sighed. "We discussed it once, and I said I didn't particularly want children. We've never talked about it since."

"Maybe you ought to have a serious discussion about it one evening? What if he asks you to move in with him or something, and he wants kids at some point? Maybe he thinks you'll change your mind."

Daisy couldn't imagine being with someone and not talking about that stuff. She and Greg had spoken about having a family, several times.

Jess looked a bit sheepish.

"What's up?" Daisy asked.

Jess sighed again. "I haven't brought the subject up again, because I'm afraid to. What if Simon really wants kids, and I don't? Where will that leave us? I love him so much, but with something that big, there's no compromise. I can't expect him to stay with me and be childless." Jess's eyes filled with tears.

"Oh, Jess. I don't know how to solve this. But what I do know is, you have to talk to each other about it. It's unfair, to both of you, to get more deeply involved, without Simon knowing how you really feel on the subject. We know you're not pregnant, so why are you being sick? Maybe you need to see the doctor?"

"It's probably just a virus. If I'm still unwell in another week, I'll go to the doctor, I promise."

Daisy was satisfied with that response. "Okay. Do you want to take your lunch break again? Go on, go get some fresh air. Greg won't mind. I'll sit on reception."

"Thanks, Daisy, you're a pal." Jess picked up her lunchbox and for the second time that afternoon, she walked out of the door.

When she got back twenty minutes later, she said to Daisy, "About this running lark, I can't be bothered. We'd have to bring our running gear in, run around the park in twenty minutes, then quickly eat our lunch. I think I'd rather cut out all the rubbish I eat, such as chocolate and crisps, and do an exercise DVD when I have time at home. I don't want to give up my lunch times with Simon either. Sorry." She gave Daisy a rueful grin.

Daisy smiled. "That's okay, I'm quite relieved actually, as I wasn't looking forward to it. You're right, it's probably better to just cut out the rubbish we eat. I'll do some sit ups and things at home. How did you explain not seeing Simon this lunch time?"

"I texted him and said I was working through it as we had some paperwork to catch up on."

Daisy raised her eyebrows. "You really need to talk to him, you know."

"I know. I've decided I'm going to do it tonight. I'll tell him I had a pregnancy scare and say that if he really wants kids, we better break up now, before we get any more involved, because I don't want any. I wasn't sure before, but this scare has made me realise that I definitely don't want a family."

Daisy thought it was sad. But then Jess was twenty-eight. It wasn't as if she was a teenager. She obviously didn't feel broody or anything, so knew what she wanted – or rather didn't want.

"Good luck, Jess, I hope you can come to some conclusion."

Jess smiled sadly. "So do I."

***

When Jess arrived at work the following morning, she went into Daisy's office.

Daisy looked up as the door opened. "Jess, how's things? I was thinking about you last night."

Jess flopped into the chair opposite Daisy, and smiled.

"Everything is fine. More than fine. Life is great." She grinned.

Daisy blew out her breath. "Thank heavens for that. So, what happened?"

"I invited him round for dinner, and after we'd eaten, I said I wanted to have a serious talk. You should have seen his face, he thought I was going to dump him."

Daisy could imagine Simon's poor little face. "Aww, bless him."

"Yeah, it was sad. Anyway, I told him I'd had a pregnancy scare, then went on to say that I know without doubt that I don't want kids, so if he does, it'd be best if we separated now."

"Blimey, Jess, you didn't pull any punches."

"Nope. Like you said, it was best to be straight with him."

"What did he say?"

"He was quiet for a long time, and I was really worried, but then he said he'd rather have a life with me, and no kids, than a life with someone else and kids." A big smile appeared on

Jess's face.

"Really?" Daisy smiled too. "Aww, I'm so pleased for you. I'd have been devastated if you two had split up."

"You would? I'd have cried forever. I really love him, and the thought of losing him was awful. I'm glad you persuaded me to talk to him though, it was horrible having that hanging over me."

"I bet. You silly thing, you should have spoken to him sooner."

"I know. I was just scared. Anyway, guess what?"

"What?"

"He asked me to move in with him."

Daisy's eyes lit up. "Oh, Jess, that's wonderful news. We should celebrate. When are you moving in?"

"Well, as you know, Simon's flat is only small, so, we're going to look for another place – one that will be ours, not his or mine. As soon as we find something suitable, we'll move in."

Daisy got up and hugged her friend. "That's fantastic. Well done. Having that talk was definitely the right thing to do."

"Yep, all thanks to you. I got you these."

Jess took a box of Maltesers out of her bag and gave them to Daisy. She knew they were her favourite chocolates.

Daisy laughed. "Ooh yummy, thanks, Jess, but you didn't have to do that."

"I know. Thanks for being such a good friend."

The girls hugged each other, and Jess headed for the door.

"I'd better get some work done. Thanks again, Daisy. Hey, it'll be your turn next."

"What do you mean?"

"To move in with Greg."

Daisy shrugged. "I don't think so. We're happy as we are for the moment."

When Jess left, Daisy thought about her comment. She was a little bit jealous that Jess and Simon had made the commitment to live together. She was happy with things as they were, but if Greg asked her to move in with him, she'd say yes in a heartbeat. But he'd never mentioned it. In fact, they didn't really talk about taking their relationship further. They spoke about getting married and having children one day, but it was always that – 'one day'. Greg never talked about the immediate future.

Daisy was a bit like Jess, afraid to bring the subject up for fear of scaring Greg off. She didn't want him to feel obliged, or that she was trying to tie him down.

She sighed. He was always telling her how much he loved her, and she loved him too, more than anything, so she'd have to be content with that for now.

***

Greg looked at the calendar on his laptop. Easter was early this year, the end of March. Damn, the weather wouldn't be particularly warm, and he'd have liked it to be a nice day for the plan he had in mind.

He could set it up for later in the year, but he didn't want to wait that long. He'd waited long enough as it was. He could have done something at Christmas, but Easter was perfect for his surprise. He grinned to himself as he imagined the look on Daisy's face. He reached for the phone. He still had a couple of months yet, but he wanted to get the ball rolling now. He had quite a few contacts, in different occupations, one of them would know who to put him in touch with.

Chapter Twenty-Seven

It was mid January, and Daisy and Jess were trying to come up with ideas for Valentine themed brochures for the agency. Greg wanted to use the occasion to encourage more people to join up.

"We'll get a mention in the paper anyway, because of George and Mary's wedding, but see what you can produce. I'm sure between the pair of you, you'll have some great ideas."

Then, as an incentive and knowing what chocoholics they both were, he'd said, "If you can make a suitable design, there'll be a huge box of Belgian chocolates in it for you."

The two girls had squealed with delight, then giggled as Greg rolled his eyes.

"Get on with it then," he'd said, and wagged a finger at them sternly, making them laugh again.

"How about," Jess said now as they wrote on bits of paper, "The Love Shack, where all your dreams come true?"

Daisy chewed the end of her pen. "Hmm, it doesn't mention Valentine's Day though. It has to be Valentine-themed."

"Grr, this is harder than we thought. Okay, I need a coffee to think properly. Want a tea?"

"Yes, please. Oops, clients arriving."

Daisy put down her pen and sat up with a smile as a man and woman entered the foyer.

"Hello, how can I help?"

The man offered Daisy a business card. "We're from Cinnamon Productions. We make TV game shows."

Jess had overheard that and came hurrying back, full of excitement. "Ooh, sounds interesting. Why are you here?"

Daisy laughed. "Jess, let them tell us. Please excuse my friend, she gets a bit excited at times."

The man and woman laughed.

The woman spoke. "We're developing a new dating game. Unlike most formats, this one is going to be about ordinary people who can't find a partner. They may have an occupation or hobby that puts potential partners off, or be terribly shy. Anything which prevents them meeting members of the opposite sex."

"Let me add," the man said, "that we are not looking for gorgeous, fit, hot men and women. We want ordinary people."

Daisy and Jess looked at each other.

"Sounds like fun. Where do we come into this though?" Daisy asked.

"We hoped you'd have suitable people on your books who'd be interested in being on TV."

"Pity I've got a boyfriend, otherwise I'd volunteer," Jess said.

The man looked Jess up and down. "Sorry, you're too attractive."

Jess's mouth opened and closed like a goldfish. Daisy smiled. Her friend really didn't know just how pretty she was.

"I'll go and talk to the boss. He owns the company. Hang on a moment." Daisy ran into Greg's office and her words tumbled out in an excited rush.

"Slow down, Daisy. Right, did you say a TV crew are here wanting details of some of our clients?"

Daisy explained again, more slowly.

"Absolutely not."

"But, think of the publicity," Daisy said.

"I am, which is why I'm saying no. Can you imagine if people found out we were on some tacky game show, our reputation would be in tatters. Not to mention client confidentiality. No, no, no."

Daisy's face fell. She thought it was such a good idea. But now, seeing it from Greg's point of view, she knew he was right.

"I hate reality TV at the best of times. It never shows

people in a good light, Daisy. It's all about getting viewing figures, and the best way to do that is by creating tension, and sensationalising things. Do you really want The Love Shack to be part of something like that?"

"Of course not."

"Well, go out and tell them thanks, but no thanks."

Daisy was about to leave, when Greg said, "Hang on, I'll do it, and I'll point them in the direction of someone who will jump at the chance to be on TV." Greg grinned.

He followed Daisy out, and explained to the couple that he wasn't interested, then told them who he thought might just be able to help them out.

"Don't say you came here first though. Let him think you chose his agency specifically, and you'll have him eating out of your hand."

When they'd gone, Daisy asked, "Why did you tell them to go to that other agency?"

"Because the guy who runs it – Dale – is an absolute idiot. He's so up himself, he thinks he's the best thing around. He'll jump at the chance to get his agency mentioned on TV."

Daisy cottoned on to his way of thinking. "And, you're hoping he'll end up being a laughing stock?"

"Exactly. And then where will people go? They won't want to be associated with his agency, so…"

"They'll come here instead. Nice one." Daisy high fived Greg and Jess laughed.

"Mr Hanson, that's devious," Jess said.

"Hey, all's fair in love and war," Greg said, and the three of them fell about laughing.

Later that day, the girls were still trying to come up with ideas for new brochures.

"Okay, we need to mention Valentine's Day and the agency. Just how we do that though, I have no idea," Jess said.

"Hmm. What do we associate love and Valentine with?" Daisy asked.

"Cupid?"

"O—k-a-ay. Let me think. How about something like: 'Let

Cupid fire his arrow at your heart this Valentine's Day. Find him at The Love Shack?'" Daisy suggested.

"Maybe: 'Meet him at The Love Shack' would be better? Ooh and I've just had an idea. When we put the words 'The Love Shack', instead of the letter O in love, it can be a heart shape with an arrow through it."

"Jess, that's brilliant. Let's draw something. What colours shall we have?"

"Dunno. We can have a little Cupid with his bow, flying just underneath the wording though."

"Yep, that's good, but we need to think about colouring," Daisy said.

"The obvious colours are red and black."

"Hmm, but we don't want to copy everyone else, and red and black are quite sexy. I'm not sure that's the image we're after?" Daisy raised her eyebrows in question.

"No, it's not. Okay, the only thing we have red, is that heart shape with the arrow through it. We need other colours that will stand out."

"Google the colour indigo," Daisy said, remembering the earrings Jess had bought her. Although they were sapphires, they were lighter than the usual sapphire blue.

Jess looked at the images that came up. "Hey, that's perfect. That would definitely stand out."

"Right, here goes. We could have the background in indigo, the wording in cream, with the heart shape in red, and Cupid can be cream, but wearing a red loin cloth to match the red heart?"

Jess smiled at Daisy. "That's going to look brilliant. Call Greg out so we can show him."

Greg was impressed with what the girls had thought up.

"That's fantastic, you two. The advertising agency wouldn't have done much better. Daisy, can you contact the printers, get them to make up a batch for us. I'll ask Frank if he'll print one in the paper too. Well done, girls. You've definitely earned that box of chocolates."

"You better make it the largest box you can find. It would have cost you a fortune if you'd had to pay someone to come up with an idea." Daisy winked at Jess.

"Yep. A box each too, I don't share. And advertising agencies charge hundreds of pounds, so you got this on the cheap," Jess added.

Greg laughed and held his hands up. "Okay, okay. I'll see what I can get you."

***

The brochures looked fabulous. Daisy had a couple of samples made up in matt and glossy paper. The glossy ones were best. The indigo colour was rich, and the cream wording stood out well against it. The red heart and cherub's loin cloth made a striking feature against the blue.

Greg had got the girls their boxes of chocolates, and also given them a bottle of wine, because as Daisy had pointed out, it would have cost him a lot more to pay a professional.

The brochures, and picture in the paper, seemed to do the trick, because they had loads of new clients joining up.

Daisy had shown Jess how to look up profiles, and she was now helping out when she wasn't busy. Greg had made the software programme available on her reception computer, so she could look people up during quiet periods. She didn't interview people – she couldn't leave reception – but she was proving quite good at searching out potential matches.

"That doesn't mean I have to pay you more though," Greg told her.

Daisy knew he'd give Jess a bonus at some point; he didn't take people for granted.

***

Daisy and Jess were talking whilst they had a tea break. Simon had found a large two-bedroomed flat for rent, and Jess was going to see it with him that evening.

"If we like it, we can move in this weekend. Just in time for Valentine's Day next week." Her eyes shone at the thought of living with the man she loved.

"You better have a house warming party, and invite us," Daisy said.

"Of course. We said we'd do that before we bought any new furniture. It won't get trashed then."

"Oh, thanks a lot. We don't trash things." Daisy looked hurt.

Jess laughed. "I didn't mean it like that, but accidents happen when people are drunk. Oh, you know what I mean." She laughed at the look on Daisy's face.

Daisy giggled. "Yeah, I know. Who else will you invite?"

"You, Greg, Kris and Romeo – if he's not working. Talking of Kris, how's his mum?"

"She's had two more sessions of chemo and, fingers crossed, it seems to be going well. She's lost her hair, but that's the least of her worries, I guess," Daisy answered.

"Bless her. I'd hate to lose my hair." Jess shook her head.

"So would I if mine was like yours. You do have beautiful hair, Jess."

She did. It was a rich, copper colour, thick and curly, and shone with health and vitality.

Jess beamed. "Thanks. I like the colour, but it drives me mad being so curly."

"Don't ever change it, it's gorgeous. I wish mine was curly."

Jess sighed. "Never happy, are we? It's good about Kris's mum responding to the chemo, though. Does that mean the cancer will go?"

"We don't know for sure, but her oncologist is optimistic. Kris said when she's a bit better – when she's finished the treatment – he's going to take me to see her, as he talks about me, and she said she'd like to meet me."

"Not hoping you'll get together, is she?" Jess frowned.

"No." Daisy smiled. "She's accepted that Kris is gay, she knows about Romeo. In fact she spoke to him when he answered Kris's mobile the other day."

"Oops, bet that was awkward."

"She apparently went a bit quiet when she asked who it was answering, and he said, 'I'm the boyfriend of Kristof'."

Jess couldn't help it, she burst out laughing.

"Yes, that's what I did when Kris told me," Daisy said with a giggle.

"Sorry, it's just the image it conjured up – Romeo answering the phone in his broken English, and this shocked woman on the other end, ha ha."

They had a laugh about it, and then Jess said, "I wonder how that old couple are finding married life."

"George and Mary?"

Jess nodded.

"I expect it's wonderful being together after all those years apart. Their reception was lovely. There wasn't hundreds of people there, just both families, and a handful of friends, but it was nice. I was so embarrassed though, when George made me stand up, and said it was thanks to me they'd found each other again."

"Aww, that's so sweet."

"It wasn't. Everyone clapped, then offered to buy me a drink. It was so embarrassing."

"You're a real life Cupid, aren't you?"

Daisy laughed. "That's what a lot of clients call me. I suppose I am, in a way. I love this job."

The door opened and for a moment, Daisy thought she was seeing double, and shook her head. She realised she was. Walking toward them were identical twins.

"Hello ladies, how can we help?" Daisy greeted them.

The twins looked young – nineteen or twenty – and it was impossible to tell them apart.

"I'm Katie and she's Kylie," one of them said.

Jess tried not to snigger. That was imaginative, both names beginning with K and ending in IE.

The other twin spoke. "Or am I Katie and you Kylie?"

The first one rolled her eyes and laughed. "Sorry, we do that all the time. It's great fun confusing people."

Daisy didn't laugh, she just smiled and waited.

"Oh, erm, we saw one of your brochures, and thought it would be fun to join up."

"Yeah," said the other girl. "We can have a right laugh with a blind date. First Katie can turn up, then I can arrive and say I was supposed to meet him, really confuse the guy."

Her sister nudged her. "Shut up, Kylie."

Daisy had had enough. "Look, girls. I don't know what sort of agency you think we are, but we don't match people for fun. This is a reputable, serious agency and our aim is to find a lifelong partner for someone."

"We are serious. Sorry I was just messin" about. We do want to join up, don't we, Katie?"

"Yeah," her sister agreed.

Daisy wanted to get rid of the two silly girls as soon as she could, and she knew just what would do it.

"Okay. Our fees for joining, are seven hundred pounds for six months on the standard service, or a thousand pounds for the premium service. Now, shall I sign you up to the premium service? I think that would be best for you." Daisy gave them her biggest smile.

"Oh erm, I've changed my mind. Maybe we'll come back another time," the girl called Katie said, and she rushed her twin out of the door.

"Yes, come back when you've grown up," Jess shouted after them.

"Jess, shh," Daisy scolded.

"Well, stupid immature girls. That's the sort of client we can do without."

"I agree. But you can't go around shouting at potential clients."

Jess pulled a face. "Sorry."

"That's okay. Actually, I'm glad they weren't serious, I could do with a break for a bit. What are you doing for Valentine's Night?"

"If we like this flat, and we can move in this weekend, we're going to get a take-away and have a bottle of fizz in our new home, just the two of us. I bet Greg's taking you out somewhere special?"

Daisy's eyes gleamed. "Actually he isn't, so neh." She laughed. "He was going to book Rialto's, but I don't want to spend it in a restaurant, with other diners. I'd like to be alone, just us for our first Valentine's together, so, we're staying in too. I haven't a clue what we'll eat though."

"Get a take-away."

"Yes, we may do. I'd be happy eating chocolate and drinking champagne, as long as I had Greg with me."

"Aww. Aren't we a soppy pair. It's lovely though, isn't it?" Jess said.

Daisy agreed. "Do you know, it wasn't that long ago, that I was moaning to Kris that I'd end up being left on the shelf." She giggled. "Kris and I even made a pact that if neither of us were married by the time I was thirty-five, we'd marry each other."

"You didn't – were you serious?"

"We were at the time, yes. We even said we'd have kids, but it would have to be a turkey baster job."

"Oh my word. I wonder if anyone's actually done that?"

"What, used a turkey baster?" Daisy wrinkled her nose.

"Ha ha. No, married their gay friend so that they wouldn't be alone."

"Hmm. I don't know. I'm sure it's happened. I don't know if we'd have actually done it. We'd have probably just carried on living together. I could think of worse people to spend the rest of my life with," Daisy said.

"Well, luckily, you've got Greg." Jess smiled.

"Yes, but we aren't living together are we? I know I stay round there most nights, but it's still not the same as living with him." Daisy sighed.

"He's obviously not ready to make that commitment yet." Jess patted Daisy's hand. "Don't worry, hun, he will do, when he's ready. Anyone can see he adores you."

"I guess. I'm looking forward to our first Valentine's Day together though. Right, better get some work done. I can't believe how busy we've been. Those brochures sure worked."

Daisy went back to her office. Her mind whirling with all sorts of thoughts, one of them being, what were they going to eat on Valentine's night? Maybe she could cook a special meal. She decided to look up recipes online.

Greg had been thinking about Valentine's Day too, and had arranged for Rialto's to make his and Daisy's favourite dish, which he was going to collect late afternoon, and cook in the evening. He was keeping it a secret until Valentine's Day. He'd get her a box of chocolates, and already had a bottle of champagne, so he was all prepared. Greg was a man of detail. He liked to plan things in advance, so that nothing could go wrong.

***

Daisy had a wonderful Valentine's Evening. She was stunned that Greg had gone to the trouble of asking Rialto's to make them a meal.

"This beats a take-away, any day," she said as she tucked in to her limoncello pudding. "Have I ever told you what a fab boyfriend you are?"

"Mmm, a few times, but tell me again," Greg said with a smile.

"Only if we can take the rest of this champagne, and the chocolates, to bed?" Daisy asked as she seductively ate off her spoon. "Mmm, delicious." She made eyes at Greg across the table, and ran her tongue across her lips.

Greg put his spoon down, went round the table and pulled Daisy to her feet. Then he kissed her, long and slow, then harder, and more frantic.

"Oh heck, never mind the chocolates, we can have them after," Daisy whispered as Greg started to undress her. They left a trail of clothing as they made their way to the bedroom.

Later that evening, Daisy got up, got the chocolates and went back to bed. She fed Greg a chocolate, and ate one herself. She leaned back against the head rail, and sighed.

"Happy?" Greg asked.

"Very," Daisy replied.

Greg hoped that in a few weeks, she'd be even happier.

"I wonder how Jess and Simon are getting on in their new

flat."

"Bet they're not having as much fun as we are." Greg nibbled her ear.

Daisy laughed. "From what Jess tells me, I bet they are, and then some."

Greg's eyebrows shot up. "She doesn't talk about their exploits – does she?"

Daisy laughed again at the look on his face. "Yes, sometimes."

"I hope you don't tell her what we get up to." He looked decidedly uncomfortable now.

"Greg. How can you even think that?"

"Sorry, I know you're not the kiss and tell type. But I also know what you women are like when you get together."

"Well, not me, thank you. You ought to know by now, that I keep my private life well and truly private."

Greg dropped a kiss on top of her head. "I'll make some coffee – tea for you," he said and Daisy admired his lean naked body as he got out of bed.

Who cared that they weren't living together. How many other women had such a kind, caring, generous boyfriend? Not many men would order a special meal from Rialto's and cook it themselves at home. Nothing much could top how Daisy felt at that moment, She was loved and cherished, she had a great job, and some fab friends.

She wondered if it was wrong to be so happy, then got a bit fearful. How long would it last before something happened to bring it all crashing down around her? She dismissed the idea quickly. She was a caring person, and she worked hard, so she deserved her happiness. Maybe it was good karma coming back at her for all the times she'd been kind to people and animals.

She popped another chocolate in her mouth, and sighed with bliss, then watched Greg as he returned to the room with their drinks on a tray. He got back into bed and started kissing her neck.

She never did get to drink her tea.

Chapter Twenty-Eight

As February gave way to March, the bitter cold disappeared, and they had a few clear days when the sun shone in an almost cloudless sky.

Greg prayed the weather would stay that way for the forthcoming Easter.

***

Jess was sitting on reception, reading a TV magazine. She saw something that made her gasp, and buzzed through to Daisy.

"You have got to see this."

Full of curiosity, Daisy went out to see what Jess was talking about. Jess handed her the magazine, and Daisy searched it, then her eyes widened in surprise.

"That's not…?" She peered closer. "Yes, it is. It's those twins who came in here."

"And it mentions the name of the agency they came from," Jess said.

"Call Greg, he'll love to see this. We have so got to watch it."

Greg came out and looked at the article, which was about a new dating game show. It showed a photo of some of the contestants, two of whom were the young twins, and it mentioned that many of the contestants had been members of Date and Mate, the agency Greg had put the production people in touch with.

"See, now do you understand why I said no? You can imagine what it's going to be like, can't you?"

"How on earth did they get it made so quickly? I thought TV programmes took years to make," Jess said.

"Not if it's a cheaply produced show. You just need a basic format, and people. They probably had it all set up ready for filming, and just needed contestants."

"Those twins must have left here and gone to Date and Mate. Ugh, even the name sounds tacky. Well, I hope it shows them up as the stupid little girls they are." Daisy turned to Greg. "They were really awful, thought the whole thing was a huge laugh. As soon as I mentioned our charges, they were off."

"Ha. I know that Dale charges less than half of what we do, and he lets people take out a month-by-month membership. He isn't particularly discerning, he'll take on anyone," Greg said with a grimace.

"We've got to watch it. Come round to the flat, we'll get some drink and nibbles in and have a laugh," Jess said.

***

The following week they were ensconced in Jess and Simon's new flat, cringing at the programme.

"Oh my word," Jess said, "I can't believe those girls are so stupid."

The twins were coming across as vacuous bimbos.

Jess howled with laughter. "Look at that one posing whenever the camera is on her. What does she think she looks like?"

"Dale Dick is going to regret his agency being associated with this," Greg said.

Daisy spluttered on her drink. "What did you call him?"

Greg laughed. "His name's Dale Wick, but he's such an idiot, he's known in the dating agency circle as Dale Dick."

Daisy burst out laughing. "I wonder if he knows what you all call him."

"I expect he does, and doesn't care. He's so arrogant. He thinks he's the bee's knees. Well, this may take him down a peg or two."

In fact, Frank – Greg's editor friend – told him a few days

245

later that Dale was absolutely fuming because several people had cancelled their membership of the agency. And that was only after one week's viewing. Dale was trying to get the show axed, but he didn't have any powers because he'd signed a contract with the production company.

Greg didn't usually like to glory in someone else's misfortune, but on this occasion he had to laugh. Nobody liked Dale, so he was getting his come-uppance in their eyes.

And, as Greg had predicted, it worked in his favour. They had more and more clients joining up, some even mentioned that they were previous clients of Date and Mate, but didn't want any association with the agency.

Greg knew the time had come to expand, the question was, was Daisy ready to go it alone?

***

Easter was fast approaching, and Greg made a few phone calls just to make sure everything was ready for his little surprise. He checked the weather forecast, and apparently Good Friday was going to be the better day.

So, on the Friday morning, he got up early, made a quick last minute phone call, then took Daisy breakfast in bed.

"Morning, sleepyhead." He kissed her. "Now, I've got a little surprise planned for around lunch time, but you'll need to wear something warmish."

Daisy sat up, instantly awake. "Ooh, what is it? Tell me."

Greg laughed. "No. It wouldn't be a surprise if I told you, would it?"

Rosie jumped up onto the bed, and Daisy picked her up, holding her against her cheek. "Mm she smells nice, and her fur's so soft. Hello, poppet, who's a gorgeous girl?"

The kitten was growing fast, and was almost twice the size she was at six weeks. She was a bundle of energy. She'd already been out in the garden a couple of times with Greg watching on, but she didn't like it, and dashed back inside when the wind got up.

Daisy put the kitten on the bed, and stretched. "I love

surprises, but I'm intrigued. Can I have a clue? Just a teensy one."

"I'm taking you out for lunch. There, that's your clue."

Daisy wondered where they could be going. Not Rialto's, as Greg had said she needed to wear something warm.

"Are we going to a National Trust property for a walk around, and lunch in the tearoom?"

"Ha, good guess, Crazy Daisy, but wrong. Now stop asking, because I'll just answer no to everything."

"Oh you." Daisy threw her pillow at Greg, which made Rosie mew in fright and jump off the bed. She scarpered out of the door.

"Oh heck. Rosie, Rosie, come here, poppet," Daisy called, feeling awful.

The kitten crept back in, looking about the room as she did so.

Daisy picked her up. "I'm sorry, darling, naughty mummy didn't mean to scare you."

Greg shook his head at Daisy's baby talk, and went downstairs.

At noon, Greg got Daisy's jacket and said, "Come on, time to go."

Daisy put her jacket on, then took it off again.

"What are you doing?"

"I don't want it on in the car. I won't get the benefit of it when I'm outside."

Greg laughed. "Okay, give it here, I'll put it in the boot until we get there."

"Get where?"

"Nice try, you'll see."

Daisy got in the car, her heart racing. Where could they be going for lunch that was outside, she wondered.

Greg drove for about twenty minutes, then turned into a narrow lane, and drove for another ten minutes. He eventually pulled up by a small lake.

"We're here."

He got their jackets out of the boot, and led Daisy off on a path to the right. As they rounded a bend, Daisy gasped. There in front of them, by the side of the lake, with willow trees overhanging the water, was a table set for two.

Daisy looked at Greg, then back at the scene in front of her. She heard a noise and turned to see a car leaving.

"Is that…was that Simon's car?"

"It may have been." Greg smiled and led Daisy to the table.

It was set with a white linen cloth and napkins. A bottle of champagne was chilling in a bucket, and there was a big Easter egg, wrapped in gold paper with a gold bow.

"Have a seat, Madam." Greg pulled out the chair and Daisy sat down.

"I'll be back in a tick."

Greg disappeared – back to the car Daisy assumed – and reappeared a few moments later, with a picnic hamper.

"Darling, this is wonderful. What made you do this?" Daisy asked.

"I remembered what you said when we were interviewing Otto that time, about what would impress you. Do you remember?"

Daisy did. She'd told Otto that she'd think more of a man who took her on a picnic to a beauty spot, than one who lavished his money on her.

Her heart melted. Greg actually remembered that, and acted on it.

"Oh, Greg, this is so lovely. You, are so lovely. But, I have to ask, why today? Wouldn't it have been better to bring me on a picnic when the weather is a bit warmer?"

Greg just smiled. "Maybe, but then the place would be full of people. I knew, or hoped, we'd have the place to ourselves today."

"And was that Simon's car? If so, why didn't he stay?"

"Someone needed to set this up before we got here. And he's got Jess don't forget. They don't want to spend Good Friday here with us."

"I wouldn't have minded," Daisy said.

"No, today is for you and me."

Greg knew he should wait until they'd eaten the hamper

food, but his heart was hammering so hard in his chest, he thought Daisy might hear it. He couldn't wait much longer.

"We can eat the food, and you can open your egg after, or you can open it now. Which do you want?"

Daisy looked at the egg.

"I had it specially made. It's a unique one-off; nobody else will have one the same." Greg knew that would do it, her curiosity would get the better of her.

"I'll open it now."

Greg nodded for her to take the egg.

Daisy carefully removed the bow and unwrapped the paper. The outside of the chocolate shell was engraved with her name in white icing or white chocolate, she wasn't sure which.

"Oh, Greg, it's lovely."

"Open the egg. It shouldn't be too difficult." Greg was watching her intently.

Daisy held the chocolate egg with both hands, and gently pulled it apart. She gazed at the little box inside, then noticed the writing on the inside of the shells.

The left side said: 'Will you', the other side, 'marry me'?

Daisy could hardly speak, she was so choked up. She glanced up at Greg then down at the little box. She picked it up and opened it, to see the most beautiful white gold solitaire diamond ring.

She gulped, and couldn't stop the tears overflowing and pouring down her cheeks.

Greg went to her. He took the ring out of the box, and got down on one knee.

"Daisy Dorson, my Crazy Daisy, would you do me the honour of becoming my wife? I want to spend every waking and sleeping moment with you, and I want to grow old with you." His heart was now beating so much he thought he might pass out.

Daisy was crying so hard, Greg wasn't sure if he'd done the right thing.

"Daisy, can you answer me please, I can't stay down here much longer." Greg's knee was starting to hurt.

Daisy laughed through her tears. "Yes," she whispered,

then she shouted at the top of her voice. "YES, YES, YES, I'll marry you."

"Thank heavens for that." Greg got up with a wince, and lifted Daisy to her feet. He kissed her tears away, then kissed her again.

"Now, let's see if this fits, shall we?" He put the ring on her finger. He had to waggle it a bit over her knuckle, but it fitted perfectly.

"We are officially engaged."

Daisy couldn't believe it. Never in her wildest dreams did she think Greg was going to ask her to marry him. She laughed.

"What's so funny?"

"If only you knew what I'd been thinking recently."

Greg held her close. "Why don't you tell me?"

"Because it's stupid now. But I'll tell you anyway. When Jess told me she was moving in with Si, I was so pleased for them, but a little bit of me was envious too. I wanted you to ask me to move in with you, but we never talk about our immediate future, you seemed happy as we were."

Greg tilted her chin up so he could look into her eyes. "And you weren't happy?"

"No, I mean, yes, of course I was, it wasn't that. I just wished. Oh, if you'd asked me to move in, I'd have said yes in a heartbeat. I never imagined you'd ever ask me to marry you."

"See, I'm a man of surprises. Daisy, I was going to ask you to marry me at Christmas. But, I wanted it to be special and unique. I wanted to ask you in a way that you'd always remember and that nobody else had done. Well, I don't know anyone who's put a ring in an Easter egg and had 'Will you marry me' written on it in white chocolate."

Daisy hugged her man. "I'll remember this day always. When we're celebrating our Golden Wedding Anniversary, I'll remember the day you proposed. Thank you, I'm so happy."

Greg kissed her. "Good. Let's drink a toast."

He opened the champagne, and filled their glasses. They toasted each other, and then Greg took a selfie of them holding their champagne glasses, then one of Daisy's hand with her ring on.

"Send it to Jess and Kris, please." Daisy had a thought. "Hey, did Si and Jess know you were going to propose?"

Greg sent the photos. "No. I didn't want anyone but you and me knowing. Well, the chocolate maker and jeweller had to know, obviously. Simon just thought we were having a picnic."

"Jess is going to be so excited."

Sure enough, as Daisy said that, Greg's phone beeped with a text. It was from Jess with the words, "OMG, WOOHOO."

Daisy laughed. Greg's phone went again. This time it was Kris. "Nice one, boss man. Make sure you look after her. K"

"Oh, I'll definitely look after her, don't you worry," Greg said looking at Daisy with a smile.

Daisy got her iPhone out and took some more photos, of her ring, the Easter egg with writing on, the table, and the view. Then another selfie of her and Greg.

She was almost too excited to eat, but she couldn't waste the wonderful food Greg had brought for them, so they tucked in, and then sat back to enjoy the view, the sun – even if it was a little chilly – and their newly engaged status.

They stayed there for an hour or so, just enjoying being together, until another couple came along, which they took as their cue to leave.

"What are we going to do about the table and chairs?" Daisy asked.

"Luckily, it all folds down, and will go in the boot and on the back seat."

"Oh, that's good. What are we doing later? Can we invite Jess, Simon and Kris around? Romeo too, if he's not working. Please? They'll want to celebrate with us."

"I thought you'd ask that, so I got some more wine in and some nibbles, just in case. Phone them when we get home, and ask if they'd like to come around about sixish."

Daisy threw her arms around Greg. "I love you so much." She stepped back and looked at him. "I really do, you know, more than I ever thought it was possible to love somebody. And thank you for today, you've made me the happiest girl on the planet."

"You're welcome. I love you too."

Chapter Twenty-Nine

Everyone was full of congratulations for Greg and Daisy that evening. Jess kept hugging her, she was so thrilled for her friend. "I want to be bridesmaid when you get married," she said.

Daisy laughed. "We'll have to see. We've only just got engaged, I haven't a clue when we'll actually get married."

Greg overheard her, and said, "I'd rather not have a long engagement. I kind of hoped we'd get married soonish."

Daisy's eyes widened. "Really?"

"Yes. I didn't ask you to marry me to then stay engaged for a couple of years."

Jess was so excited now, she was jumping up and down, clapping with delight.

"Steady on, Jess, Greg and I need to discuss this."

Greg looked worried and took Daisy aside. "Don't you want to get married soon?" he whispered.

"Oh, darling, of course I do, but weddings cost an absolute fortune, and need a lot of planning."

Greg smiled. "Only if you're planning a huge event. I have another idea, want to hear it?"

Daisy called to her friends. "Guys, we'll be back in a bit."

To whistles and cheers from Jess, Simon Kris and Romeo – who had the evening off – Daisy grabbed Greg's hand, and led him upstairs.

She sat on the bed and beckoned him to sit beside her.

"Okay, you can tell me now. I didn't want an audience whilst we discussed our wedding. What's your idea?"

Greg held Daisy's hand. "Well, you know you said you'd like to go to Italy…"

Daisy's heart quickened. She could guess what Greg was going to suggest, but hardly dared believe it. She just nodded, unable to speak for the lump that had already appeared in her throat.

"I've done some research, and it wouldn't be too difficult, or take a lot of planning to have a civil marriage in Italy. What do you think?" Greg looked at Daisy and then added, "I assumed you wouldn't want a church wedding – neither of us are religious – but if you do, then Italy is out, as it's not easy for non-Italian's to marry in church." Greg knew he was babbling, but he was nervous all of a sudden, unsure of what Daisy would say.

"Greg, shut up and kiss me."

He happily obliged.

When they came up for air, Daisy said, "I can't think of anything I'd like more in the world, than to marry you in Italy. It would be absolutely perfect."

"Thank heavens for that, as I've sort of got my heart set on it now."

"When were you thinking of?"

"How about this October?"

"This – but it's already almost April. Heck, Greg, that's not much time. I need to sort out a dress and shoes, I haven't even got a passport… I—"

"Darling, relax. You can go shopping for a dress and whatever else you'll need. Leave the other details to me. All I need to know is, would you'd be happy becoming Mrs Hanson this year, or do you want to wait until next spring?"

"I'd marry you tomorrow if we could arrange it," Daisy said.

Greg laughed. "Even I can't perform miracles."

"Oh, I thought you could." She smiled, her eyes full of love for the wonderful man sat beside her. "Why October?"

"No particular reason other than the weather. At the beginning of October, it isn't hot, but it's not cold either. I did think of September, but your birthday's then, and the summer months will just be too hot."

"Okay. October sounds great." Daisy grinned. "I'd like Jess

to be there and Kris, but they probably won't be able to afford it, and we can't have all three of us off work then." Daisy pushed out her bottom lip and looked sad. "I want to marry you – more than anything – but I'd love my best friends to be there."

"What about your family?"

"Mum and Dad will understand. We can always have a family celebration when we get back."

"Good idea." Greg cocked his head and looked at Daisy. "Don't worry about the company, we'll work something out. What if I said I'd pay for Kris and Jess to come, as part of the wedding costs? Simon will just have to pay for himself then."

Daisy couldn't believe it. "Oh, Greg, would you do that?"

"For you, yes."

"Omg, let's go tell them."

Daisy got up and literally ran downstairs. She burst into the living room and they all looked at her.

With a huge smile on her lovely face, she asked, "Who wants to attend a wedding in Italy in October?"

Jess shrieked her head off, then grabbed Daisy and hugged her, dancing around on the spot at the same time.

"Jess? Urgh, Jess you can let me go now, I can't breathe."

Jess released Daisy and said, "Are you really getting married in Italy, this October?"

"Yep, looks like it."

Jess shrieked again.

Then Kris grabbed her and hugged her. "I am so happy for you, sweetie, you really deserve this. And I can't wait to go to Italy."

"Ah, Italia, the country of amore. I wish you both the best for your marriage in my beautiful country," Romeo said, and kissed Daisy's hand, then shook Greg's.

The next hour was spent with everyone asking questions, getting worried about the cost – until Greg reassured them – and then more congratulations and the night ended with them all getting drunk and staying over.

***

The next morning, Daisy groaned as she lifted her head off the pillow. "Ouch, thank heavens we don't have work today, I don't think I could cope."

"That's what you get for drinking so much."

Yes, but it's not every day you get engaged, and find out you're getting married in Italy in…" Daisy counted on her fingers, "…seven months' time."

Greg snuggled up to her. "True. So, soon to be wife, are you happy?"

Daisy cuddled back into the warmth of her new fiancé's body and sighed. "Blissfully. Just when I thought I couldn't be any happier, you spring something else on me. You're amazing."

Greg moved away and sat up. "So, now would not be the time to tell you another little secret?"

"What?" Daisy sat up in bed and looked at Greg incredulously. "There can't be anything else, surely?"

"Well, if you don't want to know…"

"Of course I do, tell me. No wait, give me a clue."

Rosie jumped onto the bed and Daisy stroked her, making the cat purr in ecstasy.

"Erm, I can't really give you a clue. Okay, The Love Shack."

Daisy frowned as she tried to think what Greg meant. "I give up. Tell me."

"I'm going to open another agency."

"Really? Wow."

"Yep, and I want you to run it."

Daisy looked at Greg as if he'd gone mad. She was speechless for once. When she'd recovered from the shock, she said, "Me? I can't run a company."

"Of course you can. You're excellent at your job. You just have to do what you're already doing. Except, instead of me being your boss, you'll be the boss."

Seeing the worried look on Daisy's face now, made Greg wonder if he'd made a mistake. Perhaps she wasn't ready. But he knew she could do it, if only she'd have a little faith in herself.

He hugged her. "Darling, I wouldn't have suggested it if I didn't think you were capable. You're brilliant at your job, you have more talent than you realise. Look how you came up with the idea for those brochures."

"That was Jess too."

"Okay, but you're good at everything you do. I wish you had a little more confidence in yourself."

"So, where would it be? But I wouldn't see you anymore."

"No, you wouldn't, but seeing as we're going to be living together." Greg looked at Daisy and smiled. "I know that's presumptuous, but will you? Move in with me, I mean?"

"Ruddy hell, Greg, just throw something else at me, why don't you? I've had so many surprises in the last couple of days... Pinch me please, so I know I'm not dreaming. And yes, I'll move in, but can I think about the new agency? I'm not sure if I can go it alone."

It wasn't the answer Greg had expected, but he knew Daisy was just nervous. With time, she'd come round to the idea, especially if it meant being her own boss.

Chapter Thirty

The only small worry on Daisy's mind, was telling Kris she was going to move in with Greg. It was a strange, mixed up feeling. She'd been part of the 'Kris and Daisy' set-up for so long, she felt sad that it was coming to an end, but excited at her new life ahead.

However, she needn't have worried.

"Baby D, I am so thrilled for you," Kris said as they ate dinner on their evening in together.

"Really?"

"Yes. When I think back to all those times you moaned about being on your own, and never finding the love of your life, and now look at you. Engaged, moving in with your soul mate, and soon to be married. If anyone deserves this happiness, you do."

Daisy's eyes filled with tears at Kris's generosity. He really was a great guy.

"Besides," Kris said as he twirled spaghetti around his fork, "Romeo can move in now."

Daisy looked up in surprise. "Are things that serious between you?"

Kris sighed blissfully. "You know how you feel about Greg?"

Daisy nodded.

"Well, ditto. Not about Greg, obviously. But I'm crazy about Romeo, and I'm pretty sure he feels the same. We've talked about living together, but I didn't want to say anything because you and I were happy being flat mates."

Daisy tutted with mock annoyance. "Kris, you should have said. He could have moved in as well, I wouldn't have minded.

I'm at Greg's most of the time anyway."

"Well, it doesn't matter now, because things have worked out perfectly."

Kris finished his meal and took his plate to the sink. When Daisy stood up and put her plate in the washing up bowl, Kris grabbed her, held her in his arms, then waltzed around the kitchen with her, making her giggle.

They did the dishes together, chatting about their respective partners, and then Kris said, "So, girlfriend, what are you going to do about your job."

Daisy put the tea towel over her shoulder, and leaned against the sink. "Oh, Kris, I don't know. I love the idea of running an agency, but I'm scared too."

"Why? Sweetie, it'll be doing exactly the same as you are now, except Greg won't be there, and you'll have some new employees. You can do the job with your eyes closed."

Daisy laughed. "Actually I couldn't. I wouldn't be able to read the screen."

Kris rolled his eyes. "Stop being clever, you know what I mean."

"But what if I have a problem?"

"Is that all that's worrying you? The boss man will be on the end of the phone or email. If anything was that bad, he'd drive over and sort it out. Grrr, you're infuriating sometimes. I wish you'd have a bit more faith in yourself, girl."

Daisy poked her tongue out at him. "I can't help it. I'm just scared I'm not as good as everyone seems to think I am, and then I'll let Greg down."

Kris took Daisy's hand and led her into the living room. He sat her down on the sofa.

"Right, listen to uncle Kris."

Daisy giggled at the serious look on his face as he sat beside her.

"You are an amazing woman. You're bright, clever, kind, generous, and caring. You can do this job easily. If Greg had any doubt at all about your capabilities, do you really think he'd risk his company by putting you in charge?"

Daisy thought about that. "I suppose not."

"Exactly. It will be just like going to work now, but in a different office, with a different receptionist and different matchers. If you do ever have a little problem you don't know how to deal with, you just pick up the phone and ask Greg. Simples."

As Daisy sat there mulling over what Kris had said, she thought of all the people she'd successfully matched. All the thank you cards and presents she'd received, and the nickname she'd acquired – Cupid.

"I am good at my job, aren't I? I can do this," she said excitedly.

"Hallelujah, you're finally seeing sense. Yes, you can do it."

"Thanks, Kris, where would I be without you?"

"Probably living in some grotty flat on your own."

Daisy laughed and picked up a cushion, a gleam in her eye.

"Oh, you want round two of our cushion fight, do you? Right, get ready to be defeated."

Kris picked up a cushion and whacked Daisy before she had chance to get a hit in first.

That night, in bed, Daisy couldn't sleep for the thoughts that were going through her mind.

She'd tell Greg that she would accept his offer, but on one condition, and one condition only. Her mind settled, she drifted off to sleep.

***

She got to work early the next day, so she could talk to Greg before Jess arrived. She took him in a coffee, and sat down. Greg admired her legs, and met her eyes with an amused smile.

"Stop eyeing me up and down. I want to have a serious talk with you."

"This sounds ominous."

"No, just something I'd like to discuss. Will you stop that?" Daisy blushed and giggled.

Greg was letting his eyes wander the length of her body, stopping at her legs, then her breasts, then he was staring at her mouth.

"Pack it in, you're putting me off."

He laughed and sat up straight, elbows on the desk. "Right, you have my attention."

"Good. Now then. I've decided I am capable of running my own agency, I'd love to do it, but on one condition."

Greg frowned, wondering what her terms would be. "Which is?"

"I want Jess as my receptionist."

Greg pursed his lips together and sat back in his chair. Jess was a bloody good receptionist, he'd hate to lose her. But, on the other hand, the two girls worked well together, and having a familiar face would help Daisy settle into the new office. He supposed it would be a bit daunting having new surroundings and new staff.

"Okay, you're on."

Daisy whooped with delight. She ran around the desk and plonked herself on Greg's lap, then kissed him. "You're the best boyfriend – I mean, fiancé, ever."

"Thanks. You're not bad as a fiancée either." He kissed her and nibbled her ear.

"Ooh, stop it, your breath tickles, and you know what that does to me."

"Mmm, yes, I know."

Greg put his hand under Daisy's skirt, his fingers stroking her thigh, then moving higher.

"Greg, don't. What if someone comes in?"

"That's part of the fun. We haven't done it in here," he whispered as he nuzzled her neck and sought out her mouth.

Daisy groaned, and pulled away. "Stop, we can't. I'd die of embarrassment if anyone came in."

She stood up and smoothed down her skirt. "I think Jess has arrived, can I go tell her?"

"What are you going to do if she says she wants to stay here?"

Daisy was firm in her answer. "She won't."

"Before you go, we need a name for the new agency. I don't want to call it The Love Shack as well. You and Jess are good at stuff like that, see what you can come up with between you."

"Okay."

Daisy left Greg's office. She was right, Jess had just arrived.

"Morning, want a drink?" she called across.

"Hi, yes, coffee please," Jess said.

Daisy made tea and coffee. She'd already told Jess that Greg had been thinking about opening another agency, but that was all she'd said. She didn't let on that he'd asked her to run it. Daisy hadn't wanted anyone to know – apart from Kris – until she'd made her decision.

She handed Jess the drink.

"Lovely, thanks. Here, I got you something." Jess gave Daisy a bag of Maltesers.

"Ooh just what I need – a morning chocolate fix." Daisy opened the bag and popped a chocolate in her mouth.

"Mmm, heavenly. Right, Greg wants us to come up with a name for the new agency he's going to open."

"He's serious about it then?"

"Yep."

"When will it open?"

Daisy finished the chocolate before answering. "Dunno, he's been looking for suitable premises for a while. He says he has a place in mind. You know Greg, once he's got a plan, it usually happens pretty quickly."

"So, he doesn't want it to be called the same as this one?"

"No."

Daisy couldn't keep it to herself any longer. "And, seeing as I'll be running it, with you as my receptionist, it's right that we come up with a name together."

Jess's eyes widened, and she stopped, her cup halfway to her mouth. "Did you just say you were going to run it, and I'd be your receptionist?"

Daisy laughed at the look of shock on her friend's face.

"I did. Greg told me about his plans and how he wanted me

261

to run the new agency, the day after our engagement, but I wasn't sure I could do it. I've had a long think, and I told him I'd agree on one condition – you came with me."

"I can't believe it! I'd love to." Jess squealed, ran around the reception desk and hugged Daisy.

"I knew you'd say yes." Daisy hugged her back. "Greg asked what I'd do if you said no, but I was sure you'd agree."

Jess sat back on reception. "I don't think I'd want to stay here without you. I like my job, but part of what makes it so enjoyable, is working with you. It wouldn't be so much fun if you weren't here."

"I feel exactly the same, that's why I want you with me. Right then, we better think up a suitable name."

"Okay, let's put our ideas hat on." Jess chewed the end of her pen thoughtfully. "You know, I can't quite believe everything that's happened since I started working here."

"Me neither," Daisy agreed. "It's amazing, isn't it?"

"If I hadn't come about this job, I'd never have met you, or Simon. This place must be magic. It's almost like you step through the doors, and all your dreams come true."

Daisy smiled. "And, the best is still to come. My wedding, maybe yours and Simon's, and us working together."

"I can't wait. What a year this is turning out to be!" Jess lifted her cup. "Here's to us."

Daisy sighed with happiness. She had a fantastic job, great best friends, and a man she loved with all her heart. She was the luckiest girl in the world.

She turned to Jess and bumped cups in a toast. "Yes, here's to us, the new agency, and whatever the future holds."

THE END

Fantastic Books
Great Authors

Join us on facebook:
http://www.facebook.com/crookedcatpublishing

Find us on twitter:
http://www.twitter.com/crookedcatbooks

Lightning Source UK Ltd
Milton Keynes UK
UKOW04f1820051015

259881UK00002B/21/P